The Fortunes of BLUES and BLESSINGS

KAREN SLOAN-BROWN

BROWN REFLECTIONS

The Fortunes of
Blues and Blessing

ISBN: 978-0-9915517-0-5

Library of Congress Cataloging-in-Publication Data on file.

Editor: Maxine Thompson

MANUFACTURED IN THE UNITED STATES OF AMERICA

The Fortunes of
BLUES and
BLESSINGS

KAREN SLOAN-BROWN

Foreword

From the beginning, as written in Genesis 8:22, "While the earth remains, seedtime and harvest, cold and heat, summer and winter, day and night, shall not cease." The good word says everything takes place in its time and in its season. Yet, the seasons are not finite; they overlap and blend. Throughout the mixtures of these seasons, where there is the sun and the rain, we experience good fortune as well as tribulation. Described by many as the two faces of fortune, it is the blues and our blessings-one causing much heartbreak, and the other providing immense joy.

For some, it is visualized as a wheel, with our fortunes continually turning, altering our fate and destiny, taking us on a journey with periods where we are soaring on top and then others where we are pressed down on the bottom, times we can't move forward, and instances when we are forced in reverse. The ageless question is whether the greatest part of our fate is predetermined by a power much higher than our own, kismet, or if the largest portion rests within our own hands.

Dedication

This book is dedicated to my sister Helene,

for sharing all my dreams, listening to all my ideas,

and reading everything I write.

Prologue

Freetown, Sierra Leone
1827

"Get him!"

Those were the last words Zokaya heard before he was surrounded and wrestled to the ground by a gang of men in a sea of rice from his spilled cart. He had been racing against the falling night through the forest along the path to his home without the full weight of his morning haul when the shadowed figures in the dusk rushed upon him from behind the trees. It was near the end of a long day traveling to the Eastern Province from his village in the Northern Province of Sierra Leone to trade his family's harvested crops when the satisfied smile he wore from the sound of the coins jingling in the pouch at his hip turned into a grimace as he fought desperately pinned under the weight of his attackers. He could smell the stench of their bodies as they held him down, restraining his limbs and leaving him defenseless.

"Get off me, you thief!" Zokaya yelled, as he struggled against the grains of rice digging into his skin as his arms and legs were spread-eagle and pulled away from his body.

"What makes you think we want that skimpy money you holding onto?" the bulky tall one standing in the middle of his legs said with a menacing laugh.

Panic stricken, Zokaya looked into their faces, recognizing the five men as warriors from a rival family in the Temne tribe. Fighting between the tribes had escalated amid disagreements over dealings with the whites in Freetown, and the slave trade was the hotbed of contention.

"Get your filthy hands off me!" he demanded. "You know I am Nemgbana's nephew."

"Shut up, boy! You must be foolish," one of them said, looking down at him.

"Do you see any of your people here? You're at my mercy," the bulky leader bellowed, punching his chest with his fist as he looked down on him.

"I don't beg from any man," Zokaya said, spitting on the ground beside him. "If you mean to kill me, do it and be done."

"I have no intentions of killing you; you're as good as money in my pocket," the leader said as he laughed and threw the rope to his henchmen for their prisoner to be tied. "Your fate won't rest with me."

Zokaya could feel the thick rope burning its mark into his skin as they bound his hands and feet, stuffed his mouth with a cloth rag, and slung him like a piece of meat onto the back of his own cart. *It's always about blood or money in this stupid war,* Zokaya thought, *and there would be no ransom paid for a dead man.* His temples pounded with anger when he thought about how much the bargain for his life would cost his family.

"Hide him under those empty rice bags," the leader ordered to the others.

Shrouded in darkness and fear, Zokaya couldn't gauge how long or how far he had been taken. When the wheels of the cart stopped rolling, he could hear the sound of water hitting the shore before he heard the voices. He strained his neck to lift his ear toward the sounds, and then he heard the one in charge talking to someone who spoke with the tone of a white man.

"We can finish our business now," the bulky leader said as he snatched off the pile of clothes to reveal his captive.

Zokaya felt disgusted and naked as the icy eyes of the white man ran along his body. Then the white man shouted to the other one standing just behind him.

"Bring the guns, Jim."

It was dark, but Zokaya could see the one in front was older, with dark brown hair mixed with white matted strands that covered his face and hung low on his shoulders. A lit cigar hung from the spaces of missing teeth in his mouth.

"I can get a pretty price for this one," he said to the leader of the group, as the younger one he called Jim dragged a large wooden crate up on the beach and pried it open. The leader flashed a wicked grin at the sight of the weapons.

"Take nephew down to the ship for our friends here."

Two of the kidnappers pulled Zokaya down to the ground, and the other two lifted the crate up onto his cart. Zokaya's fate was now clear to him; he was being traded for guns. He pulled at the ropes that held him bound in a brave effort to struggle free as three of the men lugged him to the platform where a ship was docked. Carried prostrate, he raised his head to see three tall towers on the deck of the ship and the white sails that hung high in the darkness. He could smell the filth of rotten food and unwashed bodies all around him as he was thrown into the bowels of the vessel. In the shadows, he saw three rows of Temne and Mende men and women helplessly lying in chains. His body, tense until that very moment, crumpled in the resignation of what was happening.

He had heard about the horror from the stories of former slaves from America who had been liberated in Sierra Leone. Tales of endless toil in smoldering fields, vicious beatings, and treatment less than that given to cattle were familiar tales in Freetown. Zokaya laid in the belly of the ship full of dismay as the motion of the vessel took him far away from any hope of escape. It was a miserable voyage. Many days, he thought he would suffocate from the smell of perspiration, sickness, and human waste. He listened to the cries of sorrow and the groans of pain and wondered what could be worse than this suffering.

Zokaya couldn't reconcile the boundless life he had had only a few days ago with the awareness that he would become another man's slave. The thing most dreaded by his mother for her sons was now a reality for him, even though slave trade in Freetown had been outlawed the year he was born. Lying on the bottom in the filth of the foreign ship with his head thumping he imagined his mother's heartbreak when he never returned from trading the family's crops at the market. He had seen the sadness and hopelessness in her face for others in their village that they feared had been captured. She had never failed to caution him whenever he went to market about the ill-will of the evil krifi in their enemies and begged him to be careful.

"Your life is stolen when you're made the slave of another man," she warned. "If you lose your freedom, it's worse than death."

"No, Mama, it won't be my death," he swore under his breath. "I'll live, I'll be free, and I promise you that I will be back."

***

Named by his mother, Zokaya, meaning "the patient one who waits," was born in 1808, the same year of the affirmed death of the slave trade. The youngest of four sons, he shared in the superior status of his father and his father before him as skilled craftsmen and landowners. As a young man, Zokaya towered above his older brothers. He was lean but muscular, with flawless skin the color and sheen of dark roasted coffee beans. Every movement he made was an example of the miracles in nature, and every step he took was deliberate. Zokaya was clever and inquisitive, raised by his mother to believe in Kurumasaba, one "Supreme Being." But she also warned him of the other spirits in the world -the good krifi and the bad krifi, which have the power to change one's fortune.

His father, Ibrahim, once a warrior of the Temne tribe, was a sub-ruler to his brother, Nemgbana. Ibrahim shared the objections of Nemgbana to slave trading. Ibrahim taught Zokaya that a man must make his fortunes from his own sweat, not from the expense of another. Ibrahim raised his sons to be fearless fighters, skilled farmers, and shrewd businessmen.

Trading the family's harvested crops once a week in Freetown, Zokaya was very familiar with the other blacks who had come there as the "Black Poor" from Britain twenty years before he was born and the newly liberated slaves from America who were settling in Freetown. There, he learned enough English to understand their stories of the misery and misfortune that they had suffered after losing their freedom, being bought and sold by others, and being treated shoddier than beasts of burden.

In 1827, Zokaya was abducted from his home in Freetown, Sierra Leone, and traded as a slave. The paradox in this circumstance was that, African slave trade had been banned by the British Empire and the United States nineteen years prior. Unfortunately, though slave trading was now illegal, it was even more profitable with the capture and sale of slaves forced underground.

***

Zokaya was just nineteen years old when the American ship landed in the Charleston port of South Carolina in 1828. There, he and the other captives were inspected like an animal before he was given a thin white cotton shirt and indigo-colored pants to cover himself. Attached to a passel of slaves linked together with heavy chains, he was taken over eighty miles, most of them on foot, to Savannah, Georgia, for a public auction.

The stares from the crowd of white men that surrounded the platform where he stood reminded Zokaya of a pack of hyenas ready to strike at their prey. Then he heard the auctioneer begin his chant to sell the nigra boy from Sierra Leone. Richard Bailey Sr. was the highest bidder paying $1,300, a handsome price for the African who knew how to farm rice.

"You know any English, boy?" Master Bailey asked as Zokaya was tied to his wagon.

"I do," he answered with a nod.

"You grew rice over there in Africa?"

"Yessah," he said, remembering the response the old man who brought him the clothes had advised him to always say.

"That's good, boy, we need somebody around here who knows what they doing."

"Head on home, Joe," the white man called him. "I got what I came for."

"Yessah, Mr. Bailey, sir," Joe answered humbly.

Walking behind the carriage driven by Joe who would have been a tall black man if his back hadn't been permanently bent over, Zokaya looked to his left and right at the layout of the buildings, trees, and the curves of the road. They would be the landmarks that would guide him back to the ocean when he made his escape.

Chapter One

Standing at the ferry dock of Ossabaw Island, waiting for Richard Bailey Jr., Zokaya looked far across the water, and he could sense the shifts in the directions of the wind. Changes were coming, but he didn't know if they were from good krifi or bad krifi. He had seen it all before in his home of Sierra Leone, battles between men over the rights to enslave another. The political tides were beginning to turn, and he had even heard whispers of war. Master Bailey's coming to the island was a sure sign that something unusual was on the horizon. He had only been on the island a handful of times, and whenever he came, something was different by the time he left.

Zokaya remembered the first time he saw him. Richard Bailey Jr. was a young boy no higher than his father's belt, walking around the plantation. He took notice of the boy staring at him among the long line of slaves stretched across the rice fields, raising their hoes and pressing their feet deep into the mud on the rice seeds. Above the sound of their voices singing in unison to the rhythm of their work Zokaya heard the little boy's question to his father.

"Papa, can we call him Hercules?"

"That sounds like a good name for him, son. He's a strong nigga, and he's brought me good luck and good money since he's been here."

Zokaya listened but gave no reaction. Most important to his plan to get back to his home and his family was his survival. He remembered the first business lesson from his father: In the most opportune bargain, give the buyer what they want in exchange for that which you want.

Now known as Hercules, Zokaya had become the main authority at Bailey Grove. It was the farming expertise that had been passed down to him from generation to generation that increased his status. He showed the other slaves how to dig ditches and create dams that increased the acreage of the rice fields and lessened the depth of the swamps. In a short time, he was considered the most valuable slave on the plantation, and his skills in cultivating the rice didn't go unnoticed by Master Bailey. He rewarded Hercules with the best slave quarters on the island, and he was the only one to receive compensation after the harvests. He worked hard from season to season, which added up to year after year with the hope he would one day buy his freedom and return to Sierra Leone. That was twenty years ago, and Zokaya, now known as Hercules, was no closer to getting back to Freetown and his grief-stricken mother than the day he arrived.

Hercules had gotten up early that morning to make sure everything was in order on the plantation before Master Bailey got there for his visit from the mainland.

"Sit down, man. Rest yourself, and eat your breakfast," Rachel chided as he paced around the small eating area in their living quarters.

Rachel was Hercules's wife, although they had not had an official ceremony to mark it. She had come to Bailey Grove thirteen years earlier as a young field slave. Bailey Sr. had acquired her before his death as payment for a gambling debt from Eliot Butler, a cotton planter from a neighboring plantation.

"No sense in worrying 'less you know what you got to worry about," she said, pouring him a cup of hot coffee.

"I can't help it, Rachel. I like things the way they are round here now. I don't want him to think he need to get a new overseer to lord over us."

"Why he need to do that fo'? You been running this plantation for nine years since the yellow fever got Captain Ferguson, and you making more money for dem than he ever did."

"It ain't never enough. You know dat," he said, sitting down at the table.

Rachel knew that very well. She had been raised on the Butler cotton plantation, where the slaves were put to work as soon as they could walk straight. She had spent the better part of her life working from sun-up to way after dark, if there was a full moon, with a cotton sack heavy around her neck that either held seed in the spring or cotton in the late summer.

When she was six years old, she watched her mother's heart break when her older sister and brother were taken away to be sold. When she was eight years old, she was a witness when her father was beaten with the whip to the point where he passed out and never woke up again. She became a motherless child when her mama was sold away from her when she was around ten years old. From that time, it seemed that anybody she attached herself too was taken away from her by death or the auction block. Rachel became sullen as a teenager, and for that, she had felt the lash of the whip on her back more than once. She was only a few days from putting her life on the line in an escape plan with a group of slaves headed for the Underground Railroad before she was traded to erase her master's run of bad luck.

Hercules wanted Rachel from the first time he saw her walk

onto the Bailey plantation. She reminded him of his mother. It was somewhere in the way she moved and held her head, proud but vulnerable. He was twenty-eight years old then, and she was nineteen, the same age he was when he first arrived on the plantation. Even though she wore a faded dress and a torn head rag, he could see Rachel was good-looking. She had deep brown skin and eyes and softly curved features on her face that continued over her whole body.

"What's yo' name?" he asked her when she was sent over to him by the overseer, Captain Ferguson, to see what her assigned chores would be.

"Rachel," she answered strong and defiant, refusing to look in the face of this tall dark figure in front of her. She had never heard of a black man being a foreman.

"You ever work in a rice field befo'?"

"No, I's worked in cotton fields all my life."

"Well, I's gwine teach you all about rice farming. Stick by me, and you won't have no problems."

That's when she first looked into his eyes, and he felt the agony of her life. It was the same look he imagined was in his mother's eyes when he never returned home that day in Sierra Leone. He was determined to do whatever he could to take that sadness from Rachel, the same sorrow that he knew his mother still carried in his absence. That was the day that all his thoughts of escape or buying his freedom were pushed back by his desire to love and protect this young woman.

Rachel maintained her distance from Hercules, never having known a man she could trust in this world. She kept to herself, not wanting to be close to anybody ever again. Despite her efforts to be rude and aloof, he kept a close eye on her and lightened her load whenever he had the chance. Hercules's need to protect Rachel was heartfelt, but the truth was there's only so much protection a pretty slave woman could get on a plantation.

Rachel had barely learned how to seed in the rice fields before she fell victim to Captain Ferguson's proclivity for taking liberties with the slave women. By the end of her second harvest on the plantation, she was pregnant. The following spring, she gave birth to a baby girl she named Maia, another of several mulattos that were born on the Bailey plantation over the years. After that, Hercules kept her and the baby next to him in his quarters at night, and the security he offered them gradually turned into a shared love over the years. Two years later, when Captain Ferguson got sick and died of the fever, it was like Sunday morning on Ossabaw; it was truly a day for them all to rejoice.

"Thank God, trouble don't last always," Hercules said, sipping the palm wine he had learned to make as a youth back in Sierra Leone.

"Alleluia," Rachel said, with her feet dancing for joy.

"You are my wife now, Rachel, Maia's my chile, and I'm gwine build us a fine house."

Hercules built a tabby cabin at the far end of Bailey property. Even as the new overseer, he wouldn't accept any help from the other slaves, wanting it to be constructed from his hands alone. He used oyster shells mixed with sand, lime, and water, the way he learned back in Sierra Leone. It was the largest cabin on the property. It had three rooms and, to keep away the bad krifi, he painted the ceilings the color of the blue sky on a clear day. It took him months and a good portion of his savings for his freedom to complete it, but the expression of joy and appreciation that shone on Rachel's face told him it was worth the effort and the cost.

***

Hercules held the reins of the horses and watched as the ferry glided to the shore and pulled into the dock. Master Bailey stepped off and climbed onto the waiting buggy.

"Afternoon, Masta Bailey," Hercules said, slapping the horse's rump with the lines to start him on the way back to the plantation.

"Any problems I need to know about, Hercules?" Richard asked, settling back in the buggy behind him.

"No, sir, things going along just fine," Hercules answered with his eyes faced forward.

"That's good; I've always said you are the best rice driver in the Lowcountry. How many slaves I got living on the island now?" he asked.

"There's 108 on Ossabaw, sir, 137 all together."

"We must not have lost too many in the cholera epidemic last year. Some other rice planters down here were nearly wiped out."

"We was fortunate, Masta Bailey. Yessir, we were."

"That's why I'm down here today, Hercules. I need to take an inventory and get things straight. The biggest auction that Savannah has ever seen is scheduled at the end of winter, and I'm gonna sell half of all the slaves I got before the next calamity comes."

"Yessuh, Masta Bailey," Hercules said, his shoulders slumping down under the burden of his words. His mind flashed back to the day he stood on the auction block, with all the white faces staring at him like he was an animal.

Richard Bailey Jr. was no different than most of the white slave owners in the Lowcountry, he rarely spent time on his rice plantation on the island, fearing the malaria from the bite of the mosquitoes in the swamps. Unlike his father, he was uncomfortable with the very notion of slavery, but he was very much accustomed to the accoutrements that the free labor afforded him. Richard also feared having the bulk of his assets tied up in dying commodities. The abolitionists were gaining power in the North, and he planned to drastically reduce the number of slaves he owned while the market was good. The ferry trip to the sea island was to categorize which slaves would be sold.

Richard Bailey had always been more of a dreamer than a businessman and had spent the better part of his youth searching for an escape that would relieve him of his legacy and the responsibility to his father's land. He had been fortunate enough to find one when he met his wife, Eliza Barren, while he was abroad in England. They had met by chance in the London Library—he a student at the University of London and her studying at Queens College.

Eliza was a native of Charleston, South Carolina, a woman of above-average intelligence. After convincing her father that she would find a husband of substance at the university, he indulged her desire to continue her education. Eliza's true ambition was to build something of her own and prove herself far more worthy of her father's favor than her three brothers. The couple had been drawn together by the qualities lacking in each other: He was attractive and carefree, and she was plain and more practical. After notification of his father's death in the fall of 1845, Richard, as the sole heir of his father's will, proposed to Eliza. Then they returned to Savannah to run the Bailey rice plantation.

Eliza had a good head for finance and managed the business more efficiently than Bailey Sr. ever had. It was due more to her influence that he had gone to the Bailey Grove plantation to get a jump on the auction. The one contention within their household was his yearning for more children. Richard had been an only child and was hesitant to inflict that lonely existence on his own flesh and blood. After four years of marriage, he and Eliza still had only one child, Daphne. It had been a difficult birth that had left her unable or unwilling to sustain another pregnancy, so the only thing she and Richard did in their marital bed was slumber.

Richard Bailey's arrival on the plantation always caused a stir.

The slaves usually kept to themselves in the fields or hunted in the woods as far away from the big house as they could get, wary of the master's visit. Maia was the only one in sight when the horse trotted up to the front of the mansion. She caught Master Bailey's eye in fleeting glance when he got out of the buggy before she disappeared around the side of the house. Hercules set off to put the horse away, and Richard walked inside the unlocked front door straight to his father's old study next to the parlor.

"Rachel bring me a glass of bourbon," he yelled, knowing she was in earshot. "Tell Hercules to get me the slave ledger."

"Yessuh, Masta Bailey," she said, moving hastily, curious to see what he had on his mind.

It was the book where the purchases, births and deaths were recorded. Hercules brought in the heavy book, and they exchanged a few words before Hercules walked back out of the study.

"What he say he here fo'?" Rachel asked in a low voice.

"It ain't good, sweet pea. He say he gon' sell half of everybody here."

"Oh no, I can't go thru this again!" Rachel said as she rushed out of the back door. She didn't stop running until she got to the refuge of her little house.

Richard went over the ledger book, choosing the families for the sale, not by name but by the number of members. He had no attachment to any of them and knew few of them by name, preferring to distance himself from the daily running of his property. He considered himself above sullying his hands in the dirty business of agriculture; he was much more suited to the higher class of culture and arts.

Eliza had advised him that whole families should be sold instead of them being broken. She didn't trust Geechee slaves and was wary of the juju or the witchcraft that she knew they practiced. She even insisted that the Bailey slaves on the mainland be Christians and attend weekly church service, aside from the fact that some had been Christians before their enslavement and worshiped in their own way.

"Hercules," Richard called out, knowing that he stood just beyond the opening of the door. "Come look at this list. Tell me if you can seed and harvest without these negras."

Hercules eyed the list of names of those who would suffer the misfortune of being sold, knowing each of the hearts that would break with home and dignity tossed like the bones from a carcass. Slaves on the Ossabaw Island didn't want to be sold; whenever anyone was put up for sale it created a pall over the Grove that always cut into the Baileys' bottom line. Now Richard planned on selling more than 71 slaves within a year's time.

"Suh, less hands, less harvest; but we make do," he said.

"Fine," Richard said before asking. "By the way, who is the young gal with the light brown hair, wearing the white frock in the courtyard?"

"That there's Maia, Rachel's girl," Hercules said with the hairs on his neck rising up in alarm. Beauty wasn't considered a blessing for a female slave on a plantation. It attracted unwanted attention. That was one of the main reasons he didn't want another white overseer coming on the island.

"Tell Rachel I'm gonna take her to the big house where she can occupy Daphne. She's lonesome," Richard said.

"Yes, suh, Masta Bailey," Hercules replied. "I'll get her things and have her at the ferry when you leave, suh."

Hercules had sympathy for the families that would be uprooted and sold, but taking Maia off the island was cutting his own family. He had never fully comprehended what it meant to be a slave until this day. He was her Tata, the Geechee word for "Daddy." He had raised Maia as his daughter from the moment Rachel gave birth to her. And even though the recorded papers said she had been born a slave, Maia had never been treated like one; she knew nothing of hard work and had been allowed to roam the plantation unrestrained as a child.

He relived the details of his lost youth in stories he told her about his homeland. He described his memories of the markets in Freetown; his village; and his mother, father, and brothers to keep them vivid in his own mind. She felt his longings for home, but she had no understanding of what he had lost, and he prayed she never would. Her freedom was his freedom. He tasted it fresh everyday as he watched her run along the shore while he fished at the edge of the ocean.

Maia loved the sea, and though the only schooling she had came from Hercules, her mind was sharp and she dreamed of the world on the other side of the sea that he often spoke fondly of when he took her hunting with him in the woods of Ossabaw. But she also feared the other world just a ferry ride away from the island, revealed in the horror stories of other slaves. The water between the worlds protected them from more cruelties, but it also kept them from being free.

Maia listened more than she talked, absorbing insight and knowledge from everyone and everything around her. Mostly she was fascinated by the emotion and the release of the Sunday worship and the shouts for deliverance from a distant savior, because for Maia, God was in pieces of the world around her. She felt His connection in the heat of a summer day. Maia even heard the voice of God in the wind and through the sound of the waves. She felt His touch in the raindrops, the underside of a leaf, and when she dug deep into the earth. As long as she could hear and touch God, in her mind all was well.

Hercules drug his feet in as he walked to the house that he shared with Rachel on their acre of land. Of all the unpleasant tasks he had performed on the plantation, this fell among the worst. He loved Maia as his own and loathed the thought of her out of the range of his protection to the point that all the muscles in his upper body tightened in anger. He could see Rachel outside tending the garden outside of the cabin they shared as he approached, and he searched his mind for the words to soften the blow.

"Rachel, Masta Bailey wants Maia to come to the big house and wait on Miss Daphne for a while. He wants her on the ferry going back today," he said quickly.

Rachel froze as still as a statue as Hercules's words skipped through her brain. Slowly, she lifted her head, and her face under the shielding straw hat was exposed to the sun. Hercules saw a faint smile creep over her lips.

"I'll get some things for her to take," Rachel said, as she turned and ran toward their home.

Hercules was stunned by her reaction.

"Praises be to God," she whispered, as she stuffed Maia's sleep shirt into the knapsack.

Rachel was happy that her child was getting out of the swamps. From the time she got there from the Butler plantation, she hated the mosquitoes, snakes, and the crocodiles. She wanted better for her child. To Rachel, the big house was a step up out of the field. All she could think about was that it would give Maia an easier life than she had had. Life at Bailey Grove for Rachel had been better than the cotton fields; but the work was hard and filthy, and she couldn't abide planting in the wet fields. Maia could stay clean and dry in the big house.

Hercules didn't understand Rachel's peace with Maia leaving. He knew what life was like in the big houses, and he preferred to live on the island with only Allah to watch over him. A girl-child had nowhere to hide in her master's house.

Hercules had been ready to bear the burden of Rachel's sadness, but now he felt useless. Rachel burst out of the doorway to find Maia, and now it was Hercules's turn to stand still in his tracks. They both knew where to find Maia, at the Point on the edge of the plantation where you could see the farthest distance into the ocean. Rachel ran ahead to give her the news.

"Maia, Masta Bailey wants you to keep company with Miss Daphne. You going to the big house across the river," Rachel said, as she grabbed her daughter's hand to make the mile walk to the ferry.

"Mama, I don't wanna leave the island," she cried. "Tell him you need me here. I'll work in the rice fields," Maia pleaded.

Maia was afraid of what might be waiting for her on the mainland. She wasn't stupid. Once she left the island, she might fall victim to the misuse that she overheard the other women murmur about. She wanted to stay near her protector, her tata; he had never let anything or anyone trouble her.

"I don't wanna go, Tata!" Maia begged, as they approached the ferry. "Don't let them take me away!"

Hercules had always been Maia's savior, and there was no question in her mind that he was made in God's image, so strong and powerful with a voice that reached deep inside of you and vibrated. Surely, he could help her, but Hercules had no words; the decision had been made.

Hercules's hands trembled. The only thing he could do to stop Masta Bailey from taking Maia was murder. He could have easily done it, but it would only be a temporary solution, and the consequences would be an apocalypse for every slave on Ossabaw.

"You'll be fine there, chile, and you can come back here and visit from time to time," Rachel said to comfort her. "You gwine be better up there, and you gwine have more."

Hercules and Rachel stood at the base of the river watching the ferry drift away. They could easily see Maia among the few slaves on the top level of the ferry making the short sail. Hercules tried to locate the silhouette of Master Bailey on the lower level of the boat, feeling like the sight of him would explain what the buckra wanted with Maia on the mainland. But it would have shown nothing, because not even Richard knew why he was so connected to the young Maia.

Maia stood with one hand on the railing, the other holding her knapsack, as tears rolled down her cheeks. Her salty tears settled on her lips and tasted like the sea she loved. Her gaze stayed fixed on the island until it faded into the horizon. She had never traveled across the water before, and she had no notion of what lay ahead for her in the master's house.

Richard had told them he was taking Maia up from the Lowcountry island as a playmate for his young daughter, Daphne, in the spring of 1849. But the truth was that he had been spellbound by Maia from the very instant he had laid eyes on her, as she leaned against a column at the front of the mansion, gazing into the skies on that fateful afternoon. Having seen the young girl, his thoughts of business were waylaid. It no longer mattered to him what other slaves existed on his land or about the planting season. He only knew that when he returned on the ferry to the mainland. He would not leave without her.

Richard was struck by Maia's demeanor and expression as her eyes searched within the clouds, and to him it seemed that she was not of this world, that she had been misplaced or thrust out of the heavens in which she now searched. This young girl was a goddess, he mused, with beauty that was beyond a mere mortal, reminiscent of those he had read about in the Greek and Roman classics that had captivated his imagination while he studied in London. To him, her skin glowed like the sun, and her brown wavy hair danced in the breeze like branches on a willow tree.

Richard watched Maia out of the side of his eye and was inexplicably enthralled by the untamed spirit that lay just under the surface of the young girl's profile as she stood at the top of the ferry. In his mind, he knew she was still only a child, but he was attracted to her. She moved him in a way he had never felt before. On paper, she already belonged to him, but he pledged to take whatever time it took for her to give her heart to him.

Chapter Two

Maia walked with hestitation as she got off the ferry. She had never set foot on the mainland before; to her it was strange and foreign, even the air smelled different. Each step took her further from her lack of restrictions as a child on the island to her subservient existence as slave on the mainland. Nervously, she tightened her grip on her knapsack and kept several steps distance between her and the man who had snatched her away from the life she loved. Among the carriages just ahead of them, she could see an older white-haired black man wearing a hat shuffling toward them.

"Welcome back, Masta Bailey," the old man said, as he took the bag from Richard's hand.

The man wore a tattered dark blue jacket and matching pants and walked with his back curved, probably from carrying bags all the time, Maia supposed.

"Joe, fetch the gal with the sandy hair," Richard said, as he walked to toward the carriage. "She's going to help Mammy and tend to Miss Daphne."

Joe was taken aback, but he knew his place; he never asked questions. He had been a slave on the Bailey plantation for fifty years and couldn't recall any of his childhood before he was brought there. He had been Bailey Sr.'s driver, and now he was the same for Bailey Jr.

"Yessir, Masta Bailey," he answered, taking the young girl by the hand, as they walked behind him. Maia kept her eyes on the ground as they walked with her hand dangling loosely in the hard curves of Joe's long fingers.

Eliza had ridden in the carriage with Joe to pick up Richard from the ferry, anxious to hear how much closer they had come to releasing the inheritance that was tied up in their large number of slaves. She had dreams of leaving Savannah and the godforsaken swamps of the rice plantation, and she had planned financial investments that she considered to be more profitable and more sterile. She wanted a life free of slaves. She didn't trust them, and they made her uncomfortable.

Eliza's anticipation of her plan moving forward vaporized as Richard approached the carriage with Joe and a young girl walking behind him. A low boiling rage began to rise in her chest; there was no reason she could think of that would be to her liking that would explain the presence of this child with Richard. She, too, could see the glow that emanated from the young girl and the promise of beauty greater than her own.

"Good evening, Eliza," Richard said smugly, as he climbed into the carriage.

Without responding to his greeting, Eliza demanded, "Who is that child, Richard, and why have you brought her from the island?"

"I've brought her back to be company for Daphne," he said. "Her name is Maia."

"I can't believe you would bring a heathen around my daughter against my wishes!" Eliza shouted.

"I've told you, Eliza, on many occasions that I wouldn't have my daughter grow up alone like I did," he said, as he turned away from her gaze. "You made your choice, and now we both have to live with it."

Eliza was vexed, but Richard had boxed her into a corner where she had no defense. She knew she had lost this battle, but she had no intentions of losing the war. She was no fool. She had grown up in a household where she had seen her father and brothers lay with female slaves regularly, and that was the main reason she forbid the presence of more than one slave woman in her home. Mammy, whose birth name was Mary, was the only slave woman Eliza allowed in the mansion. Mary was Joe's wife, and she had been born on the plantation nearly sixty years ago.

In the back of her mind, Eliza had pushed out thoughts of Richard bedding down with slave girls, even though her fears of having another child kept Richard at arm's length. At other times, the thoughts persisted, and there were occasions when she wondered what price she would have to pay for her continuous denials. Eliza knew that she wasn't among the loveliest of women, but she wasn't plain, she dressed and carried herself well, and she was careful to keep the young and pretty of their social circles off the estate and at a distance.

Joe and Maia sat silently atop the carriage as they approached the entrance of the big house, their thoughts running in opposite directions. Joe was happy for the child's company for him and Mary and the fresh energy that comes from youth. Their children had long been gone, a few dead and a few sold. But Maia was unhappy to leave her Mama and Hercules, her home, and her precious sea, the only comforts she had ever known.

Mary heard their approach and she stood at the door with Daphne at her side. She had raised Richard after his mother, Hannah, died in childbirth; and now she had the burden of single-handedly running the big house, cooking, cleaning, and looking after Daphne. She first saw the girl-child that sat beside Joe; and then she saw the contrast of emotions on all of their faces: Richard's elation, Eliza's irritation, Joe's amusement, and the child's despondency.

"Oh, Lord, what do we have here?" Mary asked, as she gingerly walked down the entrance steps with Daphne in hand.

"This here's Maia," Richard said as Joe pushed Maia forward. "You getting old, Mammy, and she's going to be here in the house for a while to help you tend to Daphne."

"Can she stay in my room, Daddy?" Daphne asked excitedly.

"Whenever you want, sweetheart," Richard responded, gratified that Daphne was happy about the child.

Eliza brushed quickly past the group, disgusted with the circumstances.

"Well, hello, Maia. My name's Mary, and this here's Miss Daphne," Mary said as she placed her arm around the shoulder of the young girl and pulled her close. "I bet you want something to eat, come on to the kitchen."

Richard stayed on the veranda for a smoke, and Joe left to put away the horses. Walking through the house, Maia was fascinated by all the pictures on the walls as they made their way to the rear towards the kitchen. In all her dreams, she had never imagined such places or the people who loomed high within the clouds.

"Here's you a plate of greens, rice, and cornbread to eat, chile," Mary told Maia, as she sat down at the table across from her.

Daphne giggled with delight as she watched Maia gobble down her food from nervousness and hunger.

"You sho' are a pretty one," Mary said in a low voice as she looked at the child with the burnt gold hair, skin, and from across the table and wondered what her fate would be.

Mary had seen so many things over her lifetime, and what she had discovered was that a black woman's lot was sealed in heartache at birth. She prayed silently that Maia would escape the troubles she had seen, and she vowed to cover her as if she was her own.

"Now that you've ate, I'm gonna show you my living quarters.

They right here just off the kitchen."

Mary lived better than most slaves in the South. She had a small sitting area outside of her sleeping room. Inside her sleeping room, she rolled out a mat and covered it for Maia.

"You'll sleep in here wit' me, chile. Next, we gonna put Miss Daphne to sleep in her bedroom," Mary told Maia as the three of them climbed the long staircase hand in hand.

Daphne bounced up the stairs excited to have a guest in the house, someone she could play with besides her dolls.

"This here is where Miss Daphne's nightgowns are kept, and this is where to hang her dress," Mary said as she showed Maia the girl's closet. "I'm gonna show you how to brush her hair and tie it in a ribbon for the night before we say goodnight."

"Can Maia stay with me tonight, Mammy?" Daphne pleaded. "I don't want her to go."

As Mary lips prepared to explain, Richard came through the door and said, "Sure, doll face, she can sit while I read you your bedtime story."

Maia sat down with hesitation, uncomfortable in her new surroundings, but the idea of hearing a story lessened her uneasiness.

Richard preferred Roman mythology over the customary fairy tales for bedtime reading to Daphne. He didn't want to fill his child's head with the nonsense of romance and happy endings that didn't exist in the real world. Richard sat in the rocking chair at the foot of the bed, and Maia took a seat on the floor on a rug beside the bed.

"Jupiter was the king of all the gods," Richard began, and soon Daphne closed her eyes and drifted off to sleep. Richard usually continued the story for his own enjoyment after Daphne fell asleep, but this night, he had Maia's attentive ear. She loved hearing stories, and listened intently to this one about Jupiter, Juno, and Io.

It had been a long eventful day, and Maia drifted off to sleep with the images of little Io swimming across the sea to Egypt. Richard kissed Daphne sweetly on the cheek and resisted the urge to do the same with Maia, but he couldn't stop himself from touching the skin on the back of her hand. He found it smooth and warm, not much different from his own, and then he left the room. Early in the morning when she awoke, Maia crept back to her mat in Mary's quarters for another nap before they began the chores of the day.

***

"You getting more comfortable round here, ain't you?" Mary asked Maia after a few months.

"It's all right, but this big house is lonely and quiet all the time. I miss my mama and tata and the noise of the island," Maia told her.

Things were not as bad as Maia thought they would be on the Bailey estate. She liked working with Mary, and she had been good to her; but she felt unsatisfied and penned in. She missed the voices, singing, and underlying rhythms that were the background of her existence living on the rice plantation. The slaves' quarters and fields on the mainland were smaller and isolated many acres away from the big house.

"I know they miss you too, chile," Mary sighed.

"I mostly miss the time when I could go off by myself," Maia told her.

Maia longed for the freedom and solitude that she had had on the island, where she could ramble through the swamps on the edge of the island, finding new places and things where she could see God.

"Do you know how to look for God, Miss Daphne?" Maia asked on one of their afternoon walks.

"No, how do you do it?" Daphne asked inquisitively.

"You see that hummingbird over there, how his wings move so fast we can't see them?"

"Yeah," Daphne said, fascinated.

"That's God. If you look at all the special things in the world, you'll see Him, just like that woodpecker up in that tree."

Seeing the birds take flight at their whim or when they sensed danger made Maia envious. She couldn't count the times that she wished she had wings that would carry her back home or wherever she wanted to go.

In the past year, she had only been back to the island three times to visit Rachel and Hercules: when Master Bailey went to inspect the summer harvest, Christmas when the master and mistress took Daphne to visit her family in Charleston, and when Master Bailey brought the ferry to fetch the slaves that were sold in the big auction.

***

In spite of Eliza's watchful eye, Richard was becoming more entranced by Maia as her beauty blossomed more fully each year. He creatively searched for more opportunities to be in her company by spending more time with Daphne.

"Daphne's six years old now, and it's time to start her schooling," Maia heard Richard tell Eliza at the dinner table. "I'm going to start giving her lessons after breakfast in the mornings."

"We can hire a private teacher or governess for her," Eliza said suspiciously.

"With your aversion to having guests in the house, I thought you would be pleased," Richard replied with some sarcasm.

"Do what you want, Richard. In a few years, I'm sending her off to boarding school anyway," Eliza said, leaving the room in a huff.

Richard's motivation was to include Maia in the lessons, even though it was against the law to teach slaves to read and write. It would be an opportunity for him to make her feel at ease while he reveled in her company. He didn't see her as one of his slaves; she was the mortal being that connected the breach between his reality and his imagination.

When their first lesson ended, Richard announced, "Now we'll have reading and story time, and we will all take turns."

"I know a lot of stories, Master Bailey," Maia said eagerly. She had heard and memorized quite a few fables from the island, where animals embody human characters.

"Soon you'll be able to read all the stories you want," he told both of them.

Maia became more comfortable, and she and Master Bailey often traded stories after the lessons: his, Roman mythology; hers, Geechee. They shared their fascination of persons and creatures with mythical powers. Their interest in the supernatural stemmed from their mutual desire to leave their present circumstances for another reality. Richard wanted a life outside of the South with the woman he loved and a home filled with growing children. Maia wanted a life where she could be free to go where she wanted and do whatever she wanted.

***

Over the next five years, Master and Mistress Bailey rarely entertained. Neither wanted to provoke any interrogations related to the pretty slave girl in their kitchen. Without exception, they left the estate for all of their social interactions with friends and relations. As Maia grew older, the distance between the couple grew wider. Richard was more blissful, and Eliza more bitter.

"There are other things to do besides playing with Daphne all day. She's nearly ten years old and will be going to school soon," Eliza said, displeased with Richard's unevenly divided attention. "Somebody's got to handle the finances of this family, and you don't seem at all interested."

"Would you have it any other way?" he asked, giving her a long inquiring look.

"I think we understand each other by now," she added.

Eliza had been focusing her time and efforts on transferring the Bailey investments from slaves and rice to cast iron with associates they met while they studied in England. The profits generated from Eliza's investments had already far surpassed the losses they had suffered from the decreased rice harvests from Ossabaw with just under seventy slaves. She looked forward to the day when they would leave this part of the country and the wickedness that thrived in the midst of slave owners and heathens. Then she and Richard could find their way back to the people they were when they had met in London.

Mary had treated Maia as a grandchild over the past six years. They had worked side by side as Mary had taught her how to cook, clean, and keep house. Maia had truly been a blessing to her and Joe, giving them as much joy as any child of their own would have.

"Gon' and give us a Scripture for tonight," Mary said to Maia as she rubbed her feet from a long hard day. "I wanna hear that one from Matthew."

"Alright, Nana," Maia said, opening the Bible. "Come to me, all you who are weary and burdened, and I will give you rest. Take my yoke upon you and learn from me, for I am gentle and humble in heart, and you will find rest for your souls. For my yoke is easy and my burden is light."

"Amen," Joseph said. "I wouldn't mind hearing one of those stories of yours tonight, Maia."

"Let the chile be, Joe, she's tired too," Mary said. "Go on to bed. We be up early in the morning."

"Yes, Nana," Maia said, rising from the floor and going out to her room near the back parlor that Master Bailey had given her a year ago.

"I's getting worried about that chile," Mary said, fearing the inevitable. "Ever since Miss Eliza say she don't want Maia sleeping by Daphne's bed no more, Masta been going to Maia's room with his books."

"She getting older, Mary. She's a woman now. With Missus resisting Masta, it ain't nothing to be done about it."

Richard had contained his urges to sleep with Maia out of respect for Daphne, until she had left the house for boarding school. It was because of her that seven years had passed before he touched Maia, who was now 18 years old. He could see no need to restrain his physical desires to possess her any longer. The loneliness of his nights had transformed him over the years, and he hungered and fantasized about things that he swore he would never do. He courted Maia with private moments in his library, allowing her to take books from the library to her room. She was carried away by the stories of Apollo and Cassandra and the adventure of the Trojan Horse.

"What are you reading?" Richard asked, coming into Maia's room.

"It's a story about Adonis; he was hunting a wild boar. He took aim and let his spear fly. He thought it was dead, but when he got closer, it rose up and killed him," she answered, closing the book when he sat down on the bed beside her.

"I've always loved you, Maia," he confessed as he removed her scarf and pulled his fingers through the golden hair that had caught his eye.

Maia sat frozen and quiet. That thing she had dreaded years ago on the ride over from the ferry, the thing she thought she had fortunately escaped, had trapped her, and like the wild boar, was about to ruin her.

He kissed her gently on one side of her mouth. "Don't be frightened, Maia. I would never hurt you. I only want you to feel what I feel."

Maia stiffened like stone, as if she had looked into the face of Medusa. Richard didn't want her this way. He rubbed her back to loosen her rigid muscles and then he left.

"Masta, says he loves me, Nana, but I don't feel nothing for him," Maia said the next evening as they cleaned up the kitchen after supper. "I love reading the books and telling the stories with him, but the rest makes me like an animal with its foot in a trap."

"That's one thing they can't do, chile, make you love somebody you don't."

"He wants to get in my bed and love on me now," Maia said, keeping her eyes on the floor. "I knew he would a long time ago when he brought me here."

"You ain't got to like it, child. It's just one more of the chores you got around here, nothing more. Many a black woman got to do the same work."

"That's why I need to be free, Nana."

"Use your mind, chile, like you do to tell dem stories. Let it take you far away."

"I do dream of having a man to love," Maia said with a shy smile. "He just ain't Masta."

"I knows, chile," Mary said, wearing a smile of own. "I'm old, but sometimes I dream of me a young thang that ain't Joe."

"Shame on you, Nana!" Maia laughed.

Mary couldn't help but laugh, too. "Chile, the feeling of needing somebody don't die until you die; and for all I know, they don't die even then."

Richard began coming to her room and sitting close to her as they took turns reading the pages of Pyramus and Thisbe and Orpheus and Eurydice. The bond that developed between Richard and Maia was not love; it was an escape for both of them from their mundane existences on the flights of their imaginations. Maia lost herself in the intrigues of the characters, and Richard lost himself in the tenderness of Maia's flesh. Richard's passion for Maia had been loosed, and he invaded her nightly dreams of freedom and fancy with violations against her young body until her innocence had vanished uncelebrated.

"I thank God Daphne is out of this house and away at school!" Eliza said, storming into the dining room for breakfast.

There are few secrets under one roof, and Master Bailey's bedding down with Maia was no exception. Mary kept her silence. She knew her place. Joe was content knowing that Maia wasn't being beaten or mistreated.

"Not feeling well this morning, my dear?" Richard asked, keeping his eyes fixed on his plate of eggs and hotcakes.

"How would you know, being that you don't frequent our bedroom?" she said with a salty tongue, too much of a lady to make mention of the sins that Richard committed under the same roof where she slept.

"Let's have a pleasant breakfast," he said, dismissing her comments.

Eliza recalled how her own mother had turned a blind eye to the immoral fornications of her father with his slaves. She swore she would continue on her slow and deliberate plan to liquidate all the assets and sever business relationships that connected her family to Savannah. Her day of redemption would be when they packed up and left this place never to return again.

Yet seeds sown in fertile ground yield plenty. The spring of 1857 began with the buds of fresh fruit on the trees and a new life growing in Maia's womb.

"I'm having a baby, Nana," Maia said to Mary as they washed clothes in the yard.

"I knowed befo' you ever spoke a work, chile, probably befo' you knew," Mary said as she wrung the water from the clothes.

"What am I gonna do?" she asked.

"Nothing, chile. Nature will take its course."

Maia had hidden her belly with the shame she felt, but time had revealed what she had attempted to keep secret. Richard was careful not to let his happiness over the baby show, but Eliza was livid, and she wasn't one to hold her thoughts in her head.

"Don't take me for a fool, you scallywag!" Eliza screamed furiously behind him as he walked out the front door. "You and your wench are not going to raise a bastard under my roof!"

"Whatever happened to the lovely genteel woman that I took for my wife?" Richard asked without turning around as he stepped into the waiting carriage.

"I'll show you!" she shouted after him. "This isn't the end of it!"

There was no way Eliza could make peace with the fact that his slave whore was carrying the seed of her husband. She spent most days spewing venomous tirades at Richard to the point that he welcomed every opportunity to leave the house and her presence.

Planting season was fast approaching, the time Maia usually went to the island with Master Bailey and visited with her mama and Hercules.

One afternoon, as Maia and Mary sowed the seeds together for the summer garden in silence, Maia stopped short in her row and said, "Nana, I don't wanna go home like this."

Mary grabbed her hand, and they walked up to the back porch to sit down.

"It's not yo shame, chile," Mary said as she lit her pipe and held it at the side of her lips. "That how things be. Yo mama love you and yo baby. You not the first and won't be the last gal that they masta laid wit'. Yo mama's masta laid with her."

Hercules met Master Bailey at the ferry, as he usually did before planting season, eagerly looking for Maia, who came back to visit whenever Master Bailey came to the island. Seeing her on the top of the ferry, his heart sank as he saw that his greatest fears had been realized. Maia was no longer his little girl; she was a woman who was owned by another man.

"Good afternoon, Masta Bailey," Hercules said, feeling more like a slave than he had in all his years as a rice planter.

He spoke to Maia with his eyes, telling her of his love and regret; and she gave him a quick smile before she looked away. He lifted her to the top of the carriage, feeling her grip on his arms that said she didn't want to let go. This child he had raised as his own, his baby, had been violated by the master who owned both of them. He had been powerless in preventing the wrongdoing, and now he had no rights to avenge the transgression. They were Master Bailey's property. He held back his hand and his tongue for the safety of his family, lest they all be killed or sold.

"Hello there, Hercules," Richard said as he climbed into the carriage for the short ride to the mansion. "How's the size of the seedings for the crop this season?" he asked, filling the awkward silence that enveloped them.

"Half the usual, suh. You know we barely have 60 slaves left working the land here at Bailey Grove," Hercules reminded him.

"Somehow we gonna have to increase the harvest for the planting season," Richard instructed. He needed a bigger harvest to raise his cash flow.

Eliza had heavily invested in ventures back in London because of the financial panic that gripped the country. She had switched their liquid assets to gold, and he needed money that was out of her control.

Maia leaned back against the seat of the carriage, smelling God in the salt air from the sea that engulfed the island. She felt as if she were free again whenever she returned to the island, where Eliza's watchful eyes couldn't follow her every move.

***

Rachel sat on the veranda rocking back and forth, waiting for the carriage. Her ankle twitched like the seconds of a clock as the minutes creeped by.

"I need to see my chile," she told Hercules fretfully that morning.

"She'll be here afterwhile. Stop yo' fussing."

So many friends and their family members had been sold over time on the island, and fears about never seeing Maia again had started to wake Rachel up at night. She had taught herself to close off emotional attachments when her first child, a boy, had been sold off at seven years old. But Maia had looked different to her each time she visited the island, and she wanted to carve her face in her memory, just in case they were separated.

When the carriage pulled up and Rachel saw Maia was big, she felt a pinch on the bottom of heart; but the joy of seeing her quickly loosened its grasp. She passed Master Bailey and Hercules without a glance as they went inside the big house.

"Come, chile, I want to feed you," Rachel said as she grabbed Maia's hand as she stepped down.

With their hands still clasped together, the two women walked to the cabin as Rachel told Maia all the things that happened since her last visit.

"I sees you got a youngun coming," Rachel said, leaving so many other intimate words left unspoken.

"Yes'm," Maia said, not looking her mama in the eyes to conceal her shame.

"I had your life, sugar," Rachel said, "but I lived it in the hot sun of the field. I was just your age when I carried you. You a pretty girl, and no masta was gonna leave you to yourself. But at least you don't suffer in the heat and filth of the swamps."

"My life is here with y'all here on the island," Maia said, walking into the house. She smelled the okra and shrimp stewing in the pot of gumbo and the hot kush that she knew was fried especially for her.

The two of them relaxed and ate while Maia shared another story with her mama. Telling the story pushed away the qualms that filled the air of the tiny home.

"I'm going for a walk," Maia said after the meal.

A swift pace carried her to the ocean to hear the voice of God and to feel His touch in the waves as they rolled over her feet. The glorious freedom she felt was short-lived as she caught sight of Hercules and her mama coming for her.

"It's time to go back, Peaches," Hercules said with more regret.

When Maia stepped back into the carriage, the pinch on Rachel's heart returned when she realized that she wouldn't be there to care for Maia when her time came.

Richard was anxious to head off and get back to the mainland; he was uncomfortable with the knowing looks he got from Hercules. His relationship with Maia was in conflict with his sensibilities, but his craving for her only grew stronger as she became a woman. He had made the trip more for Maia's benefit than for business. He hoped that seeing her people and the island would raise her spirits and warm her heart.

Richard still loved Eliza, but she had turned cold. Maia was his passion, and now she was having their child, giving him the immortality through another life that Eliza continued to deny him.

***

The summer months were fleeting. Like the dewdrops left from midnight rainfalls under the morning sun, they were soon gone. But lush greens that covered the grounds and the trees bore wit-ness to their effect. Growth and increase were evident all over the

Bailey plantation. The rice harvest had come in, and Master Bailey was pleased with revenues from the ton of rice that Hercules was able to create with so few workers. Eliza's London investments were burgeoning with profits from industrialization, and Maia's belly had grown tight with the impending birth of a new life. She lived under the vigilant eyes of both Mary and Eliza.

"Nana, help me! The pains are coming!" Maia cried out in alarm late one September evening while she and Mary were cleaning up in the kitchen.

"My Lord, chile!" Mary said, startled by her words. "Take my hand. We gon' take us a walk."

Richard was out of town on one of his many jaunts to Atlanta, where he circulated among their acquaintances. Eliza had chosen to stay close to home.

"Squeeze my hand hard when it pains you," Mary told Maia as they walked around the rear of the kitchen house back and forth until the pains came harder and closer together.

Mary's mother had been a midwife, and she had seen her birth many a baby and had delivered many herself.

"I'm scared, Nana," Maia said between the pains.

"No need, chile, I done this many times befo," Mary said as she hummed a tune to calm both of their nerves. "I can see the pains is getting close. Let's get you up to your room now."

"I want my Mama," Maia said with fear as she sat down on the bed.

"I know, I know, but I'm here for you. Now chew these roots, chile," Mary said, placing an ax under the bed to cut the pain.

The two of them sat on the bed holding hands and swaying in a circle as the pains grew stronger. Mary prayed, "Be wit' us, Lord."

"Oh God, help me!" Maia screamed when the pain and pressure mixed deep inside her womb. "Mama, come and get me from here!"

"Mary, why didn't you come and tell me?" Eliza said, stomping into the room.

Maia had tried to hold in her cries, but it was to no avail. Eliza realized from the noise and turmoil that Maia's time had come.

"I can see the head," Mary said with anticipation. "Push hard as you can, chile."

The labor wasn't a hard one with Mary's knowledge and skills and Maia blocking out the pains with images of Aeneas being tossed about on the seas of Italy in her mind's eye.

In all the commotion, neither Mary nor Maia paid any mind to Eliza. She had backed up and stayed hidden in the shadows of the corner near the door. She watched the two of them and grew more frantic with each grunt of pain from Maia. If only she could have stopped this day from coming.

"One more hard push, chile, and that should do it," Mary said to encourage Maia.

Maia closed her eyes to summon all her strength and squeezed down.

"Relax and take a deep breath," Mary said.

Except, no sooner had the baby been pulled from Maia's womb and the life cord tied, when Eliza darted across the floor out of the darkness and swooped the baby out of Mary's arms and dashed out of the room. The only sound that she made was the swishing of her dress against her legs. Mary stood in shock as Maia reached out her arms to hold the child she had just pushed out into the world. Mary's throat locked up, even though there were no words to answer what had just taken place. Only moments had passed, and Maia was becoming distressed in the midst of her fatigue. She hadn't heard her baby's cry or seen Eliza grab the child.

"What de wrong, Nana?" she asked, worried.

"Missus took the baby, chile," Mary said finally, as she hopelessly searched her mind for words of comfort to soothe the young girl.

"Oh help me, God!" Maia screamed as if she had been cut by a blade. She fell back onto the bed in grief. "Missus gon' kill my baby."

"Have mercy on us, Jesus!" Mary said as she climbed into the bed with Maia and held on for the girl's dear life, trying to share her pain and hold on to her sanity. But throughout the night, Maia cried enough tears for her own personal sea as her body rocked and contorted like a small boat tossed by a thunderstorm.

Exhaustion set in, and Mary calmed Maia in the early hours of the new day with songs from another time and place. And even though the events of the previous night ruled their thoughts, they never spoke about it. The horror of what possibly happened to the baby was too much.

When Richard returned to the house and saw Maia's empty belly without the baby in her arms, he assumed the worse that their child had died. Mary knew better than to cross her mistress and kept her silence.

"Somebody took my baby from me," Maia whispered to Richard when he came to her room.

"It's my fault. I should have been here," Richard said with his voice full of guilt and disappointment. But he wondered what he could have done.

Eliza had warned him on several occasions once the pregnancy had become evident that she would not suffer the humiliation that plagued her own mother. She would not have his bastard child living in the house with Daphne when she came home for the holidays, and as usual, Eliza had not wasted her words. Richard spent the nights reading the story of Romulus and Remus to Maia to ease the torment of not knowing what happened to their own flesh and blood.

***

Over the next three years, life on the Bailey plantation was as predictable as the seasons. Hercules presided over the ever-shrinking rice plantation along with fewer and fewer slaves. Rachel lived for the few visits from Maia with growing regrets for giving her blessing to circumstances that only gave her child the blues. Mary and Joseph tended to the master and mistress of the mansion as they grew older and less concerned with their own lives.

Then there was Maia, whose bed and womb were filled by Richard, only to leave her heart and her arms empty. She had borne him two more children that she had never laid eyes on, all taken from her within minutes of their births.

"I don't want you to tell her anything," Eliza insisted to Mary again after the third child. She's not to know anything, not even the sex of the babies."

Maia laid in her bed for more than a week, heartsick with grief. When she thought about her babies, she wanted to die, but she was determined to live just in case they were alive.

When Mary brought some food up to her room, Maia rolled over and asked, "Are my babies dead, Nana?"

"I's so sorry, chile," Mary said, filled up with sympathy for the young woman. "Your babies was first a son, a daughter, and then a son. That's all I know."

For Maia, they had no faces or names that she could recollect in her lonely hours. Her days were torture that was exaggerated in the nights, unable to hold the flesh of her flesh. What had she done to bring on such pain? She stopped looking for God in the sky, in the earth, or in the air beneath a bird in flight; and she could no longer hear His voice over the roaring waves of the ocean.

Chapter Three

In the fall of 1860, the tides in Georgia were shifting, and repercussions were seen from the richest households to the most humble of slave quarters. Abraham Lincoln's election as president caused a swell of rumors of war in Savannah.

Maia listened intently to the conversations between Richard and Eliza at mealtime. From what she heard from the other side of the door, there was a reason to hope that soon they would be leaving, and she would be able to go back to her life on the island.

"All this political upheaval is for naught," Richard said to Eliza, reading the morning paper. "We all knew slavery was bound to end one day, one way or another."

"I'm ready to cut all of our ties here and take a train north or sail overseas as soon as possible," she replied, fearing the violent insurrections that had spread through other Southern states would eventually erupt in Georgia. "It's only been two days since the election, and the whole city is crowded in the center of town, protesting and calling for Georgia's secession from the Union."

Richard wasn't nearly as concerned. "I hope there will be a peaceful end to the controversy, where the slaves will eventually be offered their freedom and given the opportunity to work for fair wages on the land."

"It's too late for that, Richard; the Georgia military has already been armed. War is practically inevitable; we might as well leave the country as soon as we can."

"I have no desire to escape to Europe. I'm past the point of dreaming the dreams of a young man," he told her matter-of-factly. "I'm satisfied with my life as a Southern gentleman."

"The fact is I plan to take Daphne and sail across the Atlantic with or without you, Richard," she said with disdain. "You can do whatever pleases you. It no longer matters to me."

"Then I won't trouble you with useless persuasions, my dear."

What he didn't say was that he couldn't imagine his life without the sweet warmth of Maia's body next to his on most nights. His connection to her had driven a wedge between him and Eliza, and any overtures he made to her received a cold reception. Richard had never planned for this to happen, and he struggled as to whether it had been his fortune or misfortune to see her on that spring day eleven years ago.

The new year began with the planter associates of the Baileys in Savannah celebrating the state's secession from the Union and furthering their campaign to preserve their way of life. But restlessness and uncertainty spread across the Lowcountry islands as Union gunboats gathered along the coast. The slaves on Bailey Grove were split in their reaction to the rumblings that traveled from neighboring plantations.

"So many folks are talking about running off," Hercules told Rachel as they sat outside their cabin, catching some of the cool evening air. "They thinking it's a good time to escape north while the slave trackers are distracted in the fights."

"I hear some want to join them colored units in the Union army," Rachel said as she weaved on a new basket.

"Most of them refuse to work now anyways, and it ain't no matter to me. I'm here to help whoever wants to prepare for their own survival on Ossabaw."

Hercules had been a trained warrior in Sierra Leone before his capture, and he knew the war between the Confederates and the Union could drag on for longer than either side had considered, maybe even years. They needed to store provisions for the winter with the blockades on the island ports.

On the mainland in Savannah, only a few slaves worked during planting season. Black families were leaving the plantations in the darkness of the night in numbers of five or more, crossing over enemy lines, searching for solace among Union troops.

"By harvest time, there's only gonna be you, me, and Maia," Joe said to Mary in the kitchen of the big house.

"I know Masta Bailey be leaving soon, too," Mary told him. "He say he doubt Fort Pulaski can hold back the Union Army."

Richard had gradually come to accept that the life he loved as the rich Southern gentleman would never be the same and that the legacy of his father hung in limbo. Looking out over the land that had been in his family for generations, he tried to press the images in his memory that would probably have to last him a lifetime. Richard had delayed leaving Savannah because of his attachment to Maia; he felt she was an extension of his soul, as if he had been joined to her in another life. But now even before his departure, the distance between them was already in place.

***

The seasons were changing, Maia could see that the clouds that had kept her from experiencing the full joy of her life were breaking up and moving out of her atmosphere. The possibility of returning to her sea island without having to come back to the mainland came closer to reality with each passing day, yet a weight hung heavy in her heart and pulled it apart.

"I'm pregnant again, Nana," she said, feeling distraught.

"Least the missus is gone, and you don't have to worry about her taking it away from you," Mary said to relieve her mind.

"It's not that I'm worried about the missus. I'm not sure if I want this seed of Masta's to come to fruition. I don't want to bring the evidence of my sin back home with me to Ossabaw. It's my chance to put all this behind me and start over."

"Why you thinking of such things, chile?" Mary said. "Don't nobody blame you for what happened here. You was a slave gal under her masta. Was nothing you could do different."

"I need you to help me get rid of it, Nana," Maia said seriously.

"I don't want to, but I'll help you, chile. You done been through so much."

Maia hoped it would slide out on the slippery trails from the inside of the okra pod that Mary had placed inside her, but the stubborn seed continued to grow.

"Don't worry, chile, it'll only be a matter of a week before all the crops are gathered and maybe another week of canning," Mary said. "Then you can catch the ferry back to Ossabaw, to freedom, to your mama and Hercules. They gonna love you and the baby."

"I guess that's the way it'll have to be," Maia said, having resigned herself to the child in her belly. "At least I'll be home for good."

***

Subsequent to him receiving word that the last of the rice planters had abandoned their slaves and plantations on the Sea Islands, Richard was appreciative of Eliza's business savvy and forethought to sell most of their slaves and put their small fortune into profitable investments. He wondered more about the extent of the damage done to their marriage and if she would allow his indiscretions to be left in the past among the ruins that would surely be born out of this war. Richard packed up his most treasured mementos of his life and family in Savannah and asked Mary and Joseph to sit with him in his study.

"I want to tell you both that I'm leaving while I still can. I have free papers for you, and I want to give you some money to help you get started on your own. I owe you at least that."

"This is the onliest home we ever know, Master Bailey. Where are we going to go?" Joe asked. "We ain't got enough time or strength left for us to start a new life somewhere else. We was both practically born here on dis land, and dis is where we gonna to die."

"If it's what you and Mary want, you have my permission to stay on the estate. The only request I have is that you both agree to be caretakers of the property and maintain the burial plots of my dear mother and father until we return. I'll see to it that Maia is safe aboard the ferry to Ossabaw this afternoon where she can have sanctuary."

"That's what we want," Joe declared, and Mary nodded.

When the time came for Maia to tell Mary goodbye, her eyes burned, and the tears that flooded them couldn't quench the fire. This woman had been her lifeline, making her existence bearable in the big house. Her nana had held her together on the many occasions she had been broken in pieces. She would always be grateful, but she had to go.

"I love you, Nana. You too Joe," Maia said before she climbed into the carriage. "I'm going to miss y'all so much."

"I gon' miss you the most, chile," Mary said, holding her fists tight, full with the cloth from her skirt as the carriage began to roll.

Joe drove them to the ferry. Maia was as quiet on the ride as she had been as the child riding to Bailey Estates on her first trip to the mainland. She had never felt love or desire for Master Bailey; she had simply endured. For Richard, Maia had been his rainbow over nearly twelve years, and he hoped that he had given her some measure of the happiness that she had brought to him and that it was not just the sordid use of a slave by her master. Their parting was awkward, and neither was able to find the appropriate words to end their story. The silence overwhelmed them, and the simple gesture of a wave of their hands said the goodbye that neither could muster.

"It jus' be you and me," Joseph said to Mary after he returned from driving Master Bailey to the train station. Richard was headed to New York, with plans to unite with Eliza and Daphne in London for the duration of the war.

Hercules and Rachel didn't know the circumstances on the mainland or that Maia was coming home. The sight of her walking in the sunset of the evening with her knapsack over shoulder was more like a mirage seen by a parched man in the desert whose thirst had driven him mad.

"My baby is home!" Rachel said, running to Maia in bare feet and pulling her close to her breast.

"We are whole again," Hercules said when he reached them. "I promise you, Maia, I will die before I let you be a slave to anyone on this earth again. Let's go inside and celebrate your coming home. I got maluvu for everyone," he said, talking about the wine he made from the palmetto tree.

Mary and Joseph closed up the mansion on Bailey Estates, satisfied to live in their quarters in the kitchen house. The initial days had been lonesome; but from time to time, slaves fleeing from other plantations sought temporary refuge at Bailey Estates on their way to forts occupied by Union forces. They exchanged the comfort for company. There were times even Union soldiers occupied the mansion. By year's, end the Union navy had landed on the Sea Islands, and the slaves left there were the first in the South to be freed.

***

"I prayed everyday that I would be a free man again," Hercules confided to Rachel, sitting at the table. "I dreamed about it most nights, but I never thought it would come this way."

"Thank God, your prayers and mine were answered," Rachel said, stirring a pot of gumbo.

"I always thought in time I would buy my freedom with the money I earned; now I can truly look forward to the day I return to my family and my home in Sierra Leone."

"I'm just glad to be back home on the island," Maia added.

"You stay here for as long as you can, Hercules," Richard had advised him. "Work the land for your own profit for as long as the Union soldiers will let you."

"I've big plans for the next planting season," Hercules said as they all walked across the plantation after supper. "But first, we enjoy this time of jubilation."

Hercules spent the winter months building a new room on the house for Maia and her baby. When the chills of the winter subsided, Maia sat on her peak of the earth, listening to waves roll in, watching the navy ships in the distance, and feeling the new life in her belly tumble back and forth. That's when she got her revelation.

"Mama, when this baby is born, I'm going to be reborn too," she said when she got back to the cabin. "Its new life will be a new life for me, too."

Maia had decided that she would have a fresh start, and she would find her purpose in this world. Each day when she did her chores and when she walked among nature looking for God she released her inner pain, her hurt, her resentment, and her shame. She prayed it out, sang it out, laughed it out, talked it out, and even sweated it out.

"I don't want the first baby I nurse and care for to taste the bitterness inside me," Maia told her mama.

In time, the glow of the sun kissed her face again, and her soul's joy was restored. All the accumulated love that was meant for the other three babies who were taken from her would be showered on this special one.

On March 17, 1862, Rachel was where she had wanted to be for the other three births, at her daughter's bedside, helping to deliver her grandchild. When Maia heard the baby cry, it was music to her ears.

"You got a pretty baby girl, Maia," Rachel said, wrapping the baby in a clean cloth.

"Give her to me before somebody steals her away," Maia said, still a bit suspicious from what had happened three times before.

"I'm here, sugar. Nobody's gonna take your baby."

"Her cries sound like she's singing, Mama," Maia said, holding her baby tightly.

"Let's hope they stay like that," Rachel laughed.

"I going to name her Diana Portunus, after the Roman god of doorways between the past and the future," Maia told her Rachel and Hercules at dinner. "She's the child who brought me back into daylight."

Diana's birth was the opportunity for happiness given to her from an importunate liaison. Diana was her fortunate aftermath to an unfortunate situation.

"Isn't she perfect, Mama?" Maia would say as she stared into her face for hours at a time, amazed by the flawlessness of her eyes and the miracle of her mouth and the sound of her voice.

"Having you both here is all I ever wanted," Rachel said. "I ain't never been this happy."

"Right now, all she needs to survive flows from my breast

because I'm her mama," Maia said, satisfied. "But sometimes late in the night, my heart hurts for the ones who were stolen from me."

Maia worked hard to push that sadness out of her mind by morning lest it crowd the delight that Diana brought to her life each day. She barely allowed anyone else to hold her baby, and sleep was able to steal only the smallest hours from her time with her. When Diana was less than two months old, Maia used her knapsack to tie her across her chest and took her everywhere she went. She carried the baby to her peak on the island by the ocean, through the woods, into the grassy fields, and into the swamps. She showed her the wonder of God in the raindrops, His perfection in a rose, and His sweetness when she touched her baby's lips with sugar cane.

Maia held her baby in her lap, looked into her eyes, and said, "I lived my mama's life, but you won't live mine. You'll never be anybody's slave, little Diana. I promise you'll always be free to make your own choices."

Chapter Four

"There're almost more Union army and Union navy on this island than us who live here," Hercules said to Rachel when he returned home from his early-morning fishing. "And the men folk are enlisting to fight with both of them as fast as they can write their names."

"Folks around here is doing all kinds of things they ain't done before," Rachel remarked, stirring a hot pot of rice. "All this hope and freedom in the air is contagious."

The former slaves of Ossabaw were on the move, preparing to join in the fight against the Confederate army and getting book learning, the two things they believed in their hearts and minds would improve their fortunes.

"I'm going out for a walk," Maia said, tying Diana around her chest after breakfast.

Among the unfamiliar faces on the island were the Unitarian missionaries who arrived from the North and started a school for the newly freed slaves, even as the battles of war raged on. On her daily treks, Maia found herself lingering around the new schoolhouse, listening for the sounds of the words that filled the pages of the books of the teachers. She missed the library of the Bailey mansion and the many worlds she explored in its books.

"Hello, I'm Laura," one of the missionaries said, introducing herself. "I've seen you around here several days. Would you like to join the class?"

"I can read and write," Maia answered proudly.

"Well, that is good news," a finely dressed black woman at the head of the classroom said. "We can surely use your help." She stretched her hand out in a welcome toward Maia. "My name is Charlotte Forten, and I'm one of the teachers in this school house, and I could use an assistant."

"My name is Maia. Can I bring my baby with me?"

"As long as she is quiet," Charlotte replied with a smile.

Charlotte took Maia to the corner of the room with the younger children and handed her a reading primer. Maia opened the book, turned to the first page, looked into the ready and enthusiastic faces of her students, and found in them her reason for living. When the learning day was over, she rushed home to tell her parents her news.

"Mama and Tata, I'm an assistant teacher at the schoolhouse!" she announced at the door. "There were five children in my class today. It felt so good to help somebody learn to read."

"That's good, peaches," Hercules said, pleased to see that bright light back in her face.

Maia was up early with Diana tied around her chest, and she never missed a day at the school. As Diana grew, she competed for her mother's attention during the lessons, until Maia had to leave her home with Rachel. That's when Hercules and Rachel knew how much being with the children at the school meant to their daughter. Hercules and Rachel were thrilled to see Maia back to her old self again as her passion for teaching grew more each day.

"I'd like to come to the school and get some learning for myself," Rachel said at the supper table. "I don't want to be the only one around here that can't read for theirself."

"Come soon, Mama. There are some older than you who want to learn," Maia encouraged.

"That'll be good for you, sweet pea. You'll need to be able to figure with all the money we making," Hercules said to Rachel. "It won't be long before we have enough money to travel that sea on home and purchase some land where I can run my own plantation."

Unexpectedly and fortunately, the war was turning into a huge money-making prospect for Hercules. He sold the provisions from his hunting, fishing, and crops grown side by side with Rachel to Union soldiers. It seemed as if they worked harder than they ever had as slaves, but it felt good to them to be their own beneficiaries.

"That sounds like an awful lot of working for us," Rachel said, shaking her head. "I guess I'm gonna work in this life until I take my last breath."

Rachel indulged Hercules in his ideas, but she didn't have a desire to leave this country for a world she knew nothing about. Having been sold once, she only wanted to dig her roots in deeper where they were finally free.

***

"How you do, ma'am?" the heavy voice of a man called out as Maia was stepping into the door of the schoolhouse.

Maia turned around to face a well-built young man about her age standing there. He was fine-looking, with deep brown skin and thick black hair that grew all over his face. She stepped back out-side to greet him.

"Hello, I'm doing well, thank you," Maia replied. "Are you here for lessons?"

"No, ma'am, I can read and write. I'm a carpenter. I work fram-ing the living quarters for the soldiers. I was just taking a walk. My name is Aaron."

"Pleased to meet you, Aaron. I'm Maia. I haven't seen you around here on the island before. Where are you from?"

"I was born to free parents in Macon. My daddy trained me in carpentry. I was working on some building projects some years back in Augusta, when was kidnapped with the group and sold as a slave. I worked in the cotton fields for a while, but the masta was greedy and thought he could make more money hiring me out to do carpentry jobs on other plantations. I had finally saved enough money to give myself a good start on building something of my own when the war started. I made my way over to Savannah, jumped on a ferry to find a safer place off the mainland to wait it out, and here I am."

"This is a safe place. I was born and raised here on the island," Maia told him. "I'm helping the missionaries here teach the children and anybody else who wants to learn."

"I don't know many people here. Would you mind if I stopped by to say hello sometime?" Aaron asked, captivated by her kindness and even more by her pretty face.

"I'll look forward to that," Maia said, smiling.

"Then I'll be back tomorrow," Aaron told her as he turned and walked away.

Intrigued, Maia watched him from the doorway. To her, his body was a fortress, something that could keep you safe, tall and broad with square angles on his shoulders and jaw lines. His muscular arms from handling heavy lumber strained the sleeves of his shirt when he swung his arms as he walked exposing the strength that was hidden under his loose overalls.

The next afternoon at the end of his work day, Aaron waited outside the schoolhouse for Maia. "Would you take a walk with me?" he asked with an extended arm.

"Yes, I would like to," Maia answered, looping her arm around his. This walk was the first of many.

Their courtship began with their walks after the school day and then later with him coming to suppertime at the house.

"Mama and Tata, this is Aaron. He's a carpenter helping with the building for the soldiers," Maia said, introducing Aaron on his first visit to their cabin.

"Pleased to meet you. Come on in and join us for supper," Rachel said, admiring Aaron's good looks.

Hercules eyed Aaron, giving him a stare that let him know that any hurt to Maia would lead to his destruction.

"This is my daughter, Diana," Maia said, picking up her daughter from the pallet on the floor where she was playing with a rag doll.

"She's as beautiful as you are," Aaron said.

"Let's all sit down before the food gets cold," Rachel said happily.

Maia shifted Diana to her hip before sitting down, and Aaron sat next to her. Rachel poured the mixture of sausage and shrimp with potatoes, corn, onion, and boiled eggs in a huge bowl and set it in the middle of the table.

"Bless this meal before us, Lord" Rachel said quickly. "Now let's eat."

"Is the Union army paying you fair for your work?" Hercules asked Aaron while he spooned a healthy portion onto his dish.

"I don't know if it's fair, but it's better than nothing," Aaron answered, following suit.

"That's because it's something they don't think they got to have," Hercules explained. "There's things they can't live without, and for those, they pay whatever they got to pay."

"What do you mean, sir?" Aaron asked. His interest was piqued. He had always been ambitious and learned at an early age the power of money when he saw another slave buy his freedom.

"What we doing right now; they got to eat, young man," Hercules said, pointing to the food on his plate. "I need some help if you have some extra time," Hercules offered. "I hunt, fish, and grow whatever crops I can to sell my wares to the military on the island."

"I'll make time, sir," Aaron nodded as Diana climbed from Maia's lap into his.

"Well, I'll be," Rachel said. "Maia usually don't allow anybody but me and Hercules to hold her chile."

"Diana went to him on her own, Mama," Maia said, watching her baby pull at the thick beard on Aaron's face.

Maia felt the greatest attraction to Aaron when she saw how easily he could make Diana laugh out loud. He danced and made animal sounds that tickled Diana whenever she became restless.

"I'm used to being around lots of kids. I come from a large family," Aaron told them.

Maia could see that Aaron was kind and gentle. He asked nothing from her, and she found herself wanting more from him. Just one year older than Maia, Aaron was her complement. He was hard where she was soft; and while she seemed to walk on air, his feet were firmly planted on the ground. Slowly, Maia let Aaron into her heart and felt a love for him that had no shame.

"I wanna to marry, Maia," Aaron said to Hercules one early morning as they sat waiting for the fish to bite. "I love her."

Aaron's feelings for her had grown with each passing week, and he knew that Maia was the woman he wanted to be with him as he worked hard to find his place in the world.

"Maia and Diana are all me and Rachel got. She been through a lot of hurt, and we want her to be happy. If you promise to make her happy, then you have our blessing."

Hercules liked Aaron. The two men found they had much in common. They were both smart and trustworthy, had been lost to their families, and had a dream of buying land when they found their true home on this earth.

"I'll spend the rest of my life doing that, I promise you," Aaron said with his chest filling with hope. He, too, had struggled and seen too much bad, but Maia reminded him of the good that was left in this life.

On Diana's first birthday, Maia and Aaron were married at the edge of the sea by a black preacher in a Christian ceremony which was attended by the school missionaries. They were both dressed handsomely: he in a black suit, and she in a white dress trimmed in lace. When they stood side by side, it was the picture of all God's good blessings. It was a happy time for them for so many reasons.

"Now, go on and jump the broom," the preacher told them.

Aaron grabbed Maia's hand, and they jumped as high as they could. Everyone in attendance there surrounded them and they began to sing songs of happiness, they gave praises to God, and some of them even shouted in the circle of love.

"This is the happiest day of my life!" Aaron said to Maia as they danced in the center.

"We'll have a lot more," Maia said, seeing God in the eyes of the man she loved.

Even while the terrors of war raged on the mainland, they celebrated this marriage on the island with a huge feast of goat, rice and shrimp, collard greens, and corn. They drank wine and danced until late into the night. Not many of the wedding guests noticed when Maia and Aaron slipped away to be alone in the rooms that Hercules had built for her and Diana.

Diana lit a small candle in the bedroom near the head of the bed.

"Honey, why are you lighting a candle. I can feel you in the dark," Aaron said, encircling her with his strapping arms.

"I want to be sure I can see your face."

Maia was afraid that being with her masta in the past would be a cloud over their bed. She also feared that the mind she had trained so well to wander whenever she was touched would abandon her again and she wouldn't be able to please her husband.

"I'm not a ghost, Maia, I'm your husband."

"I know that, Aaron," she whispered close to his ear.

He pulled her to the bed and kissed her deeply and passionately, and she warmed to him.

"Aaron, Aaron," she murmured over and over with pleasure as she responded to the touch of the man she loved.

She hadn't been damaged. She was present in mind and body.

***

The spring planting season and the new season of marriage for Maia was interrupted by the announcement of a draft that would be held in June in Fort Pulaski and Ossabaw Island. Aaron wanted to stay on the island with Maia and Diana, but even more, he wanted to fight for their freedom.

"This is my chance to stand up and be a man for the first time in my life," he told Maia at the kitchen table.

"You always been a man, and you don't owe nobody nothing," Hercules said, knowing the price of war can be more than it's worth. "You already done your work for free."

"I want to stay a free man," Aaron answered. "That's why I'm gonna fight."

"That's all I got to say. Every man makes up his own mind," Hercules said before he stood up and walked out of the house. He couldn't stand the thought of Maia being hurt again if Aaron didn't live to see the end of the war.

Maia didn't protest. She had read of the motivation that drew a man to war. She poured as much love and good times as she could into the two weeks before Aaron would leave as a member of the Third South Carolina Volunteers regiment.

"Come back to me the same way you did when I first saw you," she said, hugging him tight at the door of their room.

She didn't want him to carry the burden of her worry and melancholy on his back as he left with the other freed men on the boat that would later consolidate with the Fourth South Carolina Infantry to form the Twenty-first US Colored Infantry.

Aaron kept his promise to write letters whenever there was a pause in their work:

> Dear Maia, My life was blessed the day I hid on board the ferry to Ossabaw. If I had not had the chance to go there, I would not have found you in that schoolhouse. I never hoped that I would find a woman as pretty as you to be my wife. I thank God everyday for the opportunity to love you. Everything I do now is for us and our family, and nothing will keep me from coming back to you. Love Aaron

During the rest of 1863 and the following year, Maia lived for the sparse letters from Aaron that described the miserable conditions for the black volunteer soldiers who had gone to Florida. He wrote that they handed the black men shovels for back-breaking labor instead of guns to fight. He wrote about the Union soldiers and how he wondered how they could fight against slavery and hate black men, the unfair treatment they received as soldiers, and how they hadn't received any pay for over a year.

Aaron moved her with stories about the thousands of freed slaves who followed the Union army, desperate for food and protection from being recaptured by the Confederate army. Maia cried through the letters that said his clothes barely held on to his back, they were so ragged, and how his stomach groaned for food after eating the thin soup they were given.

Maia shared Aaron's letters with Hercules and Rachel about the colored soldiers who had resigned out of the army in Jacksonville in protest over the equal treatment they had been promised. At the start of 1864, Aaron wrote that he was tired of the sound of the musket, the sight and smell of death of white and black men, and his dreams—when he could sleep—were filled with the horror of the many men who had been killed. Halfway through the year, his letters changed, and only relived the time they shared together and how much he missed the fresh smell of the island flowers, Maia's smile, her touch, and the tenderness of her skin.

Diana was getting close to three years old, walking and talking and following in her mama's footsteps. Her independence was already showing as she forced Maia to loosen her protective hold on her. She loved to go to the garden with Granny and sing with her while she worked, and every chance she could she loved to go fishing with Poppa and sit quietly as they waited for a catch.

***

"Rachel! Maia! It's over! It's done!" Hercules roared as he ran through the field where they gathered the fall harvest. "The Union army marched all the way from Atlanta to Savannah. The Confederacy has been defeated."

"Thank God!" Rachel said, clutching her muddied hands to her chest.

"Hallelujah!" Maia said, relishing the news with anticipation. "That means Aaron will be home soon. Thank you, Lord! I'm so happy my baby won't ever be owned by another man."

Georgia's legacy of slavery had come to an end. There was both disappointment and jubilation with Abraham Lincoln's Emancipation Proclamation. As for blacks, the prayers of the numerous generations of slaves in the Lowcountry, where slave trading had originated, had finally been answered—a day envisioned and hoped for by multitudes, but expected by few.

The new year began with the Special Field Order No. 15 from General William T. Sherman on January 16, 1865. It authorized the Freedman's Bureau to redistribute the land abandoned by white planters and confiscated by the Union army to the newly freed black families on the coastline and thirty miles inland. More rejoicing followed General Robert E. Lee's surrender to General Ulysses S. Grant on April 9, 1865, signaling the end of the Civil War.

Ossabaw Island was buoyed with a spirit of celebration as the local blacks who had never even owned themselves became the owners of forty acres. On the mainland, some farmers were loaned mules from the army to help them work the land. That was the first time freemen new to the island had planted a crop to harvest that would be their own. Maia was anxious to get a place of her own where she and Aaron could raise their family.

Aaron felt vindicated at the war's end, but as a soldier, he lacked the victorious elation of those back home. He felt as if he were a different man, a man who had witnessed too much ugliness and experienced too much evil. He wondered what he had inside himself to take home to his new family. He covered his emotions with a steel façade when his troop, the Twenty First US Colored Infantry, was the first to march into Charleston, the city where the wretched had war started some four years earlier.

"Glory, glory hallelujah. Glory, glory hallelujah. Glory, glory hallelujah. As we go marching on." Aaron sang strong and loud as they marched, feeling his humanity rising with each liberation song from the depths of his soul, where it had been buried. The war was over, and he had survived. He was humbled as his commander accepted the formal surrender in the presence of the heroic 54th Massachusetts Infantry and other colored troops.

"This whole city has been destroyed," Aaron said to William, a fellow soldier, when they saw the burned-out buildings and broken-down homes.

"White folks here been long gone. Now we got to bury their dead," William said as they worked on their assignment to dig up the mass graves of Union soldiers.

"Every man deserves a proper burial. It's the least the living can do," Aaron replied as he worked on a fenced-in cemetery that they would name the "Martyrs of the Race Course" in honor of the sacrifice those men had given with their lives.

The ceremony was attended by the white missionaries and teachers who had come to the city to teach the former slaves to read.

"After this, they ain't gonna have no use for us," William complained when the dedication of the cemetery began.

"Good, I'm ready to go back to my wife and family."

Aaron watched the schoolchildren bring flowers and sing songs as they marched ahead of the great mass of black women and men honoring the dead. After the memorial service, the people ate in the fields and watched the ceremony of the colored infantries as they marched around the gravesite.

***

On Ossabaw Island, the colored soldiers were welcomed back as heroes as they slowly made their way home from the mainland.

"It won't be long now," Rachel said to comfort Maia when she and Diana came home alone again.

Maia had taken Diana with her to the pier at the end of every week to bring Aaron home. Finally, after a month of trips, she saw him standing on the ferry.

"I see him, Diana! Your Tata is finally home!" Maia said, picking Diana up so she could see him getting off the ferry.

It didn't occur to her to tell Diana about Richard Bailey being her father. Maia considered her life at the Bailey mansion a closed book. Aaron was the only father Diana would ever know and the only one she would ever need.

Even though Aaron had been gone for only two years, Maia could see the physical changes in her husband. There were stress lines on his face, and his shoulders were slumped down as if he were toting a large sack of rice. Unbeknownst to Maia, Aaron had seen that winning the war didn't make the difference that they all had hoped it would. He had seen black men having to work like slaves for pay that couldn't sustain themselves, much less a family. He had seen black soldiers who had served valiantly for freedom be slaughtered in hatred after the war. He had come home discouraged, knowing that the black man's fight would have no end.

"Aaron, here! Over here!" Maia yelled toward the group coming off the boat.

Aaron smiled at the refreshing sight of his girls, and it lifted his spirits as he moved through the crowd to get to them.

"I'm so happy to see y'all!" Aaron said, grabbing both of them in is arms.

Maia hugged Aaron around his shoulders to push off the burdens that sat on his back. They both blinked away the tears of joy they had in for seeing each other again.

Little Diana curiously watched them before Maia said, "Diana, this is Tata. He has come home."

"Y'all look so good, and you have gotten so big," he said as he picked Diana up with one of his arms.

"So much has happened since you've been gone, Aaron. Folks are getting their own land and planting their own fields."

Maia talked the whole mile walk to their farm house. She told him all that had gone on in his absence: who had left, who had come back, what the soldiers had done, what went on at the school, and how much they all missed him.

"How do things look over there on the mainland?" Maia asked, wondering what amount of damage the war had done.

"I just want to hear about you and what good food y'all have for me to eat," Aaron said, eager to put the dreadful experience behind him.

"We missed you back here, Aaron. There's so much to be done," Hercules told him over the evening meal."

"Let the man rest for a minute. He just got back," Rachel said. "We just glad you all in one piece and safe."

"So am I," Aaron said. "So many good men have died."

"That's all behind us," Maia said. "Now we can go back to living our lives."

"That's right. We all free now," Hercules said, "That means we got to register with the Freedmen's Bureau."

"We got to have a family surname," Aaron reminded them.

"I want my own name," Hercules said. "I ain't never been no Bailey."

"I don't want to be called Bailey, either," Maia added. She certainly didn't want a constant reminder of her life in the Bailey mansion.

"I like the name *Liberty*," Aaron said. "It's what I fought for, and every time we say it, we'll think of the sacrifice that has been made by so many so we can be free."

"I like it, too," Hercules said. "From now on, we are the Liberty family."

Aaron and Maia registered with the government for a homestead of their own. And by the end of the summer, when the bulk of the harvest season was over, they started building a house on their land, not more than a half mile from Rachel and Hercules.

"You've been scarce lately," Hercules said to Aaron when he joined him one early Sunday morning at their favorite fishing spot. "There's still a lot of money to be made from the land."

"I'm so busy helping people get settled in their houses and

repairing the church that was damaged by the Union soldiers that I haven't even had time to work on my own house," Aaron replied.

When Aaron left the island to join the war, it was as an outsider. But he returned as a favorite son and was looked on as a leader on the island with Hercules.

"You may not have to worry about that for much longer," Hercules said. "The struggle ain't over. Word is that only after one harvest, the President is giving the land back to the Confederate planters. Black folks being forced off the property they been given."

"We should have known that they ain't gonna give us blacks folks something. We got to buy it if we want to keep it."

"I doubt that many of 'em white folk want to come down on the island to live," Hercules reassured him. "They never wanted to be down here before the war."

The blacks on Ossabaw, as well as on the other Sea Islands, had a certain level of independence from being isolated from the mainland. Most white men and their families were afraid of catching the fever from the swamps.

"That's true, but we got to keep our eyes open. They making up black codes and rules to control us now that we free," Aaron said cautiously. "The Ku Klux Klan is making life hell for blacks trying to have something of their own on the mainland. They say gangs of them ride through the night, hiding their coward asses under white sheets, stealing, burning down folks' property, and killing anybody who dares to stand up for hisself. If they come down here, we need to be prepared to defend ourselves.

"I was born a warrior, son," Hercules said unwavered. "I'm prepared to die as one if need be."

Chapter
Five

"I can barely tell the difference between things now and the way they were before the war." Aaron said to Hercules as they worked the field in the early morning hours. "Here it is two years later, and only a few fortunate black folk got the 40 acres and a mule they promised us."

"I ain't never known nobody to give me nothing. What I got I had to pay for," Hercules said matter-of-factly. "That's the only way you can say it's yours."

"You sure are right about that. More white planters have come back south to claim the land and then hired the same families as sharecroppers to work the fields."

"Black folks here don't have much luck. Fortunate for us, Bailey gave me permission to use the land as long as I want, and he ain't come back," Hercules said. "I done hired as many of those who was uprooted to work on this land. They know I'm gonna pay them more than them slave wages the white man offer."

Over the next few years, even with the drought of 1867 and the floods of 1868, Hercules made money. His experience as a farmer had taught him to shift and rotate his crops between growing rice and sugar cane.

"Seems like the struggle for most of the families left on the island is too much," Aaron said over breakfast one morning. "Their numbers are slowly falling down as they move back to the mainland."

"There's barely enough people around here for planting and harvesting to make a decent profit," Hercules told him. "Rachel and me, we both near the end of our fifties, and we can't work the hard long days that we done in the past years."

"There's still money to be made, but not on the island," Aaron told them. "Soon, we'll need to make plans to move to the mainland. Me and Maia are having a baby."

"Thank you, Jesus!" Rachel said, raising her hands and looking up into the blue ceiling, "We being blessed right here."

"I keep telling him we got everything we need right here on Ossabaw," Maia said. "There ain't nothing but more trouble and heartache on the mainland from what I hear."

"My family's growing. I got to think about the future," Aaron added.

"Not much we can do about the future, son," Hercules remarked. "It usually takes care of itself."

"One thing that war has taught me is that a poor man ain't never gonna be free," Aaron said defiantly. "There's no such thing as emancipation without money, and I can't provide for my children on the island much longer."

Hercules had made enough money to leave the island, maybe even enough to return to his home in Sierra Leone. But he realized that whatever he had left after the ill-fated circumstances had robbed him so long ago, time had gone on and taken the rest. He didn't have the get-up-and-go to start all over again in a new place. He accepted the reality that he and Rachel would probably never leave Ossabaw.

Hercules repeated the words he would often tell them at supper: "When I die, toss me in the sea, so at least that way I can float back home."

Rachel laughed and said, "When I die, bury me twice as deep, so I can't be moved."

"Neither of you can go anywhere now that we have another baby coming," Maia declared.

Maia stayed busy teaching at the schoolhouse through the final months of her pregnancy. She was at peace carrying the baby of the man she loved; it was so different from the other times when she felt ashamed. Wanting to have the child of the man you loved made all the difference.

Aaron worked hard, long days at the lumber mills on St. Simons Island between his building projects in Savannah. He was trying to earn as much money as he could before the baby was born. The bigger Maia's belly got, the more pressure he felt. He wanted more for his children.

"Things are changing around here," Aaron said at the end of a long day. "Reconstructing the South has raised the demand for lumber, and the pay is good. But we're running through the forests, and the work will dry up once the trees are gone."

"You can always go back to working with Hercules," Rachel said to stop him from worrying. "He could use some help planting for the new season."

"I'll give it some thought," Aaron answered, but his mind was already fixed.

Aaron didn't want to upset Maia, since Ossabaw was the only place she had known as her home, but he didn't want his children to grow up isolated on the island. He wanted their lives to be bigger than his, and he wanted his children to go to a quality school where they could be well educated.

On the morning of May 24, 1870, Maia went into labor before Aaron had time to leave for work. He hurried over to get Rachel and Hercules, his heart thumping against his chest with anticipation. They returned in a flash, and he and Hercules occupied themselves feeding Diana breakfast. When they heard the baby's first squall, it was the proudest moment of Aaron's life. His first child, his baby boy, had been born.

"I want to call him Apollo," Maia said.

"Apollo Liberty. That has a nice ring to it," Aaron said, repeating it. "I like it."

Apollo's birth motivated Aaron even more. He felt the urgency to move on where he could build something for his family and leave a legacy for his son. He couldn't bear the thought of them spending the rest of their lives on the small sea island, the same land where their mama had been a slave.

"Maia, it's time to give our children the chance that we didn't have," Aaron said, trying to convince her that their world extended beyond Bailey Grove.

"They already have much more than we had. You've done a good job providing for us here. Why do we need to leave?"

"I understand your feelings about the mainland, but this isn't enough for me," Aaron said.

He just needed a little more time to earn enough money to put with the war wages he had saved to get them started. He was determined that he would get them a home of their own. Deep inside, this gave him the justification he needed to get Maia to break her bond to the island.

On Emanicipation Day in 1871, that evening after dinner, Aaron started the conversation about leaving again.

"Maia, we can't stay where we been slaves. We won't know real freedom unless we move on," he said.

"I hear some places on the mainland are worse than war times, and the colored man is the enemy now. The children are safe here, and we're at peace here. Why do we need to look for trouble?" Maia replied.

"We're not looking for trouble, honey," Aaron said. "We're looking for a place where our children can have a better life."

Maia looked at them in front of her. Diana was almost nine years old and Apollo was just pulling up to learn how to walk. They were happy, and she was comfortable here. Maia gave it some more thought after the children were sleep.

"I have to admit that even though I feel safer on the island, I do dream of going to faraway places that I've seen in the books in the big house and at school," Maia whispered to him in the night. "It's the stories that I've read about free blacks catching hell on the mainland that make me hesitant to leave. I just need a little more time to get used to the idea."

"We won't make the move until the time is right," Aaron said, pulling her close. "I've met some powerful black men at the Freedmen's Bureau, and we're making plans. I know we can have a better life in Savannah."

Aaron was determined to join his new friends in the fight to elevate their race with political influence and prosperity. He was becoming more politically active in the community, taking every opportunity to encourage blacks on the island to register to vote after the new amendments were made to the Constitution. He knew that was the only way for them to have any real power to change things.

Over the next few years, life became simple on Bailey Grove. Hercules and Rachel kept a small garden outside of their cabin and a few animals for their own use. Hercules still loved to go fishing, and Rachel would go with him so she could pick sweetgrass to sew into baskets as they enjoyed the newfound peace together. Maia still taught at the schoolhouse. Her students loved the stories that she told them after the lessons of the day, and she could see God was there when an old man or woman from the evening classes would read from a book or write words on a slate.

Diana was a now eleven years old, the same age Maia was when she left Bailey Grove. And all the people living on Ossabaw said Diana's singing was as melodic as that of the indigobird, and even when she spoke, a song could be heard. Apollo was a handsome boy of three, showing all the charm and curiosity of his mother, and he was his father's pride and joy.

Aaron and Maia hadn't made the move to the mainland, but he had already begun living a life separated from the island. The lumber mills on the Ossabaw were now closed, and he worked at the lumber mills in Savannah for weeks at a time. Word of his skills as a carpenter had spread throughout the city, and he was a much sought-after builder during the mass reconstruction after the war. Aaron had trained several men from the island to work with him as a construction team in Savannah, and they returned to the island at the end of each week.

Although he was spending extra time in Savannah, whenever he could to work on the home he was building for Maia and the children, Aaron was also meeting more of the successful black men who were the movers and shakers on the mainland. A fellow carpenter named James Simms brought him into the mason brotherhood at the Prince Hall Masonry of Georgia and Eureka Lodge, and he also joined the Workingman's Friendly Association of Savannah.

"The lumber business is really growing in Savannah, now that the islands are nearly cleared of trees," James said to Aaron after one of the meetings, "The number of black churches in the city is growing fast, too, and they need buildings."

"I'm ready to make my move," Aaron replied. "I'm tired of being away from my family so much. It's time I started my own business."

"It's going to be hard," James told him. "There's no place to borrow money right now."

"I've got what I need," Aaron assured him. "Fortunately, I didn't have my money in the Freedman's Bank before it collapsed, and I bought some prime land from another associate who found himself in dire straits."

"This life is like a see-saw. When one man's up, another one is down," James commented, happy for Aaron but sad for the other.

"I can't argue with that. I'm just glad to have my turn to go up," Aaron said. Then, across the room, he saw Bishop Henry Turner, the pastor of the church he was working on. "We'll talk soon, Brother Sims. I need to speak with the bishop."

Aaron felt that if he could find a position for Maia in Savannah, it might help ease her reservations about moving.

"Good work so far, Brother Aaron," Bishop Turner said, extending his hand for a shake.

"Thank you, Brother Turner, I'm doing my best for you. I was wondering if you knew about any schools in Savannah where my wife might be able to teach?"

"There is a school; it has been run in secret by Jane DeVeauxes long before the Civil War," Bishop Turner answered. "That might be the perfect place for her."

"I'll look into it. I appreciate all your help, Brother Turner," Aaron said.

"If we don't look out for each other, none of us will make any progress," the bishop added on his way out.

Now that everything was in order, Aaron shared the good news with Maia on Christmas Day.

"Baby, I have a special gift for you and the kids. I've built a new house for us in Savannah. It's time for us to move into it. I can't wait for us to begin our new life on the mainland. 1874 is going to be our year."

"I thought we were going to wait until the time was right. Things haven't changed for black folks; it's just a different kind of war."

"Our children have a right to live anywhere in this country," he said to her. "I want Apollo to get the best schooling; and Diana's voice is a gift to the world, not meant to be trapped on Ossabaw Island for only us to hear."

"I don't want us to spoil the day for the kids talking about this. Let's enjoy this Christmas if it's going to be our last one on the island."

"We'll settle it next week. I can't put it off much longer."

Maia didn't share his excitement and was upset after learning of Aaron's gift of a new house in Savannah. It wasn't that she didn't appreciate all he was doing for them. Maia just didn't want things to change; she didn't want to leave her family or the children at the school. She knew how cruel whites could be off the island.

A few days later when Aaron went to work on the mainland, she took the children to visit Hercules and Rachel.

"Mama and Tata," Maia said, bursting through the door holding both Apollo and Diana's hands, "Aaron built a house for us on the mainland and wants us to move now."

"Maia, you're worrying the younguns," Rachel said, pulling them away in her arms.

The children sat down quiet on a couch, unnerved by their mama's fretfulness.

"That's not so bad, peaches," Hercules said to calm her. "You're young, and there's a big world out there off of this island. You need to go and find your place in it."

None of them understood the ordeal she had suffered on the mainland. They didn't know the agony she felt having her children snatched away before she even laid eyes on them. Why didn't they understand the pain waiting for her on the other side of the water?

"My place is here, Tata."

"That's not true, Maia; your place is with your husband. The life you had there before is not the life that's waiting for you now."

Maia let her tears fall like rain and prayed they would wash away the fears. It was her nightmares that really scared her. There on the island, she had pretended that those years in the big house were just a bad dream.

"Everything I wanted for you, chile, may not have been good for you, but I only wanted you to be happy and have better than I did," Rachel said as she avoided looking into Maia's eyes. "But I know Aaron will take care of you and the children."

"If things don't work out, you can always come home," Hercules promised as he hugged her face tightly against his shirt to dry her tears, "As much as we will miss you and the children, you shouldn't be in opposition with Aaron. He's a good man."

"I know that, Tata."

"He's been a good husband and father, and he's never stood in the way of whatever you wanted."

"I know that, Mama. I won't fight it anymore," Maia said, prepared to accept the inevitable. "From now on, I'm going to give him the same consideration."

***

Two months later, the small community of Ossabaw was filled with mixed emotions to see Aaron and Maia go; their whole family had been a warm bright light on the island. Aaron, Maia, and the children had packed up their belongings and were taking the short ferry ride to the mainland.

Maia's mind flashed to the first time she had ridden on that ferry and then again to the last time when she returned home to the island. The short journey had been the turning point in her life.

Unexpectedly, once her feet touched the soil of the mainland, she felt an intense desire to return to Bailey Estates.

"Would it be alright if we stopped at the Bailey house? I want to see if Mary's still there." Maia asked Aaron.

It had been so long since she had thought of Mary and Joe, but secretly she thought of her babies most every day. She wondered if they were still living, if they knew who their mama was, and if she would even recognize them if they passed her on the street.

"Whatever you want, sweetheart," Aaron said obligingly, gratified that his plans for his family had finally come together.

Aaron hired a driver to take them to the estate. Surprisingly, when they reached the entrance to the grounds, it appeared that the mansion was in good condition. Maia had always come through the side entrance of the piazza, so she approached the door there and knocked. The door was finally answered by an old black woman, but Maia could see through the years that had gathered on the woman's face that it was Mary.

"Is that oonuh, chile?" the woman asked as she strained to see.

"Yes, Nana, it's me," Maia uttered, trying not to choke as the flood of love she felt for the woman rose from her heart to her throat.

"Come close to me, chile!" Mary said as she held out her arms for an embrace.

Maia held Mary in her arms and absorbed the tenderness and yearning that encircled her body as they stood together in the foyer.

Speaking softly in her ear, Maia asked, "Where is Joe, Nana?"

"He went on to glory some few years after the war, He was so tired he just lay down, amen," Mary said as her loneliness spilled from every pore, and Maia's heart knew her pain.

"Nana, this is my husband, Aaron, and our children, Diana and Apollo. He's built us a house, and we've come to live on the mainland. I want you to come stay with us."

"Bless you, chile, but I ain't gwine nowhere. I gwine die here with Joe. Besides I got Miss Daphne to care fo."

It was then Daphne made herself known in the doorway to the parlor.

"Hello, Maia," Daphne said as she walked toward her. "I have missed you and wondered about you on so many occasions."

"Daphne, I'm glad to see you are well. What about your mama and papa?" she asked, politely hoping that they weren't in the house.

"They live in London; my papa suffered a stroke three years ago and is confined to a chair; my mama is in good health. I prefer the States to Europe, so I returned after the war was over to live here," Daphne replied.

The whole truth was that Daphne had come back to escape the interference in her life from Richard and Eliza. She had grown up in boarding schools without their constant attention and was now much more comfortable without it. The inexhaustible attempts of Eliza to find her a suitable husband when she favored a life of solitude had made it impossible for her to remain in London. Her parents had vowed to cut her off financially, but she earned a stable income from the rental of properties and land on the estate and was happy to spend hours fulfilling her passion for painting landscapes.

Daphne was still young, not yet thirty years old. She enjoyed the company of suitors for conversation and as escorts to the theatre, but she had doubts that she would ever marry and provide an heir to the Bailey fortune that Eliza had toiled so to enlarge.

"Well, we only stopped by to speak for a moment and have to go. Its been good seeing you again," Maia said.

"Before you go, I have a letter to give you from Papa," Daphne said, giving her a knowing look before she rushed from the room to the library to get it.

When she returned, the letter stuck out from the pages of a small book called *The Hymn to Aphrodite*. Maia took the book and dropped it into her bag, gave Mary a hug she hoped would last forever, and directed Diana and Apollo to do the same.

"Goodbye," she said to them and to the memories she had of the Bailey Estates. That season of her life was over.

"I'm here if you need anything," Daphne said sincerely.

Aaron tipped his hat, and the Liberty family climbed into their carriage and left.

"I don't want anything from that house except what was taken from me," Maia said bitterly as she gripped Diana and Apollo tightly in her arms. "That's something that I don't think anybody can give me."

Chapter Six

"The house is beautiful, Aaron!," Maia said, looking around in wonder at the work he had done. "It's much more than we expected."

"It has four bedrooms. One for us, one for Diana, one for Apollo, and one for your parents when they come to visit," Aaron said. "Only the best for my family. And since we're going to be living here, I've built two more houses down this same road. I'm calling it Liberty Street."

"A street named after us, Tata, I can't believe it!" Diana said, running up the stairs behind Apollo to find their rooms. Maia and the children were more than pleased, almost overwhelmed by the fancy home that Aaron had built for them.

"You never cease to amaze me, honey," Maia said, giving Aaron a big hug. "You are so good to us. I'm sorry for being so contrary."

"I only want to make you as happy as you've made me."

Aaron and Maia enrolled Diana and Apollo at the Beach Institute, a private school near their home for black students. The children quickly adapted to their new surroundings and met new acquaintances at the church and at school.

Aaron introduced Maia to Susie Baker King, a woman he had met at the Freedman's Bureau. She had also been a teacher before she became a nurse for the Union army and had started her own school in Savannah. Susie and Maia had an instant connection when they met; Susie had been teaching newly freed slaves on St. Simons Island at the same time that Maia began teaching on Ossabaw. Unfortunately, the friendship between the soul sisters didn't have time to fully blossom because Susie had the chance to pursue her other passion as a nurse in Boston.

Aaron and Maia attended a social gathering of the Eureka Masonic Lodge, and it was there that Maia found a new purpose for her life.

"Its story time, brothers," James said once the important announcements had been made. "Who will grace us with an interesting story today?"

The men and their wives took turns entertaining one another at the table with stories from their lives on plantations and the war.

"We want to welcome Brother Aaron's wife. This is her first time joining us," Brother James said. "Do you have a story you would like to share?"

Maia had no desire to share any tales of her life on the Bailey plantation.

"I do, if you don't mind me telling a different kind of story," Maia answered.

"The choice is your prerogative," James replied.

Maia sat up straight, leaned forward in her chair, and began her tale:

> There was a young slave boy named Basil who was visited by a mystical creature that rose out of the ocean as he stood on the shore, throwing twigs into the waves one spring day. The large creature was indistinguishable as its physical features transformed as he looked upon it. He couldn't tell if it was a fish, human, or beast. The lower part of its body was partially

covered with a dark blue smooth layer of fur that glistened in the sunlight and looked almost like skin. The creature spoke to him in strange sounds and gestures; but, incredibly, the words were interpreted clearly within his mind.

"I'm going to give you the power to transform yourself into anything you desire whenever your life is in danger," the creature told Basil. "Your freedom is yours to take if you want it." Then the creature disappeared back into the sea.

Basil decided to start right then on his journey to go far from the place where his mama had been sold away from him a year ago. He had only gone a few miles when he heard the gallop of horses mixed with mumbles of voices. *I'm a tree,* he thought, and he was. The tree went unnoticed as the slave catchers rode by. The unusual gift turned out to be the key to Basil's survival as he transformed himself into a deer to run through the woods, a black bear to fend off a wolf, and even an eagle on occasion to escape imminent perils as he traveled north and ultimately gained his freedom.

"That was an impressive tale, Sister Liberty," John Deveaux said when Maia finished her tale. "I would like to offer you the opportunity to write a series of stories in a newspaper I'm establishing called *The Colored Tribune.*"

"I would love to do something like that," Maia said readily. "I've been making up stories all of my life."

The move to Savannah turned out to be a blessing for the family that Aaron had hoped for, but most of his plans for himself were leading him to frustration. The political fire in his belly was only serving to burn him as the advances that had been made by black leaders were being reversed as Reconstruction ended. He had lost before he even had a chance to run for an office.

"I'm making the money that I always wanted to," he said to Maia in the early morning hours before they rose out of bed. "But I'm not helping anybody but myself."

"That's not true, Aaron. You've done of lot to help so many people ever since you came back from the war," she reminded him. "It's going to take a long time for us to catch up, but at least we're not slaves anymore."

"I want to do something meaningful, something where I can better myself and the people around me. I want us to have real power," he explained. "Money without power is useless. The two of them should be hand in hand."

"You are going to have to be patient, honey, things will change. They always do."

"The odds of that happening now are getting slim since Pastor Turner has been removed from the state legislature. With him out of office, I don't stand a chance," Aaron said discouraged.

"You'll get your chance; it's not good to rush things. More important, I don't want to see you get hurt. Them crazy white bigots up there in Atlanta have thrown all the blacks out of office. Abram Turner was murdered, and they beat Abram Colby in the streets with a whip."

"We don't have time, Maia. The damn KKK are lynching us every day, trying to hold us back. That's not going to stop. All the black leaders in Savannah who are working to keep black folks progressing, including my Masonic brothers John Deveaux and James Sims, are all being threatened. Now with this new poll tax, most of our folk can't even afford to vote."

"Don't get yourself all worked up this early in the morning. You won't be able to eat your breakfast," Maia said, sliding out of the bed, "Besides, you have a successful business to get to."

Aaron's construction business might have made him one of the most prosperous blacks in the community, but it left him unsatisfied and rejected. His pastor, Bishop Turner, and friend, John Deveaux, were selected as delegates for the Republican National Convention in 1876, leaving him at home out of the action yet again.

Maia enjoyed writing for the newspaper, which changed its name to the *Savannah Tribune*. She became a popular feature in the paper and was invited to public readings at events in the city. Diana excelled as a student at Beach Institute, and Apollo was growing fast and strong, with a budding talent for baseball. Nevertheless, as with the tides of the ocean that she had bonded with so long ago, Maia's fortune was changing again.

"There's yellow fever spreading through Savannah," Aaron told Maia at dinner after the children had left the table.

"Oh God, no. That's awful news," Maia said as nausea rose in her throat.

Maia had seen the scourge years before when she was a young girl on the Bailey Estate and remembered how several of the slaves had suffered and died. An epidemic was what they feared most back on the island. She knew very well that yellow fever was aggravated by the early summer's drenching rains and the late summer's sweltering heat.

"Black and white folk are already leaving the city in droves by train, trying to get away from the sickness," Aaron told her. "Everybody's scared."

"What are we going to do, Aaron?" Maia asked with her concern growing by the second.

"I don't know yet. I'm gonna have to think," he said, looking in her direction, but his mind was already in another place.

She and Aaron tossed and turned through several nights, neither wanting to ask the other to leave Savannah and both fearing for their children's health and well-being.

The days of indecision ended with Aaron's announcement one evening at the beginning of September. "Things are real bad, Maia. We're going to Atlanta."

When the morning came, Apollo shivered in his bed, despite the early warmth of the day.

When Maia walked into his room to wake him and saw the state he was in, she fell to her knees at his bedside and cried out, "Please God, don't forsake me, Lord!"

Aaron alarmed at Maia's cries, ran to the sound of her voice and found her on the floor by Apollo's bed. He knew then that their greatest fears had found them.

"Maia," he said, interrupting her pleas for mercy, "listen to me. I need you to get Diana and take the train to Atlanta as we planned. I'll nurse Apollo and when he's better, we will join you there in a few days."

"No, Aaron, I can't! I won't leave my baby; he needs me," Maia replied with clenched fists that said she would not relent.

"All right, I'll go for the doctor, but I don't want Diana to stay in the house."

Aaron rushed through the next hours getting Diana and her things on the train amid her tears and confusion. "Why aren't we all going together, Tata?" she kept asking.

"Apollo is sick. Your Mama and I are going to get him well, and then we'll join you in Atlanta in less than a week," he answered. "Andrew Frierson, one of my lodge members, and his wife, Marsha, will meet your train when you get there."

With Diana safely on the train, Aaron rushed back home to see about Apollo.

"The doctor says he'll be here as soon as he can," Aaron assured Maia when he got back to the house.

Over the long hours that followed, Maia and Aaron discovered the portion of hell that is on earth. In all the horrors and suffering that they had experienced and witnessed over their lives, nothing compared or had prepared them for the anguish and despair that plagued them while caring for Apollo during his sickness. To watch their strong young son's body wracked with pain and fever and be helpless to ease it was almost more than they could bear.

"I'm here, Apollo," Maia said as she wiped the sweat from his trembling body.

"Help me, Tata!" Apollo screamed as his body arched in agony and delirium.

"I can't take it, Aaron!" Maia wailed frantically. "Seeing my boy lying there sick, I'm about to lose my mind."

"It's tearing me up, too, baby, but we got to be strong so we can take care of him," he said, putting his arm around her shoulder. "I'd gladly trade places with him if the Lord would let me."

Maia had already had three children taken from her. She was on the verge of breaking down, when a knock at the door brought her back from the brink.

"I'm sorry it took so long to get here," the doctor told Aaron and Maia. They had called for him the day before, but he had just arrived. "Give him these medicines, and then you'll have to wait it out. Hopefully the fever will break."

After three days, Apollo seemed better. The yellow tinge of his skin had faded.

"Mama, I want some water," Apollo said, rising up in the bed. "I'm thirsty. Can we go back to the island? I miss Boy." he asked, talking about one of Hercules's dogs.

"I've got some water right here," Maia said anxiously. "We can go see Boy as soon as you are feeling better."

Maia and Aaron felt some relief and looked each other in the eyes for the first time in four days. Their son was coming through the crisis. Except, sometime in the middle of the night, Apollo began to throw up blood; and by the hour when the sun rose in the morning, the center of Aaron's heart was gone. Maia sat in a chair beside her son's bed in a daze, wondering why the Lord wouldn't let her keep her children.

Aaron and Maia buried Apollo in the church cemetery. A few friends who hadn't left the city supported them in their grief. Aaron was despondent, as his mind filled with so many questions. What if they had stayed on Ossabaw? What if they had lived in another part of town? What if they had traveled to another state? Was he being punished for the lives he had taken in the war? Why couldn't it have been him instead?

Maia was just numb. It seemed that no matter how many times she had picked herself up, life would just knock her down again. Whenever she allowed herself to feel happiness, it was taken away. She had given birth five times and had only one child. Where was God in that she asked as her body rocked to the rhythm of the train. The silence and grief between Maia and Aaron was so thick in the air they could barely breathe; and when they arrived in Atlanta, they were both physically weak.

Prince Hall Freemasons were at the train station to help the families of their brothers from the Lowcountry, and Brother Andrew Frierson was there to meet Aaron and Maia. Diana had been staying with him and his family as she waited for her parents to arrive. When they arrived at Brother Frierson's home, Diana rushed open-armed to the door to greet them, only to be stopped in her tracks by the sorrow that clouded their faces.

"What's wrong, Mama and Tata?" she asked as panic spread across her face.

"I'm so sorry, Diana. Apollo didn't get better. Your brother was taken from us by the fever," Aaron said.

Diana fell into Maia's arms as her joy at seeing them was transformed into sadness and tears. Maia struggled to hold her up, barely having the strength to support her own weight from grief. Aaron choked at the sight of them and turned away to hide his tears.

The Liberty family did their best to comfort one another as the fall months rolled one after the other. Sometime in December, the newspapers announced that the epidemic had ended and that it was safe to return home to Savannah.

"There's no reason for us to rush back. The city is deserted, and most businesses have practically shut down," Aaron said to them as they sat around in the parlor at the Frierson home.

"You know you all can stay here for as long as you need," Andrew replied.

Maia couldn't find any words to express what she was feeling, so she stayed quiet.

The holiday season came and left without anyone noticing. But when January rolled around, Maia thought about the school year beginning.

"Do you want to enroll in a school here in Atlanta?" Maia asked Diana.

"No, Mama. I don't know anybody here, and I don't feel like meeting anybody new," Diana replied. "I just want to be left alone."

She spent most of her time humming soulful tunes on the veranda of the Frierson home. Even during the chilly mornings and evenings, she sang without words, for she knew no words that could express the grief and loneliness that passed from her heart to Maia's and then to Aaron's.

Maia wrote a letter to Hercules and Rachel to tell them of the tragedy.

Dear Mama, I am brokenhearted again from the death of my baby, feeling pain that burns from the top of my skin to the center of my bones. I escape the horror of it all in sleep, where my mind no longer has the will to dream. I don't know if fate has been more cruel or merciful to have let me have the years to love Apollo before he was taken from me. I had vowed to protect and hold on to these children with all my strength, but I was helpless and could only stand by and watch his spirit pulled from my hands by a evil yellow fever. I miss you both so much and wish I could turn back time be there on the island where we were all together. Pray for me, Mama, for only a miracle from God will get me through this.

Love, Maia.

The elections of 1876 signaled the end of Reconstruction, and Aaron knew his dreams of holding a political office in Savannah would never be realized.

One evening, as the Christmas holiday approached, Aaron took Maia's hand and said, "Would you take a walk with me?"

They put on their coats and stepped into the winter's chilled air. Instinctively, they tightened their grips on each other's hands, and by some miracle they reconnected and looked into each other's eyes. Each saw the person they loved in a way they hadn't for a very long time.

"We have Diana to love and look after," Aaron said to Maia.

"I know that, Aaron, but Diana is fourteen, and she wants to go to college," she said. "I want to know that our life together is not over."

Aaron pulled her to his chest and held onto her as if she were a lifeline that would keep him from drowning.

"We'll be happy again," he whispered in her ear. "I promise

you."

It was on Emancipation Day, January 1, 1877, five months after Apollo had died, when Maia said to everyone at the table, "Now that we've finished eating, I have a story for you."

"In Africa, there was a pride of lions that had been traveling in seach of water during a drought. On the journey, one of the male lion cubs strayed and was trampled by a herd of elephants. The mother lioness was distressed and wanted to stay in the place where the cub's spirit had been released, but she knew that without water they would all die. In a way, she thought it would be fitting for them all to die. But that night, as she watched her other cub sleeping, she saw his life flash before her eyes. She saw him grow older and stronger, she saw his mane flow out in great glory, and she saw him lead the pride and become its most fearless protector. That lioness knew that she had to nurture and preserve this cub's life in remembrance of her lost cub. The next morning, she stood waiting for the pride to rise, and the journey in search for water continued."

"That was a meaningful tale, Maia," Marsha said to break the silence after Maia finished speaking.

"Andrew and Marsha, I want to thank you both for saving my family," Maia said, shaking with emotion. "You opened your home to us at the lowest point of our lives."

"I know you would have done the same for us," Marsha said, grabbing Maia's hand to stop them from shaking.

"I thank God for you both," Maia continued. "You have nurtured each of us, done things for us that we didn't have the strength to do for ourselves, meeting our every need. But now we must go back to our home and get on with our lives."

Diana sat quietly tapping her feet under the table with relief. Aaron coughed to clear the lump in his throat before he stood up with his arms extended to Andrew who sat at the head of the table to his right. Andrew quickly got to his feet, and the two hugged as if they were blood brothers. Marsha and Maia joined them as they all embraced. Happiness, sadness, and love were all mixed together. Tears of hope fell from their eyes, hope that they would survive this tragedy as a family.

Chapter
Seven

When they returned home to Savannah, the house had an emptiness to it that could never be filled. But each member of the Liberty family did their best to curtail their melancholy lest it spill over on another. Maia received letters from Rachel and from Daphne Bailey. She read the letter from Rachel and Hercules, which expressed their sadness at Apollo's death; and the other one she placed with the unopened letter from Richard that Daphne had given her when she visited Bailey Estates. Maia couldn't think of anything that either of them could say that would mean something to her, so she left their letters unread.

"I got a letter from my mama today. She says she's praying for us and she's coming up for a visit real soon. She wants to see Diana graduate from the Beach Institute," Maia said as she boiled rice for dinner.

"Mama, write her back and tell her I joined the church choir, and they're gonna let me sing a solo," Diana said as she dropped down in a chair in the kitchen.

"You're awful quiet. Aaron, what are you reading over there?" Maia asked.

"I'm going over some new contracts, checking if the numbers add up," he answered.

"John says I should think about publishing a book of my stories since the printers are now refusing to print any black newspapers."

"That's just what we were talking about at the lodge meeting. Things are moving backwards for black folk in Georgia," Aaron remarked. "Henry was saying that he doesn't think blacks will ever be able to raise themselves up financially or socially without political power. Then he gave this speech about black people leaving Georgia and even the United States."

"Leave here to go where?" Maia asked over the sizzling of the shrimp.

"He's talking about emigrating back to Africa, but I've got my doubts. This is the only home I know about, and I'm gonnna hold on to the piece of land I have here instead of searching for something else in a foreign country that I don't know nothing about."

Aaron's thoughts drifted back to Hercules and how he had dreamed about returning to his motherland so many years ago. He shook the thoughts out of his head. The idea that even after emancipation they were all still slaves to time and chance made him feel powerless again.

"I'm Aaron Liberty," he had said to them. "I'm free to make my own fortunes wherever I choose."

***

A dream came true for the Liberty family in the spring of 1879.

"Mama, I got my letter from Fisk University in Nashville. I'm going to be admitted!" Diana sang, waving the letter in the air.

"That's such good news, Diana. I'm so happy for you," she said, forcing a smile on her face. She didn't know how she was going to live when Diana went away to school.

They spent the summer months shopping for a wardrobe and preparing for Diana to go to college. Diana was looking forward to having a fresh start where she would be independent, her own woman. No one would know her father or her mother or about her family on Ossabaw. She wouldn't feel as if eyes were watching her every movement. She could be free of the weights of her mother's disappointments and her father's expectations.

Diana had been a loner most of her life, not because she was shy or unfriendly, but because most of her acquaintances felt she was unapproachable or were intimidated by the strong personality and success of Aaron. Diana longed to be free of responsibility to anyone besides herself, not because she had been burdened with chores, but because she felt caged or chained sometimes by the emotions of her mother, which tugged at her whenever she got her blues. Diana loved her mother dearly, but sometimes the neediness she sensed in Maia made her want to run away.

***

"At first, I wanted to take the train by myself to Nashville. But now I'm so nervous, I'm glad you two insisted on coming," Diana said as the train got closer to Tennessee.

"You know there was no way I was going to let you go up there without me," Maia said. "I think you know me better than that."

On the first of day of September, the Libertys arrived at the boarding house near the college that housed the freshman female students. Diana and the young woman who would share a room came to the door at the same time.

Diana extended her hand to the small-framed girl who seemed too young to be coming to college and said, "Hello, my name is Diana Portunus Liberty."

The girl looked up at Diana, taking in her light complexion, the quality of her clothing, and was a bit hesitant. But the sincerity in Diana's eyes drew her in; and she took her hand, smiled, and said, "Hello, my name is Lena Terrell Jackson."

"It's a pleasure to meet you," Diana said, smiling back at her, feeling she had met her first friend.

"Where are from?" Lena asked on the way to the welcoming reception.

"I'm from Savannah, Georgia. How about yourself?" Diana asked.

"I'm from around here in Nashville," Lena said. "I'm here to become a teacher."

"That's a good vocation, my mama's a teacher, but I'm here to sing," Diana said, ready to fulfill her destiny.

The two young ladies sat together and got acquainted as they chatted freely at the reception that evening with their families before each said their emotional goodbyes.

"I'm going to miss you so much!" Maia said as she held Diana in a hug for nearly ten minutes.

"Write if you need anything," Aaron said, and then he filled her hand with the Liberty nickels he always kept in his pocket.

Diana and her roommate had very little in common. Lena came from a family with nothing to their names; Diana's had become well-off owning property. Lena was serious-minded and was at Fisk on a mission to become a teacher and return home; Diana was the butterfly that had finally gotten out of its cocoon and was there to study music and see how far away from home it could take her.

Unlike Lena, Diana made friends easily with the other students. The young men were attracted to her comeliness, and the young women were drawn to her sweet demeanor. Diana could not remember a time in her life when she felt so light and carefree. She felt so liberated that she decided that she no longer needed to state it. She dropped the last name the family had taken after the war and introduced herself as Diana Portunus. She made a commitment to herself that she would stay unattached, with no one to satisfy except herself.

Diana sat in her first class of the day, bubbling up inside from the lightness she felt. She couldn't remember a time when she felt more like singing. She strained to stay focused, knowing that the auditions for the Fisk School Choir were that afternoon. This opportunity was what she had been living for; she knew that this would be the beginning of her dreams coming true if she was chosen.

"My goodness, the room is already filled," Diana said nervously under her breath when she got to The Little Theatre.

She stood among the crowd of hopefuls that lingered at the door, waiting for their chance to sing.

Once each student received a number, Mr. Spence, the choir director, said, "May we have quiet, please? The auditions will now begin." Then a singer's voice could be heard from the small stage inside.

Diana had planned to sing "Michael Row the Boat Ashore." But as she listened to the other singers, she became panicky, and her heart was thumping at the top of her chest.

"What if I forget the words?" she murmured to herself just as her number was called.

Diana walked quickly to the stage, took a deep breath, closed her eyes, and began singing, "Kum ba ya, my Lord, kum ba yah. Kum ba ya, my Lord, kum by yah."

When Diana finished, she opened her eyes and absorbed the gaze of the whole room. Then she felt the heat of embarrassment.

Mr. Spencer broke the silence when he said, "Thank you, Miss Portunus."

She slipped out the back stage door. Diana felt sick as she rushed home to her room.

"How did I sound? What did I do wrong?" she asked herself as she looked at her reflection in the looking glass. "If I don't make it into the choir, there is no other reason for me to be here."

Diana laid down on her bed and tried to drift off to sleep so she wouldn't have to think about how everyone just looked at her with blank faces. But after a few minutes Lena, came into their dorm room.

"Aren't you coming down to dinner, Di? Everybody's talking about your audition today," she said, standing over Diana.

"No, I don't want to see anybody right now," Diana answered.

"Why not?" Lena said. "The talk is you were the star of the freshman class."

"Really?" Diana asked, sitting up. "They all looked at me like I made a fool of myself."

"They were just surprised that you had such a good voice; they say you gave them chills on their arms. You're gonna make it, Di, so let's eat," Lena said impatiently.

Diana felt her whole body relax, and then her stomach grumbled. "Yeah, come on, I'm starving," Diana said, jumping up and walking ahead of Lena as her hopes and dreams came back.

Word of the magnificent mezzo-soprano in the Fisk School Choir spread to George White and Frederick Loudin, who were in the process of reorganizing the Jubilee Singers. The troupe had been disbanded by school administrators earlier in the year after three exhausting tours across the country and throughout Europe. Diana was taken aback when she saw Mr. White sitting in the parlor when she got home from class.

"Hello, Miss Portunus. I'm Mr. White. I'm working in a joint venture with Frederick Loudin to put together another group of Fisk Jubilee Singers," he explained. "We learned of your audition with Mr. Spencer, and I would like to extend an invitation for you to be part of the group."

Diana was finally hearing the words she had fantasized about over and over in her mind.

"I would love to be one of the Jubilee Singers!" she responded with enthusiasm. "It has been my dream for a long time."

"Wonderful," he said. "But you must understand that this group is no longer a part of Fisk College. We will be going on tour very shortly, and you will most certainly have to withdraw from your studies at the school."

"Mr. White, being a part of the Jubilee Singers was my only reason for being here," Diana said with sincerity.

"Well, then it's settled," White said. "We will expect you at our rehearsal hall tomorrow."

Diana's next decision was whether she should tell her parents. They wouldn't be pleased about her leaving school. It didn't really matter; she knew she was going regardless. She got to the rehearsal early the next day, singing the whole way to warm up her voice for practice.

"Welcome, Diana," Mr. White said when she walked into the room.

Diana was surprised to see how plain the rehearsal hall was; it was simply a room with chairs arranged in a half-circle. Mr. White gave her some musical arrangements to look at while they waited for the other members to join them.

"Hello, hello, hello, everyone," Mr. White said as the other singers walked in together.

Diana was awed by the arrival of original singers Frederick Loudin, Maggie Porter, Ella Sheppard, Addie Lewis, George Barrett, Jennie Jackson, Patti Malone, Robert Hall, and David Mallory.

"I hope you have some new music, George," one of them announced.

Diana listened as the singers talked and teased while Mr. White -George, as they called him- handed them the new music sheets. Diana began to notice that Frederick was the head of the group and detected an air of self-importance coming from Maggie. But it was

David, who she assumed was a newcomer like herself, who kept his attention boldly locked on her.

David's eyes spoke volumes, asking for much and offering everything. Diana sized him up in short glances. He was dressed well, tall with broad shoulders, skin the color of butterscotch, hair short and curly, and his eyes were a clear rich brown like molasses and they were stuck on her. It was only George's call to begin that gave her a welcomed reprieve from his constant stare.

George motioned for their attention. "For the new members, and a reminder to the veterans, there is a high level of commitment required from a Jubilee Singer. In our mission, the voice and tone are used to pierce the mind of the audience until they feel the words and their souls cry out from understanding the sufferings of slavery."

Then George lifted his arms to conduct. He directed them through a warm-up, and then they ran through songs from the previous the rehearsal hall was; "The Lord's Prayer," "I've Been Redeemed," "Steal Away," "Golden Slippers," "Swing Low," "Nobody Knows the Trouble I See," and "Balm in Gilead." Diana kept up as best she could, having to read some of the songs she didn't know, but she got a few nods of approval from George and Ella.

"For this fourth tour, we are adding a new song," George said. "I've given you all the arrangement for "Go Tell It on the Mountain.""

They rehearsed for about three hours until George stopped and said, "I've been moved, you all may go."

Diana was exhausted and amazed that she had actually sung with the Jubilee Singers. Her dream was coming true. The group dispersed quickly without much conversation.

A voice from behind her said, "You are one of us now."

Diana turned around to see David with his arms wide open as if he expected an embrace. Instead, she extended one hand, and he took it and brought it to his lips for a soft kiss. Diana could feel the sensual heat that radiated from all around David, and she was drawn to it as much as her instincts told her to keep her distance.

"May I see you home?" he asked.

"I would be honored," she said.

On the short walk home, Diana learned that David was born in Nashville, lived nearby with his Aunt Lilly, both of his parents were dead, and any other siblings of his had long been separated before the war.

"You and I are going to be inseparable," David told her at the door of the house.

"Oh, and why is that?" Diana asked.

"Because now that I've met my future wife, I'm not going to let her out of my sight," he answered with a wide smile.

Diana smiled back. She liked his confidence, and he had the prettiest teeth she had ever seen.

"Well, Mr. Mallory," Diana said, "you may have to keep searching. I'm not sure if I'll have time to get married. I've got a lot I want to do first."

"I'm not worried, Diana. I'm a patient man," he said as he turned and walked away.

Diana watched David's back as he strolled down the sidewalk. She never had a man pursue her before, most probably thought they didn't have a chance with Aaron around, and she wasn't sure what to do to about it.

Chapter Eight

There were only six weeks before the troupe would leave on tour, and Diana's excitement was only contained by her apprehension over not writing home to tell her mama and tata. Lena watched her plan and prepare for the trip and was happy for her, but she was sad to see her new friend leave. She couldn't help but feel envious of Diana. From the outside, it seemed Diana had led a magical life and no misfortunes had ever touched her life, and with her own long list of struggles, it seemed unfair.

"I wonder why some people get the roses and others just get scratched by the thorns," Lena wondered out loud.

"Come on, girl, and stop daydreaming. I'm starving," Diana said as she pulled Lena to her feet from her desk.

"I bet you have never seen one day without food," Lena said as they went to dinner.

Diana thought about it, and she realized that she had never been hungry. "I guess I've been blessed," she said, taking notice of David waiting to walk with them.

David was a determined suitor in his quest for Diana's affections. He walked her to rehearsals, took her to lunches and music recitals around the school, and gave her wildflowers he picked from his aunt's garden. Diana liked David. She thought he was very handsome and fun to be with, but she didn't want a relationship that might come in between or complicate her future career. She had always been showered with so much love that she never hungered for it or felt a need for it. She just wanted to sing. After much thought, Diana sat down and wrote a letter to her family.

Dear Mama and Tata, so much has happened since I saw you last. I tried out for the Fisk choir, and before I joined that group, Mr. George White, the director of the Fisk Jubilee Singers, invited me to join his troupe. It was more than I could have hoped for so soon. The singers will be leaving on a tour around the world in just over one month, and I wanted you to know I will be traveling with them. Please don't worry about me. I will be fine, and I will write often. I love you both very much, Diana

"I can't believe it!" Maia said, stunned by Diana's letter. It was hard enough for her to know that she was living in another state, much less traveling around the world.

"I'm not sure if she's old enough to go that far away alone," Aaron added.

"I ought to run up there in my bare feet and bring her back home," Maia said. But she knew what it was like to be trapped in a house with someone with love as the justification, and she didn't want to do that to the only child she had left.

"As tight as we want to hold her, you and I understand her need to be free and to roam God's creation on her own terms," Aaron said, squeezing Maia's hand.

Maia decided to put her fears in the bottom of her shoe and prayed that God would keep Diana in his front pocket.

Dear Diana, I want you to experience all the good fortune that this world has to offer you. I accept that I can't keep my precious songbird in a cage; she has to fly, and the world is waiting to hear her voice. Go with our blessings, and we will miss you until you return. Love, Mama

***

Frederick Loudin was emphatic in his objections to racism and discrimination and billed the circuit as a civil rights tour to support the Civil Rights Act of 1875. The Fisk Jubilee Singers planned to tour across the country, Canada, Europe, Asia, Australia, and New Zealand. Over the next two years, they first traveled by train out to the West Coast; up into Canada; down through the South, where Jim Crow was taking hold; and up to the East Coast.

Dear Mama and Tata, You wouldn't believe the large crowds of people who come to hear us sing wherever we go. I must also say I have never been this cold in all of my life! I have seen snow piles as high as my own head in the Northwest all the way up to Canada. We have even gone to the White House, and President Garfield gave us great compliments on our performance. I miss both of you very much. Love, Diana

Maia wrote to Diana about Aaron and the churches he was building in nearby Charleston, how her stories were being published in newspapers outside of Georgia, and that she was teaching part-time in a public school. Diana wrote to Maia about David, who wanted to court her, but she told her mother that she wanted to stay focused on her singing career. She found that she preferred the distant adoration of an audience while she stood on stage; it had its limits, and she could control it. In September 1881, Diana received a letter from her mama that made her ache to be back at home.

My Dear Diana, I pray that this letter finds you in good health and happiness, for I sit down to write with my heart broken once again. On August 27, a storm like we had never seen came over Ossabaw and my beloved Tata, Hercules, was washed away into the sea. Tidal waves taller than two men rushed past the shore, and waves flooded over and into the house on Bailey Grove, and it collapsed with most of it flowing back into the ocean. Your nana was here with me visiting when the storm began to brew, and she is safe but inconsolable. She wanted to return to the island to search for him, but we have learned that he is gone and there is nothing to return to. I hope that God has mercy and takes him far across the waters to his home in Africa. As for Savannah, there was much damage here from the fierce winds and rain; roofs were ripped from the tops of building all through the city. Many lives have been lost, and your tata has been very busy with the repairs. Stay safe my child. I miss you with all that is within me. Love, Mama

The time on the road across the states had begun to wear on the Fisk Jubilee Singers, including Frederick, who had had a wife and family at home. Even though they respected one another's talents, there were intense personality conflicts among some in the group that were aggravated by the tiring work schedule. But on stage, audiences were impressed by the excellence and professionalism of their performances.

David's feelings toward Diana grew stronger as the tour continued, and he managed to keep Diana well within his sights, and other men who made advances to her at a distance. But her indifference to him was hard to swallow at times. He began to ask himself if what he felt was true love or a need to possess someone who was unattainable. He spent hours trying to pinpoint the nature of his attraction. She was beautiful, had tremendous talent, and exuded a softness that people wanted to touch; yet she was out of his reach. There were instances when he entertained himself with other women and put forth no efforts to conceal it, but Diana remained unperturbed and even seemed relieved from his hovering.

Near the end of November 1881, an unfortunate accident occurred while the troupe performed in New York. George fell off the stage while directing the choir and was seriously injured. His conditon further irritated his rheumatism.

"Listen, everybody," Frederick said at rehearsal. "The report from the hospital is that George will probably be unable to continue on the global tour."

"So what does this mean for us?" Maggie asked above the grumblings of the group. "We're not even halfway through the tour, and we're making more money than we ever have."

"My plan is that we go forward on the tour without him," Frederick said. "We all want to perform, it's in our blood, and we can definitely use the proceeds."

"I'm in agreement with that decision, Fred," Addie said. "We need to put food on our tables and clothes on the backs of our families."

Not everyone felt the same. There was much contention. Egos clashed, and the group lost three singers; but they were able to reach a settlement. After a recess over the summer, they would move forward on the tour, with Frederick taking over the leadership position and the task of finding replacement singers to reorganize what they would call the Loudin Fisk Jubilee Singers.

For Diana, the timing was a welcome respite. She missed her family and wanted to go home and was glad to have some peace away from the group. The constant bickering between Maggie and Frederick left her questioning whether she wanted to remain a Jubilee Singer or pursue singing with another group.

"Why don't we get married over the summer?" David asked Diana, pressuring her to commit to him before they separated.

"That's the last thing on my mind right now. I'm only twenty years old," she told him before she left New York. "I'm not ready to settle down and raise babies for the rest of my life. All I know how to do is sing, and that's what I'm gonna do."

"Well, I'm staying in New York," he said. "You know where to find me when you're ready to be my wife, but I can't promise you how long I'll wait."

David's words were thrown out to hurt Diana, but they only provided her with a reprieve. She had become fond of David, maybe even loved him as much as she was able, but she knew it wasn't enough for him. He wanted a wife and a quiet and nurturing home life. She loved performing and the stage, along with the adulation from a distant and anonymous crowd. Diana looked forward to the time she would spend at home, where she could have some peace from all the pressure and his ultimatums.

***

Maia and Aaron had received the letter from Diana telling them of her return to Savannah. They had missed her so much, and they waited eagerly to hear the noise of their child in the house. Aaron had never really recovered from the loss of Apollo, and his unyielding grief had separated him from Maia. Over the years, their conversations had grown shorter, and their time spent doing things apart from each other had grown longer. Although Aaron had found a beautiful wife, built a successful construction business, and provided for his family, he was still discontent.

There were voids that Maia could not even imagine, empty spaces that grew even larger after Apollo died. Aaron had done the things that he had been warned about when he was a young boy. He had wanted too much and had wished for things he could never have. It was evident from the hollows inside him where his dreams once lived. Dreams that vanished at different times over his life, dreams of a large family of his own, dreams of becoming a political leader in Savannah, dreams of accumulating greater wealth, dreams of seeing his boy grow up to be a man, dreams of Apollo being a star baseball player, dreams of standing up at his son's wedding, and dreams of holding his grandchildren.

It was never Aaron's plan to be unfaithful to Maia; it was only a means to an end. He first saw Eve Baker serving meals at one of Bishop Henry Turner's Back to Africa meetings at the Prince Hall Lodge. She wasn't what you would call a pretty girl, but she was pleasant to look at. She made eye contact whenever she spoke, and she talked a lot. Eve worked hard to make each person feel like they were the most important person in the room. She needed the extra money that she earned from tips, and she wasn't shy about mentioning it.

"How you doing, Mr. Liberty, can I get you anything special?" she asked, flirting with Aaron, knowing who he was and how successful he was.

"I can't complain." he replied, "How about you? Would you like to get some more steady work?"

"I need as much work as I can get," she answered with a teasing glance.

Aaron watched Eve carry the heavy platters from the kitchen, taking notice of the strength in her arms and the toned muscles in her legs. He felt the energy of her youth revitalizing him.

When the meeting was over, Aaron put three of the Liberty head nickels he always carried in his pockets in Eve's hand. On his way out, he whispered in her ear, "Come over to my office soon. I have a job for you."

When Aaron took Eve into the rooming house, there was no emotion involved, not even lust. He saw her as someone who would give him another chance at immortality, someone who would bear him another child. She would give him a strong son, one who would be unbeatable by any circumstance or disease.

Eve saw Aaron as an older man. At 44 years old, he was more than twice her age, but she thought he was still good-looking. He could help her to a better life, buy her nice things, and maybe even pay for her to go to school.

Aaron was generous with Eve. He gave her whatever she asked for: a place of her own, new clothes, and money to go to beauty school. In return, he only asked her to be available to him when he wanted. It was only five months into their arrangement when Eve gave Aaron the unfortunate news.

"I'm sorry to tell you this, but I'm pregnant, Aaron," Eve said regretfully after she walked into his office. "I asked around to see where I could find a doctor who can take care of it before I came so I would know the cost of the operation."

Aaron pretended to be unnerved by her unexpected announcement, but inside he was overjoyed. His prayer had been answered. His only concern was how to keep it all a secret.

"I can't risk something happening to you by some butcher in a dark room," Aaron said as he sat down beside her. "Have the baby, and I'll take care of both of you."

***

When Diana's letter came, it was only four months before the expected birth of Aaron and Eve's baby. Maia and Aaron went to the train station to meet Diana. Their love and concern for her was the bond holding them together.

"She looks so grown up, honey," Maia said when Diana got off the train.

"Yes, indeed she does," Aaron muttered.

They were both impressed by how mature and sophisticated she looked after two years on the road with the Jubilee Singers. Tears of joy rolled down Diana's face at the sight of her mama and tata through the window as they waited in front of the train station. She had been so anxious to get out from under their sheltering, but now she couldn't think of any other place she would rather be. Having been on her own, she could see that she hadn't appreciated the tender loving care that she had been covered with.

"Excuse me, please, I need to get by," Diana said, unable to stop herself from rushing past the older man lumbering down the train steps in front of her.

"Mama and Tata, I'm so glad to be home! I missed y'all so much," Diana said as she threw her arms around them for a heart-felt hug.

"We missed you too, baby. I'm happy you made it back to us safely," Maia said.

"Yes, it's so good to see you," Aaron added.

"I've so much to tell you," Diana said.

"Well, wait until we get home. Your Nana wants to hear about all the places you've gone to; and she's made you a big feast of rice and okra, shrimp, fried chicken, and black-eyed peas," Maia said.

"I'm getting full just hearing about it," Diana said.

They rode the streetcar down to West Broad Street, wearing their smiles in silence as Diana soaked in the sights that had changed since she had last been there. As they turned onto Liberty Street, Diana noticed that the city was different to her yet familiar at the same time.

The family spent an evening of fellowship that left them all more satisfied than they had been since the tragedies began six years ago. Nevertheless, by the next morning, Diana was bored and restless and wanted to do something. Maia had given up teaching to care for Rachel after Hercules had been washed away in the storm. She sometimes submitted stories for printing in *The Savannah Tribune*, but her life had become quiet and contained, and it had been years since she had even looked for God. Rachel was 68 years old now, but she felt more tired than her age. She was tired of standing up, bending down, and bearing against the storms of her life.

After breakfast, Maia and Rachel were surprised when Diana said, "Let's plant a garden, Nana, like we used to."

"I don't know, chile, I can't grow nothing anymore," Rachel replied.

"Yes, you can, Nana," Diana told her. "You, too, Mama. Let's get out of this house and do something."

"It sounds good to me," Maia said as she pulled off her apron. "It's time we did something more with ourselves. I just might find God out there."

The three generations of women went out to work the land, and all looked different. Diana was dressed in overalls and one of Apollo's ball caps. Maia wore loose-fitting pants and a one of Aaron's old shirts with the sleeves rolled up. Rachel tied up her hair in a scarf and wore a large flowing skirt that landed just above her ankles. The women were so much alike, but they didn't know it. Each of them carefully guarded their hearts, albeit for different reasons.

Rachel learned early that close relationships and feeling too much was dangerous, and you always ended up hurt. Maia felt love deeply and shared it openly, but the losses of her children hurt her so much that she had to shut down her emotions just to get through the day. Diana had been overwhelmed by so much love that she feared it would smother her and that if she loved someone, he might also feel that way.

"So what do we need to get this garden started?" Diana asked, clapping her hands together inside the tool shed.

"Just grab something you can dig with," Rachel said, grabbing a small shovel. "We need to loosen up the soil first."

"This feels good," Maia said as they dug side-by-side, turning over the earth for their garden in the back of the house. "Now, what are we gonna plant out here?"

"We'll figure that out later," Diana said, breaking the ground around her feet with a pick.

Rachel chanted while they worked, and it felt like they were back on Ossabaw. Then Diana sang *"I'm Gonna Shout All Over God's Heaven,"* and then Maia smiled because she could see God all around her again.

The bond between the three women grew stronger as they spent the next month tending to their garden. They planted vegetables and herbs, pulled out weeds, and kept the soil moist with water. Some days, they just came out to watch the seedlings grow. But the tranquility that they created for themselves was disturbed when Diana reconnected with some old school friends at a church social. That's where she heard the rumors circulating about her father and some woman named Eve, and the baby she carried. She couldn't imagine her tata putting anyone else above his family.

Diana kept her silence for a few days, unsure if she should bring upset into the house. She wasn't even sure if wanted to be around when the hell of it broke loose after the baby was born. Finally, Diana decided that she would go straight to Aaron about the stories.

When Diana stepped into the small storefront office of Liberty Construction, Aaron could sense the reason for her visit. He now realized that a secret like his would eventually be revealed, and his fantasy of having a child without his family knowing or being hurt was far from reality.

Aaron rose from behind his desk to greet Diana and said, "You should have let me know you were coming today. We could have gone out to lunch."

"Is it true, Tata? Is that girl, Eve, having your child?" Diana asked, not wasting time with pleasantries as she looked deep in his dark eyes for an answer to why he would hurt her mama.

"I know I can't expect you to understand what I have done, but it is true. Eve is having my child. I didn't mean to hurt or dishonor my family," Aaron said, looking away, not wanting her to see his shame. "I have worked my whole life to be worthy of your mama's love and respect, but this other need was uncontrollable. I want to leave a part of myself in this world when I die, or this lifetime of hard work won't make any sense to me."

Instinctively, Diana covered her ears, not wanting to hear anymore.

"What about Mama? She's already suffered enough pain and disappointment!" Diana protested, feeling the betrayal.

"Listen, Di, I don't love Eve. But the space left by Apollo was too big, and I just needed to fill it. I'm selfish. I knew it was wrong, but I refused to think about it or how y'all might feel. I only cared about what I wanted at the time."

Diana had come there to tell Tata how horrible he was, but as she turned to leave, she realized that she felt sympathy for him and could not begrudge him any relief he got from his heartache. She didn't know what to do, but she was sure that when his indiscretion was inevitably exposed to Mama and Nana, it would not come from her lips.

Chapter Nine

"Come on in this kitchen, chile. I need to show you how to can food," Rachel said to Diana. "That way you can take something good to eat back with you when you go back on the road with the other Jubilee Singers."

"You can teach me, Nana, but I don't have room to carry any back with me. We travel light."

"The only thing Di wants to do in the kitchen is eat, Mama," Maia said, pushing her daughter out of the way so she could help clean the vegetables.

"I can cook, Mama. I just can't see myself as somebody's wife or mama for a long time."

"Take care you don't end up growing old by yourself, chile. It ain't no way to live," Rachel said, missing her Hercules.

When the fall came, the garden yielded a harvest of corn, beets, squash, tomatoes, and okra that had been made much more delicious with the added love and care that had been showered over them by the Liberty women. Each meal that was served with food from the garden felt like a celebration for their hard work.

"I'm going to start picking the vegetables with y'all in the morning," Aaron said, following them out the door. "I don't want to keep eating them without helping y'all with the work."

"The hard work was done a long time ago. Now we just reaping what we've sown," Maia said.

'That's true, but give me a chance to make it up you all," Aaron said, waiting to get started.

"You're in a mighty good mood this morning," Rachel told him as they headed to the garden.

"I guess it's all this good food I'm eating," he answered cheerfully.

The women couldn't help but notice how much happier and more relaxed he was when he got home every evening. Diana hid the smirk on her face. She knew that much of his improved attitude was because of the son that Eve had delivered on the last day of August. She had also heard that the boy was named Roman.

In late October when the seasons changed and the days grew getting shorter, Diana got a wire from Frederick Loudin. He wrote that he had filled out the troupe and that they would reunite in New York for rehearsals after the new year.

"In a few months it'll be time for me to get back on the road again, Mama," Diana said to Maia one morning as they gathered the last of their harvest.

"The time has gone by so quickly," Maia said, patting her on the shoulder. "The growing season is over for now."

Diana had enjoyed the period at home, but she was ready to leave Savannah. She felt as if she was part of Tata's betrayal by not telling her mama about his son, and it made her uncomfortable. There were even times when she wondered how her mama and nana could not know, with the word spread all over town. Anyway, it was out of her hands. She was ready to get back to her destiny: singing and performing on stage.

Diana stayed close to home and didn't attend many social functions for the rest of the year. The conversations between her and her mama and Nana had moved from the garden to the veranda and then inside into the parlor as the weather cooled.

"You meet so many people when you're traveling," Diana said as they sat in the warmth of the hearth. "Seems like they think they know you after the show is over."

"Be careful out there, Di. Men always trying to take advantage of a single woman," Rachel warned.

"David is always around; he doesn't let any of them get too close," Diana said. "He acts like we already engaged."

"I think you should look for a man who has his feet planted in one place," Rachel advised her, "not one running all over the country."

"Don't even think about settling down until you are done roaming around the world," Maia said. "Having a family changes your life. All you do will be for them until their grown."

Then Diana asked them, "What if a man spends time with other women? Is he still a good man, or should I end things with him?"

"Things like that are not so cut and dry," Rachel said. "A good man takes care of his home and respects his wife. Besides that, each wrongdoing has to be mulled over before doing anything. Sometimes a man is better than his actions say; sometimes he's worse."

"If a man and woman love each other the way they should, then there's no room for another woman," Maia said.

Diana thought about what they both said. She watched her tata carefully for a few days. She saw that he did take care and respect her mama and concluded that despite what he had done, he was better than his actions.

At the end of February, Aaron and Maia took Diana to catch the train returning to New York. The visit had been good for all of them. Diana learned more about life and love than she knew before, Maia had time to share with her baby and saw that she had become a woman, and Aaron had some of his burden of secrets lightened. The hugs they shared were full of a new understanding of one another, and their parting tears mixed with the drops of the chilly rain that blew across the tracks, marking the end of the winter season.

***

The rhythm of the train lulled Diana into a daydream; her head was filled with imaginings of the cities that lay ahead of them on the tour. She had written to David to let him know when she would be arriving, and he had assured her that he would be at the station when she got to the city. When the train finally pulled into the station, she saw him through the window. His eyes searched among the passengers getting off the train as she made her way to the exit. *He is good-looking,* she thought to herself. And while she had to admit that she did not love David as a wife should, she had missed him, she loved the attention, and he kept the other interested men out of her hair.

The Jubilee Singers spent several months in rehearsal, working to perfect the harmony with the new singers. Their voices were coming together nicely, but power struggles and petty jealousies still tore at the fiber of the group. Frederick had to put those problems to the side to accomplish the things that he knew they were capable of.

"I think we can benefit from a tour through the States to put the finishing touch on our performance before we travel to England for the first leg of the world tour," he announced after rehearsal.

"How long and how many cities?" Maggie asked. "It's a hassle touring in the States, and we don't make half the money."

"It should take about a year. And with all the responsibilities of leading the group and organizing the business affairs, it is becoming quite cumbersome for me. So to lighten the load, I've asked my wife, Harriet, to join us to assist in the management of the business end."

"I know she has your best interests at heart, but what about the rest of us?" Maggie complained in a low voice.

"We have enough problems traveling with the spread of segregation, so I hope we will at least be able to come together as a group," Frederick said, ending the discussion.

"I'm just anxious to get to all the cities and countries that I've seen in magazine pictures," Diana said to David, "even though I'm scared about sailing across the Atlantic Ocean to get to London. I've always been able to see land from the short boat trips I've been on."

"This will be a lot different from those," David said. "There will be many days with no land in sight. But don't worry, I'll take care of you."

Things were changing in cities across the country, especially in the South. For the group, finding accommodations in hotels and eating in restaurants were new problems they could do without. By the start of 1884, the Jubilee Singers were ready to leave the States and the segregation that added a sour note to their concerts.

The singers boarded a steamship sailing to England for a six-year world tour. Diana would be sharing her cabin with Annie, who was one of the more colorful members of the group of singers. She was one of the few members whose parents had never been slaves, but she had lived through some hard times working as a seamstress in Philadelphia. She had been married once, but she said he had turned out to be the wrong man for her. She hid her pain behind a happy and boisterous disposition; but when she sang, the emotions from her life experiences poured through her contralto voice and brought many people to tears.

"I'm getting tired of being stuck on this ship. It's so lonely sometimes," Diana said to Annie as they rested in their cabin. The isolation on the steamer was taking a toll on her.

"You probably missing your folks at home is all," Annie told her.

"I guess so," Diana replied. She did miss the comfort and affection of her Mama and Tata, and her thoughts of Apollo would sometimes leave her feeling downhearted.

"David is here at your beck and call. Why don't you go out and have some fun?" Annie asked. "You're young, and you don't need to be cooped up in this room all the time."

"He seems to have found some others to occupy his time," Diana said exasperated.

The normal human urges of youth were keeping her awake at night, and David's constant closeness made her feel as if she couldn't get enough air into her lungs. In his own frustration, David would sometimes amuse himself with other women, and Diana would become jealous, not of his attentions to other women, but because of his freedom to love on someone without any responsibility or risk on his part. Diana felt as if she would explode, and her curiosity had long since reached its peak.

Sensing that Annie still lay awake, Diana asked, "Annie, do you know how to be with a man and not have baby?"

Annie laughed out loud for a minute. "There are no guarantees, but there are things that you and the man can do to make it less likely."

Diana listened attentively to every word. She didn't see why she couldn't have the pleasure from a man just because she didn't want to marry.

The next evening after dinner, Diana pulled David away from the group. "Why don't you take me on a tour of the ship and then your cabin room," she said, holding his arm close to her body.

"We have plenty of time to see this ship. Why don't I show you may cabin first?" David answered, feeling the heat of her body.

Inside his room, David wrapped Diana tight in his arms, and she gave him her approval with a kiss. David had thought Diana was afraid of love and that his patience and coaxing had finally conquered her fears. But Diana, on the hand, was happy and pleased to have found that she could have what she wanted without giving up her life to get it.

Once the steamship arrived in London, the group was met with royal carriages that carried them to their hotel. Diana explored the city in the day after rehearsal, performed in the Jubilee concerts in the evening, and discovered physical pleasures with David at night. He wanted her to be his wife, but he had learned not to push and was more than satisfied with the way things were for now. Besides, he already thought of Diana as his, and they would marry when they returned to the States.

The group traveled by train to Ireland and Great Britain and was always transported in royal or imperial carriages around town. Two years passed quickly. With the Jubilee Singers appearing in concerts almost every night, they had gone from being treated like second-class citizens in the Southern United States to being treated like royalty in Europe. They had never been more sought after, and their increased popularity had led to the development of a number of imitation Jubilee Singing groups touring at home in the States.

At the end of March 1866, Diana boarded the SS. Orient steamship bound for Melbourne, Australia, for a voyage that would take six weeks. The first part of the journey was under gray skies and cold rains, and it seemed to Diana that the waves grew larger with each passing day. Her head and insides had begun to sway with the ship.

"Come on, you need to get some air," David said, standing at the door of Diana's cabin.

"Just looking at the water makes me sick," she told him, the expanse of the ocean was too much for her to take in at times, and there were days when she refused to leave her cabin.

"There's something you need to see, something you may never get a chance to see again," David said, coaxing Diana to come up on the deck when the voyage had passed the halfway point.

"This is something to see," Diana said to David when she saw the seals and the dolphins swimming in the sea, and the vision of them lifted her spirits.

The color of the water held her captive as she looked deep down into the abyss. It appeared to be melted glass in varying mixtures of greens and blues for as far as her eyes could see.

As they came closer to Melbourne, the sea had become the most beautiful of blues. David said, "I'm going to buy you a stone in this color for you to wear in a necklace, so you will never forget our time on this ship."

"I don't need a stone to remember this ship," she said, turning toward him to give him a soft kiss on his lips.

"I guess not, but I'm buying you one anyway," he said, pulling her closer to him.

The group was escorted to the finest hotel in the city, the Grand Hotel, and Diana was glad to be on dry land again. When the whirlwind of their arrival had subsided, she took some time for herself and sat down and wrote:

Dear Mama, I miss you so much and think of you and Nana often. I trust you both are keeping your hands busy in the soil. I imagine that the garden is as pretty and tastes as good as it did with our first harvest. I was so relieved to stand on solid ground when we got to Melbourne; there were many days when I didn't think I could stand another day on the ship. Yet it was all worth it. We have been welcomed as royalty and treated with great regard. It feels like a dream! We gave a private concert for the most prominent citizens in the city, and they extended invitations to us to dine at their estates. And on the last day of May, there was an unbelievable reception at the Grand Hotel before a private concert. They have a YMCA here, and we have our rehearsals there. The last concert we gave was before seven thousand people, and I almost cried when they gave us such strong applause after our performance. I wish that you and Tata and Nana could be here and see this country and its strange colored people that rub noses in greeting. Keep me in your prayers as you are in mine, Love Diana

Frederick and Harriet capitalized on the group's popularity in Australia, and the Loudin Jubilee Singers performed three and a half profitable years there. They earned close to 500,000 American dollars, which included concerts in Sidney, Brisbane, and New Zealand. The music and the singing were so powerful that even the most skeptical of patrons were moved by it. They could feel the suffering and the struggle of the negro; and for a time, they opened the doors of their cities and their pockets to the Jubilee Singers in sympathy.

Diana was mesmerized by the wealth and ambience that surround them in Europe and in Australia and toyed with thoughts of staying there and not returning home to the States. The day before they were to set sail on the tour to Asia, Diana received a letter from home.

Dear Diana, I received your latest letter today, and it made me feel a happiness I have not felt in a long time. I can see all the things that you tell me about in your letters so clearly, sometimes I think I am actually seeing them through your eyes. I'm glad you are there now; things are not so well here. I am sad to tell you that your Nana passed away. There is another civil war starting in this country, but this time it's between the whites and us negroes. There

have been lynchings and vicious attacks on us for no reason. Nana was so afraid that we might be made slaves again
that when she saw the cross burning in the church yard, her
heart just gave out. We buried her on the colored side of
Laurel Grove Cemetery. I look hard every day to see God,
and what I see most is the devil. I am so thankful that you
are blessed right now to be away from the hate and horror
that has made its home in Savannah. My love for you had
a beginning, but it has no end. I miss you more than you
could ever know. Love Mama

It was with mixed emotions that the group left Australia. It had
been a unique experience, and they had made friends they would
never forget, but there was still much ahead of them on the world
tour. On October 25, 1889, Diana boarded the *S.S. Orizaba* to Cey-
lon and Colombo, just south of India. They crossed rough waters
before arriving in Calcutta in December. Grateful to touch land
again, Diana looked into the faces of the people with fascination
as they stared back with a mutual curiosity. She remembered that
Frederick had told the troupe that they were the first negro ensemble to tour India.

They received more rave reviews and were met with even larger
audiences in Bombay. When they came to the stage in the concert
hall for their second performance, they saw that it was so full that
some of the audience members sat at the rear of the stage. The
singers were buoyed by the energy of the audience and delivered
a magnificent performance that was rewarded with roof-raising
applause. Diana was in awe. This was beyond her wildest dreams,
and she wanted time to stand still long enough for her to memorize
every detail to write back home about it.

Dear Mama, It pierced my heart to hear that Nana is gone, and it makes me sad that you have to endure so much suffering. I wish I could have been by your side at her funeral. I miss you more each day, but I am so fortunate to have this opportunity to see the world. India is the most mysterious of places; the women are most amazing. They wear a fancy dresses called saris, which are unstitched and draped around their bodies. But what catches my eye is the beautiful jewelry that they wear from their heads and ears to their necks, on their hands, and even on their feet. Mama, you would not believe the Taj Mahal, and I don't have the words to describe it. It's a tomb made out of white marble by an emperor for his third wife, and its like heaven built on earth. What is so special is that they allowed us to sing inside the temple. We sang "Steal Away to Jesus" and "We Shall Walk Through the Valley," and it was a religious experience that I am blessed to have witnessed. The next time I write to you, it will be from China. Love, Diana

As they journeyed to Hong Kong, Diana stared out into the horizon from the steamship, searching for guidance in her decisions as the world tour drew to an end. The group had filled concert halls to capacity; and thanks to Frederick and Harriet's business acumen, they had all earned enough money to be comfortable for a long time. For some in the group, the glamor of touring and performing had faded, and they were tired after six years of constant work. But Diana was the youngest in the ensemble, and her appetite had only increased for more. She also found herself spending more time trying to figure out how to break ties with David, who kept her ears filled with plans about settling down when they got home. Diana was content with the way things were. What was so wrong with traveling, singing, and making lots money while doing it?

The group sang to packed houses in China, and then in Japan, although Diana found it odd that most of the people in the Orient audiences were Europeans. On April 3, 1890, the singers boarded the *S.S. Rio de Janeiro* bound for San Francisco. The voyage back to the States was very rough, as the ship sailed into a storm that lasted for days.

Diana feared that after braving waters all over the world, she would die just a week before making it home. She lay on the bed feeling weak from being unable to eat. Next to her family, she missed the food of home. Diana had tried the cuisine of the different countries she had visited, but her tastes were firmly fixed on the flavor of the Lowcountry. When they reached the West Coast, they rested for a few weeks before continuing concerts as they moved east. It was there that Diana received a letter from her mama.

Dear Diana, I am overjoyed that you are finally back in the country. I am so anxious to see your face again outside of my mind's eye. But before you get here, there is much I must tell you. For a long time now, your tata has had a secret, something that he doesn't think I know about. For some time, he kept a young woman in the city, and she gave birth to a child before you left on the tour. I turned my head to his betrayal, knowing I could not soothe his hurts any more than he could mine. This baby boy, who is now seven years old, brought your tata back to life for a while. But now a younger man has married Eve, his mother, and is raising his son Roman as his own. What your tata thought would bring him fulfillment has left him empty. Don't

judge him harshly. We all have flaws. We are bound by the love that keeps us a family through the good and the bad.
Love Always, Mama

Diana was relieved to know that her mama knew the truth and that she would not have to keep the secret from her any longer. Diana was also certain that she would rather not have the complications of marriage and was committed to her career and going back to Europe.

"Coming back here to American is more like a splash of cold water in the face than a welcome," Diana told David as they rode south on the train. "All the adoration ends once we leave the stage."

"I'm done with the life of drifting all over the place, Di. It's time I made a home for us. We've made enough money."

"Is that what we worked so hard for, to come back home where we can't eat in restaurants or find hotels where we can sleep?" Diana asked with sarcasm.

"Maybe so, but we can be happy with each other. That's what matters," he said, putting his arms around her. "I want to go home with you to Savannah and meet your family."

"My family is having problems right now," Diana said, explaining what had happened between her mama and tata. "I think it will be better if you wait in Nashville. I'll write when it's a good time to come."

"All right, Di. That will give me some time to visit with my aunt and get things settled for us," David replied, hers was the better plan.

David gave her a long, hungry kiss on the lips before he got off the train in Nashville. Diana knew that most folks thought there was something wrong with a woman who didn't want a husband and a house full of kids, but she didn't care. It wasn't fair that she had to choose. Men could pursue their careers and chase their dreams for as long as they wanted without being judged. They were even praised for their determination and for being hard workers.

Diana watched David from the window of the train as it moved slowly along the track, knowing that she might never see him again. She loved him but not enough to give up everything that she had dreamed of having.

Chapter
Ten

Diana stepped onto the streetcar in Savannah and paid her fare. Walking to the rear, she ignored all the puzzled stares of the other riders. Diana could have passed for white if she wanted to, but she was too proud for that. She had never been ashamed of who she was. Dressed in a violet skirt, tailored jacket trimmed in velvet, and a matching hat, she had given them all something fine to look at. She took an empty seat by an open window near the back, set her bag down at her feet, and laid her parasol on the seat next to her to discourage anyone from sitting there. None of the black folks riding on the car recognized her; and like the white riders up front, they wondered who was she and why she sitting in the back with the darkies.

With the heat of the June day, the air on the trolley was hot and heavy as the afternoon quickly turned into evening. All along the ride, Diana sensed the tension between the front and the back of the streetcar, but she paid it no mind. She was grateful for the breeze that flowed through the open window that helped her relax and clear her head from traveling. She turned to the window, refusing to make eye contact with any of the other people on the streetcar, wanting to have the extra time to gather her emotions before she got to the house on Liberty Street.

Underneath the beauty of the South was an irrational ugliness, a beast that fed on the belief that it could only thrive on the conquest of another. Even though she wanted to be there to soothe the pains of her mama and tata, she was already thinking about leaving for New York move her dream closer to fruition. Savannah seemed so small and unsophisticated after Europe and the Orient, and the white-only signs that sprouted across the South reminded her that home would never be the same.

Diana could see her mama sitting on the veranda as she approached the house. The house looked the same, well-kept and unaffected by all the circumstances of the people who lived in it, but she couldn't say the same for her mama. Looking at Maia, Diana thought of 2 Corinthians 4:8-9: "hard pressed on every side, but not crushed; perplexed, but not in despair; persecuted, but not abandoned; struck down, but not destroyed." Maia stood up in anticipation as she saw Diana coming up the walk. When they were close enough for their gazes to meet, their smiles spread and caught the joyful tears that flowed down their faces. When they hugged, everything was right in the world for a moment.

"It's so good to see you, baby. I'm so happy that you're home," Maia said. "I missed you so much."

"I missed you too, Mama," Diana said, stepping back from the hug.

"We are so proud of you, baby, and we've read about y'all in the papers. But there were many nights that I tried to walk away my worry for you being so far from me. I know I've worn down the rugs in the house and the weeds in our garden."

"I worried about you too, Mama. I didn't want to think of you spending all your days in this house alone," Diana replied.

"Child, I'm not alone. Your tata is here, even though he spends a lot of time with the brothers at the lodge," Maia said, her voice trailing off. "Come inside. We've been waiting for you before eating supper."

Diana could smell the aroma of the food when she stepped inside. It was the most familiar thing to her in the house. She put her bag down in the foyer while Maia walked in to set the dinner table. She found Aaron sitting in the parlor reading a newspaper. When he saw her, he dropped the pages to the floor, jumped to his feet, and pulled her close in his strong embrace. In her father's arms, Diana could feel his life's anguish and disappointment with things in his world.

"Hello, Tata. How are you?" she asked.

"I'm fine now that you are home, baby," he said as he took her hand tightly and led her into the kitchen.

During the meal, the three talked and talked, and it took them nearly two hours to eat.

"I'm going to start writing stories for *The Savannah Tribune* again," Maia said. "John Deveaux started printing it again about four years ago. A few months back, it was bought out by Sol C. Johnson, and he's asked me to come back. I need something else to do with my life now. Not only that, I'm thinking about going back to teaching, too."

"That will be so good for you, Mama, and everybody loves your stories," Diana said. "What else has been going on around here while I've been gone?"

"Hurricanes flooded the Sea Islands again," Aaron said. "Most of the folks from down there are living on the mainland now."

"There's nothing for them on the islands anymore. They need jobs," Maia added.

"There are a lot more black businesses on West Broad, but race troubles keep growing, too. They burning crosses and setting fires whenever they get the notion. Those ornery fools dressed up like ghosts even busted out the windows of my office and Harold's grocery last week," Aaron told her. "Plus, we paying our taxes and still can't vote."

"We're spared all the hate that's here when we're on tour," Diana told them. "Even though most of the folks don't speak English, they love our concerts. I had never seen so many people in one place, and we made good money thanks to Mr. Loudin and his wife, Harriet."

"What about your beau, Diana?" Maia asked. "I didn't expect you to be here by yourself. I thought he would be coming home with you."

"Yeah," said Aaron cheerily. "Shouldn't we be getting ready for your wedding?"

Diana thought this was the right time to tell them about her plans.

"David is waiting for me in Nashville, but I won't be going there. I'm not ready to settle down and get married yet. I want more for my life than raising babies on some farm."

"You not as young as you were when you left, baby. I don't want you to miss out on your chance to have a family of your own," Aaron said. "Time don't wait for none of us."

"We just want you to be happy with someone to love," Maia interrupted. "Finding a good man who loves you and can take care of you isn't an easy thing these days."

"I can take care of myself, Mama. Besides, love doesn't last any-way," Diana said.

"Things change, life takes you through some hard things, and we make mistakes, but love does stand the test of time," Aaron said, raising his voice.

"Why should I give up the only thing I wanted to do my whole life for a man?" Diana asked. "Maybe he should be willing to do what I want to do."

"It's not about what you give up, Di. It's about sharing a life with somebody," Maia explained.

"Who says you can't still sing in Nashville?" Aaron asked.

"I don't want to end up sad and old with someone, waiting to die."

Those words stung Maia and Aaron. They both dropped their heads and stared down into their dinner plates. Diana felt awful that she had said too much and had hurt them.

"I'm sorry Mama and Tata. I didn't mean to say that; I just don't want to stop singing. David feels that we have enough money to stop performing, and we can start a business here or in Nashville. But I'm happy on stage, and that's where I plan to be for a while," Diana said.

Aaron didn't respond. He had decided to let it be. The child always did what pleased her anyway.

"Your voice is a gift from God," Maia said with resignation. "It's your life; live it in the way you choose. My joy is seeing you happy."

After they had finished eating, Aaron got up from the table and went back to the parlor and his newspaper while Maia and Diana cleared the table. All talked out, they moved in silence as they cleaned the dishes and put them away. Their pent-up emotions had run away over dinner, and they all needed time to get them settled down again.

When they finished the dishes, Maia returned to her seat on the veranda. Diana had given her some things to mull over in her mind. She thought about how much of her life she had spent waiting; waiting for someone to decide her fate, waiting for freedom, waiting for someone to come home, waiting for the pain to stop, waiting and not even knowing the reason. She realized that she had waited to live, and she wasn't going to wait to die. She was determined that from now on, she was going to make things the way she wanted in her life.

The next morning, Diana went into her mother's room to erase some of the words that were spoken the night before. She saw Maia combing her hair in front of the mirror.

Diana looked at her mother's reflection and said, "You're still so pretty, Mama, why don't you wear some of the jewelry I sent you from India?"

"It's so beautiful I didn't want it to show me up," Maia replied.

"There's nothing on this earth that could do that," Diana said. "Where do you keep it? I want to see it on you."

"It's in one of those drawers," Maia said as she leaned forward to look closer at the features of her face in the mirror.

Diana rummaged through the drawers, looking at the things her mother kept. The colored buttons in one, hair bobs in another, scribbled notes and newspaper clipping, and in the bottom she found the letters she had sent while she was on the world tour tied in a red ribbon. Lifting them out of the drawer, she discovered a book with two letters inside addressed to her Mama that had never been opened.

"Mama, why haven't you read these letters? One of them was sent fifteen years ago?" Diana asked curiously.

"I couldn't imagine what they could tell me that would change things for me," Maia answered matter-of-factly, not moving her gaze from the mirror.

"Can I read them to you?" Diana asked.

"If you want to. Go ahead," Maia said.

> Dear Maia, I have no idea how you feel about the things
> that happened between us in the past or if you even care
> to remember them. I have to come to understand that the
> years that I have relished as a beautiful dream may have

been a horrid nightmare for you. I have had time to reflect back on my life at Bailey Estates since I have been ill, and I ask your forgiveness for taking advantage of my position. My actions were driven by a love for you that I could never explain. I can only say as the Romans say, love brings more torment than happiness. I saw myself as Zeus hit by Cupid's arrow when he saw the lovely Europa, but it was a fantasy in which I escaped the tedium of my mundane life. In this letter, I hope to provide you with some measure of peace, which is the least that I owe. Eliza confided to me when I became ill that the babies, our children, did not meet any grave misfortune and were raised in a good home. I'm sorry that I lacked the courage to demand the truth so many years ago, but I didn't feel I had any rights to question her based on my own behavior. I don't have any hopes of ever seeing them or returning to the United States, yet it is my hope that you will lay eyes on them at least once. Sincerely, Richard Bailey.

Maia sat frozen in the chair, watching her own reaction in the looking glass. Confusion swirled in every part of her being. She had grieved for these children for over thirty years, so there was no more sadness to feel, but the letter brought her no relief or gladness. She was numb, as she had been during those years in the mansion, with no feelings of love or hate for the man she called Masta Bailey.

Maia, too, had escaped Bailey's impositions in her own fantasies of fictional characters that lived in and out of the books he liberally provided for her. She recalled her life before he took her with him to the mainland and saw herself as a happy, carefree child who scampered in the woods and along the beach, unearthing the miracles of God, spared from the realities of slavery by her parents on that isolated island on the sea.

It was at the big house on Bailey Estates that she learned that she had few choices and her life was not her own. She recollected the years that she merely existed for the conveniences of others and the births of three children who had no names. Then there was the year of Jubilee, when she allowed herself to hope the bad times were behind her. Unfortunately, there were more which lay ahead. More seasons with sunny days, clouds, and storms.

"Mama, are you all right?" Diana asked, bringing Maia out of her reverie.

"Yes, I'm fine sweetie. I'm just thinking about all that has been taken from me and all that I have been blessed with in my life. I'm thinking that as long as I live, it will be that way, and that's the way of this world."

Diana was puzzled. "Mama, I didn't know you had other babies."

"There was no need to talk about them; they were dead to me and I to them. What's important for you to know is that you have the same blood that they have, and not just mine."

"Are you telling me that Tata is not my father and that the man who wrote this letter is?" Diana asked. "I'm a slave master's child?"

"That is what I'm saying, Diana. But today, it doesn't matter. You have never been without a father who loves you," Maia said. "Hand me the other letter, and let all truths be told."

Dear Maia, I was glad to see that you were well and surrounded by a family that loves you. I had wished that things could have been like they were when we were young, when you took my hand as an older sister would and led me on adventures through the fields around the house. It was all much simpler then. I'm writing to inform you that my papa died in London, and my mum returned to the country and now lives with me on Bailey Estates. Her once-sharp mind now drifts, and most of the time she babbles incoherently; but there is always a subject on which she is consistently lucid. She speaks of a business associate and his wife who was unable to have children, and of having given them all three of the babies, which may be of some consolation to you. There was first a son, then a daughter, and then the last one, a son. The children were reared well in a good home. The eldest son is named Joseph, and he is a lawyer. The daughter is named Juliette and is married. The youngest is named Jack, and he is a veterinarian. Only time will tell if it was opportune or to their misfortune, but the children have been raised as white. I felt as a sister, I should tell you all that I know, it is your prerogative as the mother to decide what you will do with the knowledge. Yours sincerely, Daphne Bailey.

The world as Maia and Diana knew it had been changed forever. They set quietly in the room as they absorbed the revelations of the two letters that had been buried in the drawer for so many years. At one moment, Maia had been given a bridge that would have led her back to her children, only in the next to find she would never be able to cross over. She could only view their lives from afar, and they would never know her as the woman who had given them life.

Diana was torn as well. Her hopes of having brothers and a sister were shattered with the realization that they would probably despise her, notwithstanding the truth that the man who was her father had been her mama's master. The stillness in the room was disturbed when Diana stood up abruptly and left the room.

Maia continued to stare into the mirror, and as the minutes passed, things became clearer and clearer to her. They had no more rights to their children as free people than they did as slaves. She could see that they really hadn't found freedom all those years ago, and maybe there was no such thing. She thought about how people are always bound by something-blood, emotional ties, financial obligations, or a variety of dependencies-so different from the animals in the wild that roam freely. She thought about the cheetah that spends its life in solitude, the gazelles that run in herds for generations, the albatross that flies thousands of miles from its home, and the box turtle that barely moves a fraction of a mile from where it's born. They all were free, but it is not without its risks.

Maia began to understand Aaron's struggle, realizing that he never meant to spite her in his efforts to connect with the future. What he had yet to see, that which shone clearly in her reflection, is that we can only bond with today, and we can't live our lives through another.

Maia released the desire to find her children and confront them with her truth. There was no way she could change the past, and she didn't see herself in their futures. She looked longer and saw her family's lives in Savannah changing, the hate and resentment that were rising, lynchings that were happening more and more, walls that were slowly building around them that would enslave them again.

Just last year, three fires threatened to burn down all of Savannah. It was then that Maia got a true revelation. For the first time in her life, she wasn't going to react to the changes around her. Instead, she would make the moves that would bring about transformation and choose her own destiny. Maia thought about Hercules and the things he had taught her.

"We are all of the earth," he would say. "It's our connection to God and His blessings. Stay close to it, and it will comfort and keep you."

This was the reason Maia spent most of her youth looking for God in the dirt, in the trees, in the sky, and in the ocean. Maia stood up, put on her shoes, and went downstairs to find Aaron. She found him looking over papers at his desk in the parlor.

She went over to him and extended her hand. "Will you take a walk with me?" she asked.

"Always," Aaron said with a smile as he took her hand. They walked out into the night air, taking a few minutes to look up at the awesome light show that was the stars.

"If you have any doubts, I want to tell you that I love you," Maia said.

"I was worried that you had stopped, and it was killing me. No matter what I've done, I could never stop loving you," he replied.

"We've spent more than half of our lives together, and I don't want to lose you while you chase something you can never have. Children are like flowers. They come from our seed, we nourish them and love them, but they can't grow if we hold them too close. They have to feel the sun and the rain to get strong, and sometimes we have to be satisfied to cherish them from a distance."

"I never meant to hurt you, Maia, and I didn't want Roman to come between us. I just felt so empty after Apollo died, and I couldn't bear it. I felt you still had Diana, and I wanted someone for me. I was ashamed of what I was doing, but I couldn't stop myself."

"I could have told you that the love of another child wouldn't take away the pain of losing Apollo. I've lost four children."

"I'm so sorry, sweetheart. I was so consumed with my own agony that I forgot that you were suffering more than I was."

"Aaron, if you let me, if you hold me close, maybe I can fill some of the empty places, and we can find what we need in each other again."

Aaron pulled Maia close and held her tightly, so relieved he hadn't lost her through his foolishness.

Inside the house, Diana shook off the initial shock of the letters and started making plans to get out of Savannah. The last thing she needed was to come across someone she thought might be her brother or sister and have to act as if she didn't know who they were. She was ready to get back to work on a stage somewhere. She had heard through Annie that an all-black musical, *The Creole Show*, was holding auditions in Baltimore and that's exactly where she was headed. But, first, she sat down to write a letter to David to tell him not to come to Savannah.

Dear David, I've searched my head and my heart for the perfect words to tell you how I feel. Needless to say, I haven't found them, so I must simply say that I can't give up my dream of being the next Sissieretta Jones. I have no other explanation. Sometimes I think that I'm scared to settle down, that I wouldn't be a good wife or mother, that it wouldn't be enough to make me happy, or I don't want to need anybody. If I was able to share my life with someone, you would be the only choice for me. I miss your voice, your touch, and even your breath on the back of my neck when you slept next to me. How can I give you up? I must be a woman with no common sense, but I couldn't build a life with you on a mountain of regrets. So, I've decided to make a home for myself in New York. I'm sorry for disappointing you, but not for the time you spent loving me. I'll understand if you can't wait for me any longer.
Love, Diana

Over the next few weeks, the emotional highs and lows reached equilibrium as Maia and Aaron took care of each other. Maia was patiently waiting to tell him of her plan for the rest of their lives, but the restlessness she sensed growing in Diana was contagious. She wasn't about to sit still in Savannah waiting for the next monstrous hurricane to blow her away or the next scourge of yellow fever to boil her blood and wreak havoc in her life. Being a true storyteller, she knew that a new beginning sometimes has to take place in a different setting.

"I have a new story that I would like you to hear," Maia announced during dinner one evening.

"By all means," Aaron said, a bit surprised. It had been a while since she had given them a story at mealtime.

Maia pushed her plate to the side and began to recite the tale, with the added drama they all enjoyed.

"There was an adventurous young whale named George, who decided to run away from his pod. George always had a mind of his own and was tired of following the group and being told what to do. One day, while the others were distracted hunting and feeding deep down in the sea, he took this opportunity to ease away and swim above the surface and feel the warmth of the sun on his body. The excitement of his plan propelled him faster and faster, and it wasn't long before he had swum far away from the pod. Spinning around in the water and diving above the surface, George felt as light as a cloud. He was happy, and he was his own master.

After a while, George began to feel strange vibrations spreading through the water. Curious, he swam towards them. When he rose up out of the water, he saw the strange mammoth object floating on top of the ocean. He plunged back down just out of sight, but he followed it, for miles and then for days. It was only when he realized the waters had turned ice cold that he suddenly became aware that he was far from the pod.

He came to the surface and saw three of the large colorful objects floating. Then the creatures on the objects threw sharp spears at him, and there were explosions all around him. George was filled with terror. He was being hunted. He filled his lungs and went deep into the sea and swam away as fast as he could. He swam for a whole day before he felt safe. When he paused to rest, he felt a loneliness that he never knew was possible, a longing for his pod that nearly made him sick.

George swam for weeks, searching, and when the ocean turned warm, he sensed he was close to his home waters. One night, as he slept just below the surface, he dreamed that he was surrounded by his pod. Upset by the dream, he opened his eyes, but it was not a dream. George was back where he belonged, in the midst of his own kind, among those who loved him."

"I've told this story because we are like George," Maia said emphatically. "We've tried to survive in a place where we are preyed upon by enemies, a land that is not our true home," Maia explained. "We took the name of *Liberty* when we came on the mainland because you fought for it, Aaron. Now I'm not sure we will ever have it in this country. The rights we won are being lost more everyday. Most of us can't even vote now, and they're making news laws to make it legal to treat us like slaves. I don't want to sit here until a mob of these white crackers comes to drag you out into the night. We don't have to stay where they are killing us."

"I understand your worries, sweetheart, but I helped build this city back up with my own hands after the war, and I'm not going to be forced out by any man," Aaron said.

"It's not about being forced out, Aaron. It's about living in peace and harmony. I'm not sure if this is where we're supposed to be. I've listened to the speeches of Bishop Turner, and his message has touched me deep in my spirit. It's like an echo to the stories I grew up hearing from my tata and I want to see this place. I want to go to Africa."

"We don't know anything about Africa, and I'm too old to start my life over."

"It's not starting over; it's just moving in another direction. It may be just the place where we belong."

Aaron replayed Maia's words from last evening as he walked to his office on West Broad the next morning. He had never seen her so energized and committed before, and he didn't want to take that feeling away from her. She had supported him without question for thirty years, and he owed her the consideration of looking at her suggestion with an open mind.

Aaron approached the storefront of his office and paused for a moment and gazed at his name that hung in the window: Liberty Construction Company. He looked at the block of buildings that he helped erect, trying to sum up what they meant to him. Could he just pack his bags and leave and never come back? He had made enough money to be comfortable for the rest of their lives, so it wasn't about the money. He was proud of what he had accomplished, but was it the end of his life's work.

Aaron had never given thought to what he was going to do as he grew old, and his son Roman was only seven years old. He had planned to spend the rest of his years raising his son and holding the business for him, but that was no longer a possibility. It had never crossed his mind that Eve would have gotten married, and now another man had taken his place in Roman's life.

"Maybe Maia is right after all," Aaron said under his breath as he unlocked the door of the office and walked in.

Diana was two steps ahead of her parents in changing her destiny. She had received a letter from Frederick Loudin about The Fisk Jubilee Singers going on tour again, but she had bigger fish to fry.

Diana had seen a few of the vaudeville shows when she was on the road and was impressed with how flashy some were. They were a world apart from the prim and proper Jubilee Singers. Ten years had passed since she first went on tour with Frederick, but she was still turning heads, and she was going to use her good looks to get her where she wanted to go: center stage. She had already gone over on Congress Street and bought herself a new wardrobe to fit her new style.

"Mama, I want you to meet me for lunch today at The Garden of Eden on the end of West Broad," Diana said when she came down in the morning.

"That sounds special. What's the occasion?" Maia asked. In all their years, they had never gone out to eat together.

"I'm making some new plans I want to tell you about," Diana said, rushing past her toward the door.

"Don't you want to eat some breakfast before you go?" Maia shouted behind her.

"No, Mama, I'm late for my appointment at Breedlove's Beauty parlor to get my hair curled."

***

Diana walked into The Garden of Eden and found a table near the window, where she could see folks passing by. She had begun to look deep into the faces of people everywhere she went in town, closely examining their facial features, looking for anyone who bore any resemblance to her or her mama. Halfway down the block, she saw Maia approaching. She admired her mama's good looks, even at fifty-two years old, and thanked the Lord above for them passing on to her.

Diana couldn't resign herself to the white blood that flowed through her veins while white people treated her liked yesterday's trash. White men boldly misused and disrespected negroes as if it were a privilege. She thought about the Jubilee Singers' tour and about the restaurants where they couldn't eat, the restrooms they couldn't use on the road, and how they were shunned at the hotels that turned them away, and she could only shake her head in dismay.

Maia saw Diana gazing out of the window when she reached the restaurant, and they exchanged smiles. Diana was pleased with the change in her mama's disposition lately, and it helped ease the guilt she always felt when it was time for her to leave.

"Your hair looks good, baby," Maia said as she sat down, and they squeezed hands as gesture of their affection, "Now what are we going to eat?"

"You choose, as long as we have some pie for dessert," Diana said.

"That sweet tooth of yours is always ready," Maia teased.

They ordered the meal, and while they waited, Diana leaned forward and said, "Mama, I heard about a show that's beginning a tour in the fall called *The Creole Show,* and I'm going to take the train to Baltimore next week and try out for the cast."

"I knew you had something going on, girl. You been running around town like a chicken. Go on, child, follow your dreams, and don't worry about us," she said as she adjusted one of Diana's curls. "I'm excited for you; your happiness is my happiness, so I hope good fortune smiles on you."

"Thanks for saying that, Mama. I was worried that you wouldn't want me to go," Diana said relieved.

"It just so happens that I plan to follow your lead with an adventure of my own," Maia said, looking back at Diana.

"That's perfect," Diana replied. "Then I won't have to worry about you when I'm gone."

Diana was curious but didn't want to ask questions. She still hadn't gotten over her initial shock of the letters, and she needed to work on a song and a routine for her audition in a few days, so she changed the subject.

"By the way, Mama, how's your book doing?"

"I guess it's selling, but my mind is on other things," she answered.

They finished lunch and took the long way home since Diana never passed on dessert and didn't want to put on any extra pounds. At twenty-eight years old, she was beginning to feel the competition of the younger and prettier girls, despite the fact that they didn't have her voice. She was determined to shine like a new gold coin at the audition, and nothing was going to keep her from the spotlight.

Chapter Eleven

Once Diana said her goodbyes to Maia and Aaron and her baggage was stowed on the train, she sent a David a telegram asking him to meet her at the train station in Nashville on the following afternoon. He had been devoted to her for more than ten years. Maia had told her that she owed it to him to go and talk to him in person about her plans.

"I'm so glad you changed your mind and decided to come," David said thrilled, and wrapping her in his arms when she stepped off the train. "I've been missing you, Di."

"I missed you too, David, but I can't stay," Diana said softly in his ear.

"What are you talking about? You just got here!" he exclaimed, pulling his arms back from her shoulders as if he had been burned.

"I came here on my way to Baltimore to tell you that I can't marry you right now."

"What in the hell do you mean?" he shouted at her, "Are you saying you don't love me, that you don't want to be my wife?"

"No, I'm saying that I love you, but I don't want to be any man's wife right now."

"So you're just figuring that out now? You could have told me this a long time ago. You had your fun with me chasing after you like a dog, and now you want to kick me to the side when it no longer suits you."

"David, I've always told you how much my career meant to me."

"All you think about it that damn dream that you're going to be some famous singer. You need to face facts, Di. You might not be as special as you think you are."

"That's not what you were saying when you were lying in the bed with me."

"That's what I'm saying now, and I won't wait on you anymore. There are plenty of women who would jump at the chance to be my wife."

"You don't need to ruin everything between us."

"I'm not the one ruining it; it's you. Now you've said what you came here to say, and I don't ever want to see you again."

"Can you kiss me goodbye?" Diana asked, touching his arm and wanting to feel his lips one more time.

"You don't want anything from me. Climb back on your train and go," he said, turning and walking away.

"There's no shortage of men that would jump at the chance to kiss these lips," she hollered at his back before she tossed her hair and stepped back up on the train.

When the evening train to Baltimore pulled away from the station, Diana felt so excited that she would have wagered that she could have run the whole way to get there. She had already put the horrible goodbye scene with David out of her mind. Just the thought of getting back in front an audience made her feet tap a rhythm on the floor of the train.

***

Diana was headed straight to the Imperial Theatre on Pennsylvania Avenue, where the auditions were being held for the tour company and had her bags sent to the rooming house that her old friend Annie had recommended. She didn't need the aggravation of trying to find a hotel where coloreds could stay. She caught a streetcar to the address and nearly tripped on the steps, moving quicker than her feet could carry her.

"Hello, I'm Diana Portunus. I'm here for the auditions," she said to a white man standing inside the theater.

"Welcome to the Imperial Theater, Miss Portunus, I'm Sam T. Jack," he said, introducing himself. "This production will be the first show starring black performers for white audiences that will not be in blackface. I want to create something unique, a high quality musical comedy show with negro performers."

"That's why I'm here, Mr. Jack, and I can sing and dance," Diana replied enthusiastically.

"Well, you certainly look the part," he said as he held out his arm leading the way to the stage.

Diana snuck quick looks at the ceiling and seating around the theater. Compared to the massive concert halls she had sung in around the world as a Fisk Jubilee Singer, the Imperial was small, but it was only the beginning. On the stage, she saw a tall black man with a young white woman sitting in a chair on the side.

"Miss Portunus, this is Sam Lucas and Miss Belle Davis. He's the director and she's the star of this show."

"Hello, Mr. Lucas and Miss Davis, I'm pleased to meet you both," she said, extending her hand to greet them.

All the while, her mind kept racing with a question, what was a white woman doing performing with an all-negro cast?

"Relax. Just call me Belle," the woman said as she stood up.

Belle was tall, one of the few women Diana had ever had to look up to, and she was younger, too. She had an imposing presence. Diana even had to admit she was probably among a group of the most beautiful women in the world. She didn't want to like Belle, but she had a warmth that was comfortable and inviting.

Sam pointed to a small black boy sitting at a piano below the stage and said, "Eubie, can play anything you want."

"The stage is yours," Belle said as she went back to her chair.

Diana had to admit she was a little confused, but she was here for a specific reason, and nothing was going to distract her from that. Through the darkness of the theater, she could see that Mr. Jack and Sam had taken seats a few rows back in the theater. She set down her handbag and took off her waistcoat.

"Do you know, 'Oh Dem Golden Slippers'?" she asked the boy on the piano.

He nodded and began to play with such skill and emotion that Diana was so overwhelmed by his talent that she nearly forgot she was the one there to put on a show. Diana began to sing and relaxed in the comfort of a song she had sung so many times with the Jubilee Singers on tour, and then she began to dance with the sheer joy she felt from being on stage again. She lifted up her dress and kicked up her heels, letting the music by the boy take her where it wanted her to go. She was carried away, and after a few minutes, so was her breath. Diana stopped and gave a short bow. Her audience of four, Mr. Jack, Sam, Belle, and the boy Eubie responded with sincere applause. The two men talked quietly between themselves and nodded their heads in agreement.

"This one has it, Sam. We can start her in the chorus singing. Then when she gets the routines down she might be a featured act," Belle said.

"I agree. She's more than just another pretty face for the chorus," Sam said.

"It's fortunate that you made it into town today, Miss Portunus. This is the last day for auditions, the cast is pretty much rounded out, but I think you will be an impressive addition to the show," Sam said before he turned to exit the theater.

"You can really sing, girl, and that's what we really need," Belle said with a playful slap on her shoulder. "Dora, who you'll meet later, can dance her butt off, but she can't sing a note."

"Who's the young'un on the piano? He can play those keys to beat the band!" Diana asked.

"His name is Eubie Blake. He's like a musical genius; he plays for the auditions here to earn a little money. Come by my place this evening, and you'll meet the rest of the crew," Belle said, giving her the address before she disappeared backstage.

Diana was ecstatic.She was on her way, she was back singing again, and it would only be a matter of time before she would work her way to center stage.

***

Diana walked on air all the way to Tabitha Logan's Rooming House on North Avenue. She had seen it from the streetcar window on her way to the theater. Diana could smell food cooking a half block from the door and wanted to close her eyes and let the aroma lead the rest of the way. Her stomach started to grumble reminding her that she hadn't eaten a meal since the night before.

Diana knocked on the door. But before her she could pull back her hand, the door snapped open, and a short woman with an crisp apron over a flowered dress said, "Come on in here. I've been waiting for you."

Diana assumed she was an older woman because her hair was totally white, but there wasn't a line or a wrinkle on her face. She had skin the color of coffee with cream and a smile of perfect teeth, with one of them outlined with gold that matched the twinkle in her eyes.

"Aren't you a pretty thing!" she exclaimed, taking a good look at Diana. "Come on in. Call me Miss Tabby. I put your things in your room already," she said as she stepped to the side and steered Diana into the dining room. "Sit down at the table, and I'll feed you. I got two other boarders, but they ain't here right now. One's a Pullman porter, the other is studying at the college, and I've had my lunch already."

"Thank you, ma'am," Diana said, choosing a side chair.

The house was immaculate. Diana eyes scanned around the room at all the ornate furniture that filled the house noticing that it had all been painstakingly polished until the character of the woods glowed.

Miss Tabby followed her eyes and said, "My late husband, God rest his soul, left me this house when he died. But he didn't leave me much money, so I rent out rooms to make ends meet."

"You have a beautiful home, ma'am," Diana replied.

Miss Tabby put the hot plate of fried trout, collard greens, candied yams, and cornbread on the table and sat down across from Diana.

"Where are you from, sugar?" Miss Tabby asked.

"I'm from Savannah, ma'am," Diana answered.

"You got family?"

For the first time, Diana didn't know how to respond. Were the strangers that shared her blood family or not?

After a moment of hesitation, she said, "My mama and tata live in Savannah, and I had a younger brother who was taken by yellow fever."

"I'm so sorry. No children of your own?"

"No, ma'am."

"Well, sugar, when you write to your mama, tell her not to worry about you. I'm gonna look out for you," Miss Tabby said as she stood up from the table.

Diana cleaned her plate and accepted a small slice of lemon meringue pie.

Miss Tabby showed her to the room that was decorated in bright yellow. Diana washed up and changed out of the clothes that she had worn on the train all night. She wanted to make a good impression, so she chose her new lavender dress to wear to Belle's house. She felt good as she looked at her reflection in the mirror, even though the waist was snug after the meal she had just eaten.

***

Diana decided to take the streetcar to the townhouse where Belle was staying; she didn't want to look disheveled when she met the other cast members.

She climbed the steps and knocked on the door.

A handsome man opened the door and said, "Hello, "I'm Bob Cole, and who might you be, pretty lady?"

"I'm Diana Portunus. I was invited by Belle."

"Well, by all means come in, and welcome," he said as he offered her his arm and walked with her into the parlor.

Belle saw her and shouted, "Help yourself to the food, Diana!"

Diana was ecstatic. Everyone looked as stylish as she thought they would.

"I'll show you around," Bob said, holding her arm and leading her through the room making introductions.

Diana met musicians, dancers, and other women who were in the chorus. She also met the featured performers: Mattie Wilkes, Charles Johnson, and Dora Dean.

She felt comfortable with Dora, enough to ask, "I've been wondering, since Belle is white, why is she working this show?"

Dora laughed so loud that Diana got nervous.

"She's not white. She's as black as you and me, but that's not saying much is it?"

Diana had to laugh, too, as she looked around the room. All of the women were light-skinned, not one dark one in the room. Near the end of the evening, Sam Jack arrived with champagne.

He moved to the center of the room and raised his arm to get everyone's attention, and then he began speaking, "Folks, first I want to applaud all of you who will be a part of this history making show. *The Creole Show* will be the finest exhibition of beauty, sophistication, and talent of the negro woman ever seen on stage. I don't want to make statements about the past but rather offer a preview of what the future will be for musical stage productions. Rehearsals will begin in the morning, but first join me in a toast to our success."

The champagne corks were popped, and the effervescence of the drink matched the excitement building in Diana's chest. The party broke up quickly after Sam left, and Diana was exhausted.

"Thanks for all your hospitality," Diana said to Belle as she rushed out the door.

Diana probably wouldn't sleep a wink, but she wanted to get some rest so she could show them who she was.

***

The show was scheduled to open in less than two weeks, so rehearsals were grueling. They lasted all day with a short break for lunch. Diana was one of the chorus girls, and the costume dresses were some of the finest she had ever seen.

"This minstrel show is miles away from singing negro spirituals," Diana said to Belle as they rehearsed. She discovered that she had to sing from her gut and her loins to light the passions of the crowd, unlike when singing negro spirituals, where you sang from the heart and soul to touch the sensibilities of the audience.

"It's a whole different audience, Di," Belle said. "You'll learn the tricks in no time."

"I've been studying you, Sam, Bob, Charles and Dora, and I'm catching on."

Diana could see they were giving all they had in rehearsal as they worked the stage, using infecting smiles and subtle sexual innuendos that would possess and mesmerize the audience.

"Keep in mind that Mr. Jack may set the image for the show, but it's Sam Lucas who knows what it takes to sell tickets. He says that we'll play in Baltimore for two weeks before going up north and then touring across the country."

"I can't wait. I'm ready to get out on the road again," Diana said excited.

Blacks and whites no longer sat in the same theaters together, so *The Creole Show* opened in the Imperial Theater in front of a colored audience. The spectators were surprised and subdued at first.None of the men were in blackface, and the ladies were absolutely gorgeous. They were all dressed with such class and elegance, the very sight of them had the crowd spellbound.

The performance was beyond anything that had ever been seen by this audience. Bob knocked them out of their chairs with his comic routine. Then he and Dora brought them to their feet with their cakewalk, and it was like angels had come to take them away when the singing started. It was a magical night. Everyone under the roof of the theater, from those backstage to the last row, felt a sense of pride for the dignity portrayed. The cast was rewarded with rousing applause and a standing ovation that lasted for nearly a quarter of an hour.

"That's what I've been waiting for!" Diana said to Belle after the show. "Now I'm more determined to become a feature act before the tour begins. I've been spending my free time trying to come up something that could put me out front."

"Choose a song to sing, practice your cakewalk, and show them what you can do," Belle said to encourage her.

Diana had learned a lot from Belle and Dora. She watched them use every inch of themselves to connect with the audience, mixing their voices with the movement of their bodies to bring the crowd under a spell. Everything mattered: the look in the eye, the turn of the wrist, the toss of a hip, the stretch of a leg, and the curve of the ankle.

It was a week later, after the show, that Diana approached Sam and Mr. Jack.

"I've been working on something special that I would like you two gentlemen to see," Diana told them. "Would you both come to the rehearsal and see my number before the tour starts?"

"I'll try to get there, but I'm running short on time," Sam said.

By the time the show was ready to go on the road, he finally relented and gave her the chance she had been preparing for most of her life.

"One, two, three," Diana counted to cue the musicians. Then she started to sing "Jump Back, Honey, Jump Back," putting all her experiences into the essence of the song until she owned the lyrics.

Then Diana began to dance, throwing off all her inhibitions and letting loose on the stage. She did the cakewalk, and next she stopped singing and let her body speak with her own dance and her words said that she wanted to rule the world. Sam took a minute to gather his thoughts. He was amazed, but he had a new problem: how to reconfigure the program to include another feature act.

He smiled at her. "All right, you have my attention, and I'll see what I can do to get your number added to the show."

Diana balled up her fist and threw a punch in the air. She had won, and she was on her way to the spotlight in the center of the stage.

***

"I want to thank you, Miss Tabby, for taking good care of me," Diana said at dinner before the last show in Baltimore. "I promise to come back and see you whenever I'm in town."

"I loved having you here, sugar, and remember what I told you about them musicians. Half of them carrying that syphilis, and it makes you crazy before it kills you," Miss Tabby said, putting the fear of God in her.

"Yes, ma'am, I'll remember."

The next day before Diana left for the train station, Miss Tabby said, "Take care of yourself, sugar." She gave Diana a goodbye hug. When Diana closed her eyes, it felt just like her nana was holding her. and she had to blink back a tear.

On the streetcar, Diana realized that she had been so busy that she hadn't seen any other parts of the city--not the market, a boutique, or a church. She hadn't even written a letter home. *This is why I don't have time for a man in my life*, she said to herself.

At the train station, Diana hurried toward the members of the cast who were gathering at the rear passenger car. Her mind drifted away from the casual conversation when she saw departure times for Tennessee and South Carolina and thought of her mama and tata and even David.

The ambitious tour of *The Creole Show* started in Haverhill, Massachusetts, on August 4, 1890, with Diana having earned her own number on the program. Their opening night at the theater was spectacular with all the dazzling black women running the show, even if they were all light, bright, and almost white. It was a gamble that paid off handsomely. The all-white audience was thrilled by the show, and Sam T. Jack knew he had a hit. From there, they traveled to Boston, and then all over the Keith Circuit in the Northeast and then on the TOBA Circuit in the South for colored audiences.

Diana worked hard to hold her spot in the show adding something new and different each time she performed. She learned to reach out to the audience, making each person feel as if he or she was the only one in the theater.

"Those girls in the chorus are dancing their asses off," Belle said to Diana in the dressing room after the last show in Boston. "Dora had better watch her steps."

"They saw Sam give me chance. Now they're all bucking to take my spot."

"That'll keep you from getting lazy, Di. There's always somebody else waiting in the wings," Belle said, wiping off her make-up. "That's how it is in this business."

The cast members were friendly off stage, but on stage they were fiercely competitive. They all wanted the same thing, top billing, and there just wasn't enough room for all of their names on the marquee.

"This show is only the beginning for me, Belle; I want it all. I won't give up until I see my name in lights."

Chapter Twelve

In Savannah, Aaron lacked the single-mindedness that Diana had in fulfilling his destiny, more so because he wasn't sure what it was. His greatest confusion was on whether he had already achieved it or if it was it still ahead of him. Is the ultimate goal to be happy? And when you're happy, is that your fulfillment and satisfaction?

Aaron was torn. He knew Maia wasn't content, and he wanted her to be satisfied; but he had needs for his own satisfaction, and he was almost sure they weren't in Africa. Many days, he sat at his desk in his office and looked back over his life, and all he saw was work. He had worked from as far back as he could remember as a young boy, from sunup to sundown, it was all he knew. He spent many nights wondering what exactly he was working for.

In the beginning, he knew he wanted a piece of land to call his own and a home. Then he wanted a woman and then a family to call his own. When he had those things, he wanted to build a business, and after that, he wanted the respect that came with being a leader in the community. Then he wanted the power of a political office, a desire that stayed just beyond his reach. With all he had accomplished, he still wasn't satisfied.

"Maia, I've been giving your 'back to Africa' idea a lot of thought," Aaron blurted out over supper. "I don't think I can let go of everything here and go to the other side of the world."

"What more do you want here, Aaron?" Maia asked, feeling his frustration. "Jim Crow is not going to let you have anything more."

"There's a gnawing inside of me, Maia. So many of my ambitions are unfulfilled. You expect me to drop them all and follow you to who-knows-where?"

"Why are you so greedy? You've had more success than most men, black or white, and you only want more. As soon as you accomplish one goal, then you make another one, another building, more houses. How much money do you need?"

"It's not only money; it's the legacy I want to leave behind. Most days, I still can't even accept that Apollo's gone. Then I put my marriage on the line to have Roman, another son to follow in my footsteps. And now that situation is hopeless."

"That's life; none of us are exempt from the trials and tribulations. The only joy you'll have is the joy you make."

"I know that in my head, Maia. I know I don't have a right to expect any more. I've been blessed, but I can't stop myself from wanting more."

"That's the thinking that leaves you discontent. At some point, you have to stop and enjoy the life you have," she said, getting up from the table.

Maia was tired of Aaron's excuses; all he was thinking about was himself. *What about me?* she asked herself. *What does this world really offer and what can I count on?*

Maia was moving to place where she could envision a life for herself without Aaron. She had the feeling that something was missing in her life, something so meaningful that she would have to search until she found it. How could she know if it wasn't in Africa if she didn't go there and search for it?

***

"I would like you to go to church with me today," Maia asked Aaron on the first Sunday in November. Bishop Henry Turner, their former pastor and his lodge brother, was speaking at St. Phillips A.M.E. "I think it will do you some good to hear his message and help you to see what Africa has to offer."

"I'll come. I don't have a problem listening, but I'll make up my own mind."

Bishop Turner had gained a lot of support for his Back to Africa campaign. So many black folks in the South had lost hope that they would ever be recognized as equals, much less have the opportunity to better their lives in the country that had kept them as slaves for so long.

"The church is packed," Aaron told her. "We'll have to find seats upstairs in the balcony."

"I told you we needed to get here early," Maia said, leading the way up to the higher floor.

As the choir sang, Bishop Turner walked to the pulpit, and Aaron was shook by the appearance of his old friend. He could see the wear and tear of the years and the struggles on his face and in the thick, white hair on his head. His body had grown full and soft. Aaron couldn't help but look down at his own hands and wonder how old he appeared in other people's eyes. All of a sudden, he was conscious of his age and aware that time plays no favorites. They were all getting old, much closer to the end than the beginning. With no comfort in his own thoughts, Aaron turned his attention to the choir, as they brought their selection to its conclusion to yield to their familiar speaker of the morning.

"The negro is facing many changes in America," Bishop Turner began in his sermon to the congregation. "I caution you today that things will only get worse. I have always been a man of faith and hope, willing to work hard and make things better for my people, but I have come to the conclusion that the best thing the negro can do for himself is to seek liberty in his own ancestral homeland."

Maia reached for Aaron's hand as the bishop spoke.

"I see no manhood future for the Negro in this country, and the man who is not able to discover that fact from existing conditions must be void of common sense. Neither education nor wealth can ever elevate us to the grade of respectability."

Aaron listened to the message, and while he saw its practicality, it went against his character and temperament. He never shrank away from a fight; his response was to fight harder. This was his country as much as any other man's, and he wouldn't cut and run or be driven out. He was trying to keep an open mind for Maia's sake. More and more each day, she was being consumed by the idea that they needed to make this journey.

"Bishop, we'd like to invite you to come to supper with us," Aaron said to him after the service. "I'd like to talk more about this trip to Africa."

During the walk down West Broad to Liberty Street, Maia stayed quiet. She had said so much to sway Aaron, but so far, he had not wavered. She hoped that the bishop could better make the case for them taking the trip to Africa.

"Aaron, you are a blessed man. You have a beautiful and faithful wife standing with you. You don't know how much that means until she's no longer there. I lost my wife last year, and it grieves me around the clock. If I could have her back for just one day, there's nothing on this earth that I wouldn't do for her."

"I know that, Henry, but I put my family in harm's way once, and I couldn't stand to do it again," Aaron said.

"Fear of the unknown can be our greatest enemy sometimes my friend. It can keep us from realizing the greatest of blessings," the bishop replied. "I'm taking an exploratory trip next October and returning after one month. Join us, Aaron, and resolve all the questions in your mind. Besides, if it will keep that pretty smile on Maia's face, then it's worth the experience."

They had a great time over dinner, reminiscing and laughing over the good times they'd had years ago at the lodge. While Maia cleaned up the dishes, Aaron and Henry retired to the parlor where Aaron confided his concerns about his son Roman.

"Henry, I don't know if I can just leave this country and live without seeing my son grow up. I know I'm not able to be a real father to him, but I do see him in the schoolyard and occasionally at church functions, and Eve takes the money I send for him every month. Sure it hurts me to my heart that I can't talk to him, that he looks to another man as his father, but just seeing him fills me with pride. And as wrong as I was for doing what I did, I have no regrets. I just pray that good fortune will smile on me before I leave this world and I will get the chance to know him and he know me and know that I love him."

"Well, my brother, only you can decide where your greatest happiness comes from, whether it is with the woman who chose to spend a life with you or with a child who has his own life to lead. Bless you and your decision," Henry admonished.

Maia came into the parlor as the men rose from the sofa.

"Thank you, my dear, for a lovely home-cooked meal, and I hope to see you both very soon," he said as he stepped out.

Maia grabbed Aaron's hand as they walked up the stairs anxious to hear if he had changed his mind after talking to the bishop. Aaron could feel her wants pulling at him from across the room as they dressed for bed.

They both laid visible in the moonlight that flooded the bedroom for a few minutes before Aaron said, "Maia, I can't commit to living the rest of my life in Africa, but I understand your craving to go there and the ties you feel to Sierra Leone from hearing about it and dreaming about it when you were a young girl. It's because of that and the pledge I gave Hercules that I promise you that we will take that voyage with Brother Henry. I feel like I owe you that much, and from there we will see how things go."

"Thank you, honey," she said as she turned and gave him a tight hug. "That's all that I'm asking for right now. That means so much to me. Savannah just doesn't feel like home for me anymore. I'm out of place here; I need to go to a new place where I can see God again, even if it's just for one day."

Maia's words brought Aaron back to what Henry had said about his wife, and he closed his eyes, knowing it was the right thing to do.

***

Once Aaron settled things in his mind, the months began to pass quickly as autumn meshed into winter. The new year was fast approaching, and there were other preparations to make for the time that he and Maia would be gone. He even wondered if he should make out his last will and testament just in case they didn't make it back. A week before Christmas, while Aaron was taking inventory of his properties and contracts, Eve came into the office.

"Hello there, Eve. Come on in. I'm surprised to see you," Aaron said pleasantly. It had been months since he had spoken to her, but he was glad that she had come. "Do you need some help with a special Christmas gift for Roman?"

Roman was eight years old now, and Aaron had been thinking that he might like a train set to play with. Eve walked over and took one of the seats across from his desk.

"Aaron, I want to thank you for all you have done for me and Roman, and I appreciate your not making any problems for Isaac and me. Things have been hard on us lately. White folk been attacking the postal workers, and one of Isaac's good friends was murdered, and now he's got threats on him. He says it's time for us to get out of here. He's got family in Chicago, and they say he can get on with the Pullman Car Company there as a porter. I just came to tell you that we'll be leaving in January."

Aaron felt as if the floor disappeared from under his chair and that he would fall at any moment. Why did he have to keep going through these changes? He had been so worried about leaving the city and not seeing Roman that he never considered that this could happen.

"Eve, if it's a job that Isaac needs, I can help him find one here. I have friends that can fix it where he won't have to know it even came from me. I need to see my son, Eve. It's bad enough that he doesn't even know me, and I can't get close to him," Aaron pleaded.

"Well, that's the bed you made. You didn't want to leave your wife for me, so why should I have stayed alone, waiting for the hours or minutes you could spare to come see me or your son. Besides, it wasn't me you wanted anyway. Isaac loves me, enough to take my child and raise him as his own."

Aaron knew more about that than he had time to tell her. He, too, had raised another man's child. He also had to admit that he would have never allowed the other man to come into his home and demand privileges.

"Since you've always done right by Roman, I just thought I should let you know," Eve said as she stood up, turned, and walked out the door.

Aaron grabbed his jacket and rushed out of the office. He felt like he was suffocating in there. Eve must have taken all the air with her when she left. He started walking, then running, already out of breath, but wanting to get home as fast as he could. He needed to see Maia and to tell her that he finally knew what she was talking about all these months. He was feeling all the feelings that she had described. He wanted to tell her that he was going to sell the business and the other properties.

Aaron could see it now; they had to have a fresh start somewhere they had never seen before. He was tired. He couldn't live the rest of his life through his son. Although he would have done it without hesitation, they weren't going to allow it. He had to face the fact that the only life he could lay claim to was his own. All he had done in his life was work, and now he wanted to relax so he could breathe. He was determined to have some good times before they laid him out on a cooling board. He wasn't sure about the moving to Africa, but he knew there were going to be some changes.

When Maia heard the news, she was overjoyed. Aaron's change of heart worked like magic on them. They both felt more than ten years younger. It was exhilarating to have something to look forward to; a new reason for living that was related to them and their lives and not their children.

***

Aaron went to meet with his lodge brother James Simms. They had worked together on quite a few building projects after the war, and he had always been like a father to him.

"What are you working on lately, James?" Aaron asked, knowing Brother Simms always kept his ear to the ground and knew what was going on in town.

"We're trying to get some and land and raise some money for a black college that the Georgia legislature is close to establishing."

"Fortunate for you, I may be able to help," Aaron said.

"What's on your mind?" James asked.

"I've got a large parcel of land I own that's adjoined to other unowned land that could be bought and used as a prospective site," Aaron confided. "I'd be willing to donate it if you'll work with me on the sale of my business and rental properties."

"What's going on, Aaron? I had no idea you were interested in selling your business or any of your real estate," James asked, stunned at the request.

"Let's just say, I'm taking a trip, and I don't know how long I'll be out of town," Aaron said.

"I won't ask you a bunch of questions for now, but I do know there are several prominent businessmen who are members of my congregation who have expressed some interest in the past in acquiring real estate. I'll check into it and get back with you shortly," James said.

***

Maia and Aaron stayed up late on New Year's Eve waiting to experience the first minute of 1891.

"This is the year that could change the direction of our lives together," Maia said. "We've experienced our share of misfortune in Savannah, but we have also been richly blessed. It's time for us to turn the page and see what is next in our story."

"Things are already moving, Maia. James told me that he has offers on most of the rental properties."

"That is good news, honey. It's time to pass some of your headaches on to someone else."

"He's handling so much of the business already that I don't even need to go to the office every day," Aaron told her.

"That means we can spend some time doing things together," Maia said happily.

They started talking again and really got to know each other in a way they hadn't had time to do before. In the spring, they re-planted the garden, and in the summer, Aaron bought two of the bicycles that he saw folks riding on around River Street Market and they learned to ride.

"Maia, *The Creole Show* is coming to the Grand Opera House in Macon," Aaron announced one morning as he read the newspaper. "We can finally get to see Diana sing again."

Since Diana had left a year ago, the show had gone from Chicago to Kansas City to Dallas, and was moving through the Deep South. Maia couldn't wait to take the train to Macon when the troupe stopped in Georgia.

"They've got a good review written here, and they've even mentioned Diana's name," Aaron said proudly.

"It's about time I saw my baby up on stage," Maia told him. But even more, she had so much news to share with her daughter. "It's hard for me to believe that a whole year has flown by, and it's less than two months before we sail for Africa. I still haven't told Diana about our plans."

On the morning of the show, Aaron and Maia took the early train on the Central of Georgia Railway to the Macon station, where Diana said she would meet them.

"Look at you standing there dressed up like a woman of means," Aaron said when Diana stepped off the afternoon train in Macon.

"You're looking so good, baby," Maia said as she grabbed Diana's hand.

"You two are looking pretty fine yourselves," Diana said, noticing how rested and relaxed they looked. "I've got a few hours before the show, and I need to get my hair touched up. Can you come with me?"

"Sure, we're free to do whatever you want," Maia answered.

"If you ladies don't mind, I'll take this opportunity to meet with some of my lodge brothers while you two go to the hairdressing salon," Aaron said, tipping his hat as they headed off.

They caught a carriage ride with some of the other performers to Notasulga, at the black end of town.

While Diana sat getting her hair curled, Maia started talking, "You know, Di, I've lived my life within a fifty-mile fence, and I'm ready to see if there's another place for me in this world. My pastor has organized a voyage going to Liberia and Sierra Leone, the place where Hercules was born, and your Tata and I have decided to go."

"What are you telling me, Mama?" Diana asked, sitting up at attention and pulling her head away from the hairdresser.

"It's an exploration, a trip to see if Liberia might be the place for us to spend the rest of our lives. We'll be sailing in October from New York with your tata's lodge brother Bishop Turner, who has been organizing a Back to Africa movement for several years."

"I can't believe this, Mama. You don't know anybody in Africa," Diana said, confused.

"There are going to be over one thousand people on board the *Steam Ship of Paris*, Maia said. "We won't be alone. Chances are we might even see some people we know."

Diana could hear her Mama's anticipation, but she was more than stunned by the news.

"Would you really move out of the country, Mama, or is this just an idea that you are considering? I like the comfort of knowing that you and Tata are in Savannah. And if things get rough, I can always come home, and home for me isn't in Africa."

Diana had seen how dark-skinned people lived in other parts of the world, and to her it seemed uncivilized.

"Why Africa, Mama? There are places in Europe where blacks are not mistreated, and they are more cultured. Why would you and Tata want to live next to the jungle?"

Maia laughed and said, "First, we aren't going into the wild, and second, your Tata isn't sure what he wants to do."

"We'll talk about it some more after the show. Meet me at this rooming house," Diana said edgily, handing Maia the name and address written on a small piece of paper.

At the theater, Maia could hardly believe her eyes when she saw her child on stage. Diana was wearing make-up and a crimson outfit that was a showstopper, stylish and elegant as well as revealing. Her baby was a full-fledged woman, teasing the audience, drawing them in with her voice, and then holding them off with the kicks of her legs when she danced.

"I was so proud of her up there," Maia said to Aaron after the show.

"I enjoyed the show, but it seemed a little risqué," Aaron replied. "She was up there shaking around like some hussy. Why couldn't she keep singing respectable music with those Jubilee Singers?"

"This is what she wants to do to get her closer to her dream, honey. She's a grown woman, damn near thirty years old, and I don't see nothing wrong with it."

"She needs to start thinking about settling down before she gets too old."

"You may find this hard to believe as a man, but not every woman wants or needs a husband," Maia said, walking ahead of him out of the theater.

Back at the rooming house, there wasn't any place they could talk privately. They huddled together and spoke in the parlor for a few minutes.

"I'm worried about both of you going off a wild-goose chase to Africa," Diana said nervously. "I'm scared. What if something happens to y'all."

"Don't worry about us. We'll be fine, and we'll write to you as often as we can while we're away," Maia assured her.

"It'll be hard to get your letters since the show will be moving on to

New Orleans, Florida, and then back north to Washington and Philadelphia before we settle in New York at the Standard Theater," Diana said with mixed emotions.

"Don't worry about us, child, you keep doing your best in the show," Maia told her.

The goodbye was long and painful at the train station, with them not knowing when they would next see one another or even where it might be.

The loose ends were coming together as the voyage date approached. Aaron had made a deal to be a silent partner in Liberty Construction, along with James Sims and two others who had each purchased one quarter of the business. Maia spent the last days before their trip closing up their house on Liberty Street and packing their trunk for travel. Hercules had always told her how the weather was much like that on Ossabaw, except for the fall and winter months, when the days were hot, but the nights were cool and sometimes even cold.

Maia walked around the house re-envisioning the first time they arrived there from the island, the happy times they had there when the children were young, and the planting of the garden with Diana and her mama. She couldn't help but think of the bad times there, too. Apollo getting sick and dying, her mama dying, and the lonely days when Aaron was out courting Eve. The pain and the joy had her tied to this house, but she was determined to leave it and see what other blues and blessings this world had for her. Come what may, she was going to live her life without fear and hesitation.

Chapter Thirteen

T he train to New York arrived early on October 15, 1891, and Maia and Aaron, headed straight to the port to board the *City of Paris* steamship. They had been so caught up in the complexities of their own lives that the gravity of the decision they had made had escaped them until the moment when they looked down from the deck and saw the outpouring of emotional goodbyes between those making the journey and those being left behind.

"I guess we only have each other," Aaron said as he scanned the crowd of unfamiliar faces, young and old, saying their goodbyes.

Maia suddenly wished she had the mental picture of her grown children to take with her, and then she imagined herself saying goodbye to Diana and Apollo.

"Hercules would have given anything to be aboard a ship this and go back to his home," Maia said, reminiscing about fishing on the island with him. That was when she could no longer control the stubborn tears that insisted they be set free.

Aaron grabbed Maia's left hand for encouragement as they both waved to the crowd below. Then he asked, "Do you still think we made the right decision to come?"

Second thoughts were flooding Aaron's mind as the vessel glided away from the dock. Should he have let Roman go so easily? Should he have sold most of his business and properties? Should he have gotten aboard this ship?

"I'm sure of it," Maia answered, smiling to herself. "I'm seeing God again."

They spent a few hours on deck, watching other ships that passed them going in different directions, until the land faded into the horizon and sky and the ocean seemed to touch. When the day turned dark, they went inside to their cabin and put their things away before dinner.

"Mr. Liberty, fancy meeting you here," a man said as he stopped by their table.

"Mr. Wright, this is a pleasant surprise!" Aaron said, standing up to greet him, "Please join us for dinner. You haven't met my wife, Maia. Maia, this is one of the gentlemen from Atlanta that I worked with on some building projects."

"Pleased to meet you, Mrs. Liberty," Mr. Wright said, giving Maia a nod and taking a seat.

"Are you traveling with Bishop Turner's group?" Aaron asked.

"No, I'm here with several men from Atlanta; we're hoping to start a profitable import/export business in Liberia."

"Excuse us; we're assigned to this table," a young black man said as he and a woman sat down and joined the group. "My name is Clifford and this is my wife, Ruth. We're with Bishop Turner."

"The more the merrier," Aaron said, smiling. "Are you from Savannah?"

"No, we're from Macon. We hope to get some of the free land in Liberia and build a home of our own there," Clifford told them.

They all talked a lot, eating very little. Perhaps from the excitement of the voyage ahead or from sea sickness caused by the ship rocking on the waves. Maia and Aaron retired early, exhausted from their trip to New York and the weight of the journey ahead.

The next morning, they had breakfast with Bishop Turner and some others traveling from Atlanta. The mood and the conversation were much more relaxed as the anxiety from the departure had subsided.

"I'm going up on the deck," Maia said after the meal, leaving the men talking.

From the top of the vessel, Maia saw what looked like small dolphins diving and swimming in the smooth water around the ship. She was energized by them and the sheer joy of life they seemed to have as they darted above the surface of the sea. She saw a whale and thought about George in the story she told Aaron. It was a sign that they had made the right decision.

The voyage was not without a few scary moments. During the first week, large waves crashed against the side of the ship and burst on board the lower levels of the deck. There were long hours when the ship swayed and bounced through a storm in the night, but Bishop Henry led the passengers in prayer, and their exhilaration dominated the fears and worry as they gained confidence in the ship with each passing day.

"What do you men do in that saloon all day?" Maia inquired after lunch one afternoon.

"We do whatever we can to make the time pass faster. Some of the men wager on card games, some smoke, and others have a few drinks," he answered with a chuckle.

"You all should come in the sitting room," Maia said, shaking her head. "We have a lot of fun in there, with folks playing the piano and singing. I've seen some real talent in some recitations and readings."

After a week at sea, they reached Queenstown, Ireland, where they could step on land for a few hours before heading on to Liverpool in London where they would board a smaller African ship for the remainder of their journey to Africa.

"These white folks here are a whole lot more civilized than the ones we have at home," Aaron noticed. "They don't carry guns and weapons on the street, threatening black folks, and they seem to love learning about things."

"I hear there is a museum we should see," Maia said.

"Why not? My eyes are wide open for everything," he replied, and it was there at the museum where Aaron met more black men from other countries who were traveling on to Africa for trade.

The ship *Roquelle*, sailed for Africa on October 24. The vessel was filled to capacity, as were the many other ships headed there from England, Germany, and France. The sea waters during the trip vacillated between calm and peaceful to rough and choppy, dictated by the tempers of the winds that blew. Bishop Turner's steadfast prayers were a comfort to passengers on the stormy days; and on the blissful days, they walked or relaxed on deck and slept or read books.

Over the next week, they passed the island of Madeira, the Isles of the Blessed, and Grand Canary Island. They were told that all the islands were created by volcano eruptions, and they were visited by people from all over the world for their beauty and healing springs. It was on November 10, when the ship anchored in Freetown, Sierra Leone.

"I can't believe that we are actually about to set foot on African soil," Maia said to Aaron as she thought about how Hercules would have felt if he had made the journey back with them. "I see God all over," she said, looking up into the majestic mountains, the blue waters that ran along the white sand on the beach, and the tall palm trees that framed the backdrop of the beautiful picture that was Sierra Leone.

"I have to admit that I'm impressed," Aaron said as they disembarked. It seemed as if the city opened itself in a welcome to them,

"It's not at all like I had expected."

The skyline of the buildings put West Broad in Savannah to shame with its three- and four-story buildings that lining the pristine sidewalks and pavements. It was an unexpected relief to behold what could have been any established city in the United States, and the fact that most of it was black-owned made Aaron feel proud.

"The people here look familiar to me," Aaron remarked. "Their faces remind me of people I've seen on the island and in other cities. Probably many more than Hercules came from this area."

"I think that the name *Freetown* is very fitting," Maia said, noting that the men and the women were dressed in whatever manner suited them. Some were fully dresses in English attire, some wore pants or shirts, and others were nearly naked.

When Maia and Aaron's trunk had been cleared in the Customs House, they were directed to the guest house where they would be staying for the next ten days before traveling on to Monrovia, Liberia. Two young natives, wearing only loin cloths, carried their trunk leading them to their living quarters. A Krio woman greeted them at the door. She was dressed in a purple silk dress and fine jewelry. She introduced herself as Faren Cornell-King.

"Welcome. Please call me Faren. My husband and I are from England, but we have lived here for 18 years. He travels on business most of the time, so I offer lodging to guests from America from time to time. I'll take you both on a brief tour of the house."

She instructed the native youths to take their trunk upstairs. The house had three stories, and their room was located at the front of the house on the second floor. Maia hadn't expected to see anyone treated like a slave in Freetown and it made her uncomfortable.

"Mrs. King, aren't all the people equal here?" she asked.

Faren smiled and said, "This is a place of great opportunity, but it isn't the Garden of Eden. It's practically impossible to find a place on this earth where social class does not exist. The natives from the bush work as servants, laborers, and domestics. They do the burdensome work that most of us prefer not to do."

Aaron set about unpacking the trunk, while Maia stood at the window, looking out over the street. It didn't look like a foreign place and didn't feel like it either since it seemed that everyone spoke English.

"I want to go out for a walk," Maia said excitedly. "Do you want to come?"

"No, not now. You go and enjoy yourself. I have a lot to do here," Aaron said.

Maia was glad; she wanted a chance to experience Freetown by herself, to walk alone as she did as a child on Ossabaw.

As Maia headed toward the door, Faren called out to her, "Dinner will be served at 6:00. Don't be late."

Maia took a deep breath of the air trying to get the scent of Freetown. She thought it a mixture of the sea and saw dust, with a touch of sweetness. She headed down the sidewalk to the market area. She wanted to see everything Hercules had seen and hear the sounds that he had heard.

As she walked, she listened to the different voices, the dialects, the songs, and the laughter of the people as they stopped and talked. She saw men from the bush working, pushing people in chairs, carrying folk in hammocks, and pulling full carts from one place to the other. She saw black women in every shade wearing dresses in every color walking as if they owned the streets. A white man greeted her with a smile and tipped his hat. Another bowed, and it was then she knew she was in another world.

One market was located in the center of town, about a half mile from the house. After so much time on the ocean, it felt good to walk a ways on solid ground. Close to the market just in front of her, Maia recognized the great Cotton Tree that Hercules had told her about in his stories of Freetown. She stopped to gaze at it for a few minutes, happy to lay eyes on something he had seen a young boy. Moving on, Maia feasted on the smells of the market, even before she got close to the vendors.

There was so much to take in. *There is a bit o' heaven on earth,* she said to herself as she saw all the women dressed in lappas of every color, with their heads tied in matching head scarves.

Some women had small children at their feet, and others had babies wrapped in cloth that was tied around their backs. She was aware of voices coming from different directions, singing and shouting that blended in a strong harmony that invited her to come closer. Maia approached the women and the array of tables to see food as colorful as the women's clothing. There were tables of pineapples, mangoes, grapes, and oranges. There was plenty of rice, corn, peppers, beans, yams, and tomatoes.

Maia touched as much of the food as she could, trying to absorb every sight and smell. She was upset with herself for not bring-ing any money to buy some of the fruit to take back to Aaron. She looked around at all the vendors and wondered if any of the women or men were from Hercules's village, and if one of them could offer her any help in finding his family.

At the edge of the market, Maia noticed a woman sitting with a baby tied so high on her back, and the baby peeping over her shoulder. The woman was dressed in the bright colors of citrus fruit: yellow, orange, with splashes of red and green. Her face was pleasant and relaxed, and Maia was drawn to her.

She walked over to her and asked, "Do you speak English?"

"Yea, ma'am," the woman answered with a thick accent. The baby stirred at the sound of her mother's voice and looked at Maia.

"Your baby has beautiful eyes. Boy or girl?"

"A girl, ma'am, her name is Ramata. My name is Fatou Daramy."

"It's my pleasure to meet you. My name is Maia Liberty, and I have come from America."

"Have you brought your family with you, ma'am?" Fatou asked.

"Oh, my children are all grown," Maia answered. "I am here with my husband. I hope to find the village of a Temne man I once knew. He lived in this city many years ago. He married my mother and was a father to me. Do you live nearby, or have you come far to the market?"

"I am Mandinka, ma'am. I come from the Northern Province, where most of the Temnes live, also," Fatou replied proudly.

"He came from a family of fishermen and farmers," Maia offered.

"Look for his people in Port Loko, ma'am," Fatou said.

"I'll do that, and thank you for your help," Maia said.

On her way back to the house, the nods of greeting and the smiles of hello from the folks in the market and along the street gave Maia the feeling of a warm embrace. She felt so happy that she could have cried. It took tremendous energy to contain her emotions and not run through the streets shouting as a mad woman. She was thousands of miles from home, but it was the first time she felt as if she was accepted.

Maia was so grateful for the opportunity to do this for Hercules. It was as if she was going to repay some of the debt for all he had done for her and her mama. The happiness so lifted her heart that she knew they would find the connection to his family very soon.

Chapter Fourteen

aron was standing on the veranda when Maia got back to the house. In that moment, she saw him in a way she hadn't for many years. He was still fit, with no round belly; his muscular arms still hung from broad shoulders; and the years hadn't harmed the sharp features in his face. He looked good to her standing out there. She felt attracted to him in a way she thought she never would again after finding out about his betrayal with Eve and the birth of their son, Roman. Their love had weathered many storms, and now she knew that it had survived.

They exchanged a secret smile, and when she got up the porch stairs, they hugged, she took his hand, and they went inside to join their host for dinner. There was plenty of rice and a sauce made from fish and chicken with eggplant, okra, and fresh tomatoes, seasoned with hot peppers.

"That was delicious, Faren. Everything reminds me of the Sea Islands back at home and the meals my mama used to cook for me," Maia told her.

"Let's drink to your safe arrival," Faren said as she poured them all glasses of palm wine.

"I feel a kinship to this place. I heard about it all the time I was growing up," Maia said. "It's a common bond that was stretched over more than 6,000 miles by my tata, Hercules."

"At least all the worry I was feeling about this voyage has

passed," Aaron said, smiling with relief. "The people look recognizable, the flavor of the food is familiar, and nothing wild and hairy has come out to gobble us up."

"I agree," Maia added with a laugh. "Yet it's all much deeper than that. The beauty of the exotic orchids and colorful gardenias, the tallness of the plantain and palm trees, the sweetness of the pineapple and the sugar plum, and the blue color of the water along the beach--they are all intensified here."

"Let's see what else might be intense," Aaron whispered in Maia's ear when they retired to their room.

"I think you will be surprised," Maia said, drawing the curtains on the window.

The passion between Aaron and Maia that had waned and dissipated over the years, sometimes even buried under the frustrations of life, resurfaced and was strengthened as every part of their being blended together in Freetown. They were thousands of miles away from their heartaches and regrets; and at this moment, there was nothing separating them from the pure love that brought them together.

After taking time to relish the moment and unspoken words, Maia told Aaron, "I met a woman named Fatou in the market and she told me where to look for Hercules's people."

"I promise you that we'll get there before we sail on to Liberia," he said, wrapping her up in his arms. With those words, Maia fell asleep content.

Aaron, too, slept more soundly and deeply than he had in years. They spent the next few days rediscovering each other as they investigated every corner of the city.

***

"I'd like to go back to the docks. There are large amounts of trade going on," Aaron said after breakfast. "I want to take a look at what's being shipped out and what's being shipped in."

Aaron paid close attention to the workers, who was in charge, and how things were organized when they got there. He wanted to see how much influence the Europeans exerted.

"It makes me proud and pleased that Freetown is controlled by black men holding the political power," he said to Maia.

They noted the missionaries that flooded the area, and they attended one of the conferences of the Methodist Church, but most of the native people were Muslims. They learned that Freetown is basically a trade town, and few natives live there.

"Most of the houses are made of bamboo with thatch roofs," Maia said as they traveled on the edge of the city. "They have some rectangular ones, but most of them are round."

"I've been trying to envision what life for us would be like here, where we would they live, and what we would they do to occupy our time and energy, and I can't see it yet," Aaron said on their way back to the guest house.

"We have time, honey. There's no pressure," Maia assured him. "I've been thinking the same thing."

***

At last, on November 17, they set out for Port Loko to find the family of Zokaya, the man they had known as Hercules.

"I've hired us a guide, Maia. I don't want to get lost out there," Aaron said as they boarded a ferry that traveled along the Sierra Leone River to the Pamoronkoh River.

"I'm glad one of us is thinking," she said as the guide came to meet them.

"Hello, Miss, I'm John. I'll be traveling with you on your journey."

"Call me, Maia. You lead, and we will follow," Maia said, her spirits buoyed.

They took in the magnificent views of the coast as the boat navigated along the Sierra Leone River. It was a huge feast for the eyes, more than they could take in or digest at one time. Aaron had always thought of Africa as a hot and dry jungle with wild animals, but what they saw was a lush and tropical landscape with water flowing everywhere, across the land and streaming out the side of hills and mountains. The river was flush with fish, in the skies they saw all manner of birds, eagles, hawks, ducks, and even parrots in the trees. Throughout the rainforest, they saw monkeys, antelopes, crocodiles, and even wild pigs; but none of the elephants or hippopotamus ventured near the shores.

"The ferry ride is just under four hours, and we will arrive in Port Loko just after midday," John informed them.

When they arrived, the river market was busy with the daily trade of palm oil, rice, coffee, timber, and a cornucopia of fruit and vegetables. Aaron couldn't help but notice that there was a heavy military police presence at the Port that patrolled the roads to the various villages of Port Loko.

"The best way to find Hercules's family is to go into one of the villages and get a recital from a griot or jeliw. They're the persons who retain the history and genealogy of the village people," John said as they got off the ferry.

There were five well-beaten paths that branched away from the river market into different directions.

"Let's take this trail," John said, leading them on the one straight in the center of them all.

"It's so quiet," Maia said, surprised by the hush that surrounded them as they walked through the dense forest of tall palm trees that closely bordered the path.

They had walked for less than an hour when they saw the houses of the village and heard the sounds of a bustling community. Several dogs barked and ran around freely, but they appeared friendly.

"The men up there high in the trees are gathering cones from the palm oil trees," John explained, "The women gathered around the steaming caldrons in the center are boiling the cones."

"The houses are much larger than I thought they would be," Aaron commented as they got closer. "I don't know why I thought they would be one-room huts."

Most of the houses were round and constructed out of bamboo with steep roofs of thick thatching. All of the natives seemed to have chickens. Some had a goat or two, and several of the large ones had a few cattle. From all the colors emanating around them, those natural and manmade, it seemed to Maia that a rainbow had spread itself across the village.

Many of the natives in the village were scarcely clothed. The men wore loin cloths, and the women wore wraps around their waists. They looked at the strangers curiously, and some watched with suspicion.

"I'm going to talk with them," John said as he walked over to one of the men and spoke to him in words that Aaron and Maia didn't understand. "I have requested to speak with the chief to state our business here," John explained to them when he came back.

They were led to a very large hut that was rectangular in shape and were instructed to wait outside. One of the guards in front went inside, and after a few moments, the chief came out. He took a seat in a large straw chair on the veranda and nodded for John to speak. John spoke to him in Temne while the chief listened intently.

The chief then turned toward Aaron and Maia, met their eyes, and responded in perfect English. "I am Bai Bombolai, and I welcome you to my village as my personal guests. We are descendants of the Koya Kingdom and are pleased that you have brought word of what may be one of our lost sons. In the third hut to my right, you will find Kanta, and he will give you a recitation of our history."

"Thank you very much for your graciousness," Aaron said before the chief went back inside his hut. Then they proceeded to walk down a cleared path to meet the griot. Kanta stood at his door and greeted them as if he were expecting them.

"Come under the tree with me," he directed as he led them to a full and expansive palm in the center of the village. He called out for someone, and a young woman with a wooden xylophone appeared and came over to join them.

"The instrument she has in her hand is called a bala," John whispered to them.

John and Aaron sat on the ground in front of Kanta, and a man brought a stump over for Maia to sit on. The young woman began to play and a small group of the villagers assembled around them. The sharp tones from the music resonated with Maia's heartbeat as she listened with anticipation.

"Tell me your story, Missus," Kanta said.

Maia told him about the slave plantation in Ossabaw, where she was raised, and Hercules, the African man from Sierra Leone, who was the rice driver.

"He married my mother and was the only father I have ever known. His given name was Zokaya. He was kidnapped as a young man, traded for guns, and sold as a slave."

Kanta looked up into the sky intently, as is if he were reading words that written there, and then he began to chant. His story told how their ancestors had traveled from Guinea and became the Koya Kingdom of Temne at the start of the sixteenth century in what is now known as Kambia. Sub-kingdoms were formed and near the end of the seventeenth century Naimbanna I reigned over the kingdom in Port Loko. Kanta recited the rulers and the descendant up to the eighteenth century when Nemgbana was Obai and the last leader of the Sierra Leone peninsula before it became Freetown. He told of his brother Ibrahim, who he kept in close counsel, and how he became one of the sub-rulers in 1775.

"He and his brother objected to the continuation of slave trading. In 1788, Nemgbana unwisely signed a treaty with the deceptive British for a colony on the peninsula. Disappointed in the outcome of the treaty and feeling duped out of their land, the Koya fought the British and the Susu for more than six years from. In 1807, our people lost the war. Port Loko went to the Susu, and the peninsula went to the British."

Kanta's recitation continued. "Nemgbana's brother and sub-chief, Ibrahim was married to Abeni, and they remained in the region of Freetown. They had four sons: Berko; Olumide; Yaw; and the youngest, Zokaya, born in the year after the war in 1808. Ibrahim had prospered with the trade of rice and other goods with the British.

Seven years later, under the rule of Bai Foki, the Temne defeated the Susu and regained Port Loko. The third son, Yaw, was a fighter and sustained fatal injuries in the war. Bad blood flowed between the chiefs on trade in 1827. In that year, the fourth son, Zokaya, disappeared on a trip to market and was never seen again. It was then Ibrahim became ill and died. The elder sons, Berko and Olumide, moved their families and their mother, Abeni, to Port Loko."

Kanta went through the generations of the two brothers before he revealed that one of the sons of Berko, the elder brother of Zokaya, lived in the village and had three daughters and one son. Maia and Aaron reached for each other's hand with the knowledge that they had found Hercules's home.

"Oh my God," Maia said as she threw back her head in joy, and the tears of recognition flowed like the streams that surrounded them in the village.

This moment was a gift, something that she wanted to give Hercules. She prayed that he was with her there somehow and was pleased they had found his family. The news spread like wildfire among everyone in the village.

Maia sat on the stump crying. "My heart is so full right now. I'm so thankful that we came on this journey to this place that I never thought I would ever see."

Leaning to the side on the tree stump, Maia felt physically exhausted and emotionally drained, as if she needed to roll over onto the ground, rest for a while, and absorb all that they had heard. A woman came over to the group and beckoned them with her hand.

"Let me help you up," Aaron said as he lifted her to her feet and they followed.

Less than one hundred yards away through a clearing, they came to a semicircle of four huts. In front of them stood at least thirty people. There were men, women, and children of varying ages. Maia looked at them all and marveled at how beautiful they were. They all had deep cocoa-brown skin and stood tall and proud.

An older man extended his arms to Maia, clasped both her hands, and said to her in perfect English, "I am Yemi, Berko was my father, and Zokaya was my uncle."

After the introduction, a barrage of hugs, kisses, and questions engulfed Maia and Aaron, and they were obliged to stay the evening for a feast of celebration. In the center of the village, all the people gathered for the special ceremony. The chief and sub-chiefs wore fine robes with fine jewelry and they were adorned with ornate headpieces decorated with plumes and feathers. Many were dressed in elaborate grass costumes, and everyone seemed to be wearing their very best ensemble.

The celebration began with the honoring of the ancestors with prayer and the sacrifice of kola nuts. Then the musicians began to play and the beat of the drums reverberated against the mountains in the distance. A few musicians shook instruments that made the sound of sea shells when they were shaken. Many of the dancers had bells around their wrists and ankles that resounded with each step. Maia recognized the familiar circle dance, and she joined in. They danced counterclockwise, and the shouts of the people in the ring reminded her of the worship services at home and she could see visions of Hercules moving in the circle. Maia experienced God totally as she received the blessing of all that was happening around her.

When they finished the dance, it was time for the communal feast. They washed their hands in a bowl of water before the meal. Aaron ate with the men, and Maia with the women. A great platter of food was placed in the center for all to share. They ate cassava bread, rice, and a groundnut stew with potato leaves, beans, tomatoes, onions, red pepper, and goat meat. They ate in silence out of respect for the feast. Using only their right hands, they rolled the rice into balls to dip in the stew. After eating, everyone washed their hands in another bowl of water after the meal and thanked the women who had prepared the meal, and then they poured the libations.

"This was, by far, the most extraordinary day in all my life. Thank you so much coming and sharing it with me," Maia said to Aaron when they found each other after the meal.

"I'm the one who should be thanking you for not giving up on me and insisting that we come on this eventful journey," Aaron told her.

Yemi offered Aaron and Maia a room in his hut for the night. His home was one of the few rectangular huts. Inside, was a parlor area, a food storage room, and three bedrooms. The Temne were superior craftsmen, and the inside of the hut was well-furnished and decorated with art pieces. Aaron and Maia were comfortable in their room. The bed mat was placed on a wooden platform, and posts held mosquito netting around it. There were shelves to place their belongings, a table and a bench, and a looking glass.

In the darkness of the night, Maia whispered to Aaron, "I would like to give a gift or something to the people as a token from us and for Hercules, but I don't know what it could be."

"Sweetheart, you already gave them something priceless: the story of their lost loved one, that he was not tortured or murdered, that he lived a long life, that he was a good and honorable man who was loved. In that way, you brought him back home to them. Besides, they are proud people. They wouldn't accept a gift from you anyway."

In the morning, after an emotional farewell, Maia left Port Loko satisfied that her mission there had been accomplished. John led them back down the path to the shoreline, while the children of the village followed for a good distance of the way. They boarded the steamboat and were back in Freetown before nightfall. At the house in Freetown, Faren was eager to hear everything that had happened. Over a late dinner, she hung on to each word about their day in Port Loko.

"It's absolutely unbelievable," she told them. "You were actually able to find the relatives of your father at the first village that you visited. It's beyond good luck my friends; it had to be divine providence that led you there."

"Oh, I believe it without a doubt, Faren," Maia said. "I have been guided by God, and I have witnessed one of His miracles yet again."

"Well, Aaron, were you convinced that the next chapter of your life is in the bush of Sierra Leone?" Faren asked with her glass raised in the air.

Aaron smiled across the table, tapped her glass, and said, "The good Lord has many miracles yet to perform."

Maia laughed and said, "Amen."

Chapter
Fifteen

"I learned that there are some unresolved issues about Freetown being a colony," Aaron said to Maia as they busied themselves packing for the final leg of their voyage to Liberia. "Several folks have told me about the continuous skirmishes and fighting with the British in Freetown over it. I don't want to be caught in the crosshairs of a civil war again."

"It doesn't matter, honey. I have already decided that I want to go back home," Maia said, wrapping up their keepsakes. "We're in a different season of our lives."

"Are you serious, sweetheart? I can't tell you how much of a relief it is to hear you say that. I didn't want us to get into a disagreement about going back home. Africa is exciting and fresh, but it only offers us more work in the fields, and that's not what I want for us," Aaron said, gazing out of their room window thinking how quickly their visit in Freetown had gone.

"Twenty years earlier, it might have been just what we needed," Maia added, "But today, as much as I've enjoyed the sights, the people, the freedom, and the energy it exudes, it isn't for us. My real purpose was to find Hercules's family and tell them what a good man he was."

Aaron and Maia had long since passed the season of planting and were well past their time of harvesting. They were in a time when they needed to enjoy the fruits of their labors and relish their lives.

On November 21, 1891, they sailed on the steamship *Mandingo* to Liberia, where they were reunited with Bishop Henry Turner, who was traveling to Monrovia, where he hoped to bring his Back to Africa movement to fruition.

Maia and Aaron planned to shorten their stay and go home from there, having answered all the questions they had at the start of the journey. The two of them stood on the deck of the ship after sunset and watched in awe as the waves broke up what seemed to be an ocean made of glass. The sea water emitted its own sparkling light from what was explained to them as phosphoric animalculae. It shone like a thick layer of diamond dust illuminating the surface in the dark of night. Gazing at it, Maia knew she was looking at God.

"Liberia reminds me of home in the South," Maia remarked as they disembarked from the ship the next morning and saw the people bustling about.

"There is a tremendous difference," Aaron said, and it was the one that most intrigued him. "They have a black president, and black folks hold all the leadership positions."

English was spoken and everyone dressed in the same manner of style that they did at home in the states. Aaron and Maia were to be the guests at the home of General R. A. Sherman, the head of the Liberian armies. He was born in Savannah, and although he had lived in Liberia some thirty-seven years he was still a loyal reader of The Savannah Tribune which he had shipped over with other newspapers so he could stay abreast of the news of blacks living back in America.

General Sherman arranged for Aaron and Maia to take a tour up the St. Paul River before their arrival at his residence. "Look at the all the folks rowing small canoes along the river, carrying food and other goods to sell," Maia said, taking in the sites. "You can even see the division of the settlements in the towns."

"I can't believe it. They're named after American states and cities, like New Georgia, Virginia, Louisiana, New York, and Harrisburg," Aaron said. "You would think they would have chosen completely different names. And even the houses are built in similar styles."

"I hear Monrovia is rich in resources and food. There is so much grown here: coffee beans, sugar cane, cocoa, a variety of fruit and vegetables, cotton, and indigo," Maia said, looking along the landscape. There were animals in large numbers, both domestic and wild.

"It's just like Freetown," Aaron said, noticing again that the natives did most of the heavy lifting and hard labor work.

In Monrovia, Aaron was again surprised to meet several men he had been acquainted with back in the States. What wasn't a revelation to him was the need for money to survive in this country. He had been told that here a man could be a man, free and liberated in every sense; but without money, the struggle was still there.

After their brief tour of the area, there was no mystery that money made a difference, and it was easy to see who had it and who didn't. There were men and women who walked down the streets dressed to death, and then there were those who were shabby and nearly naked. When they reached General Sherman's house, it was obvious that he was one of the most successful in town. His three-story estate was suited for royalty.

General Sherman met Aaron and Maia at the entrance dressed in full military regalia. He was very light in complexion with straight hair and a mustache turned up on the ends.

"Welcome to my home, Mr. and Mrs. Liberty. It is most fitting that you have finally arrived in Liberia. If my mission is successful, you both will be our permanent guests."

"Thank you for having us," Aaron said graciously.

As they followed him into the sitting-room, they could see he walked with a slight limp to the right. He also kept his left arm close to body, most likely remnants of his many battles.

"Please call me Reginald," General Sherman said, offering them something to drink before dinner. "Your reputations precede you," he continued. "I am a fellow carpenter aware of the hard work and financial success that you have achieved in Savannah, Mr. Liberty. We need more men who have the knowledge you possess to grow and develop this country. And you, Madam Liberty, I have enjoyed your stories in The Savannah Tribune. It is my pleasure to meet you both."

"Thank you, Reginald. And please call me Aaron, and my wife, Maia."

"I'm sure you are famished by now. Come, join us for dinner," he said as he led them to the dining room.

Robert T. Sherman, the general's brother, and Liberia's immigration agent, was already seated at the table with his wife. William D. Coleman, a wealthy farmer and merchant, along with his wife, also joined the gerneral's dinner party. After they were seated, and properly introduced, servants brought the meal to the table.

"We're having champagne to toast the arrival of our new guests," Robert said as he poured from the bottle into their glasses. An array of liquors was served throughout the four course meal and then the lively conversation began. "What is the status of racial relations in the U.S.?" Robert asked, "Are things better or worse?"

"Much of the progress that was realized after the war during reconstruction is being rolled back," Aaron said. "The right to vote for so many in the South is being diminished, decent jobs are hard to find, and black blood is spilled night and day fueled by a hate that grows in the hearts of white men who want power over blacks."

"The KKK runs wild in the night burning crosses," Maia added. "When they burned one on the front yard of our church, my mama got so scared her heart stopped. So many blacks live in constant fear of attacks and the never-ending lynchings that are occurring in Georgia."

"There is an alternative to all that, my friends," Reginald said. "The opportunities for a man of your means are unlimited here in mercantile ventures. All of us seated at this table have made vast fortunes as merchants, with minimal investment. There is much for you to consider during your stay. However, I think we have talked about serious matters far more than is good for the digestion."

The general tapped his champagne class for attention and said, "I don't know if you all know that we have a celebrity within our midst. Mrs. Maia Liberty is a well-known published author in Savannah, a superior storyteller who has captivated audiences in faraway places she doesn't even know about. Even I have become one of her loyal readers. It would give us all great pleasure, my dear, if you would favor us with one of your tales."

"Well, I haven't prepared anything for this warm reception that you have given Aaron and me, but I have been a little inspired by what I have seen since I have arrived in this unique land of Africa.

"This story takes place in an uncharted land called Amirage. This spot on the earth was a place of wonder, where every species of animal or plant could thrive. Peace had ruled over this paradise for one hundred years, but contention and competition was brewing among the animals over who would be named as their leader. They began to separate and segregate themselves in areas they desig-nated as their own, and a pall fell over the land. The sun didn't want to shine there anymore, the rain didn't want to fall there any-more, and the trees and plants lost their zest and began to die. A period of drought and famine started to take hold.

"At the edge of this land ran a deep body of water, and about 300 yards across that water, there was an island. When they were all at their wit's end and their survival was coming into question, they called a grand meeting. The eagle spoke first, and said, 'I have found the answer to our troubles. I have been to the island over yonder, and I have found a forest of trees. Written below the trees are the words, 'Food set upon the earth for the one who is most worthy.'"

"The turtle asked, 'How do we know who is the most worthy?' They all began to argue and plead their case as to why this food was allocated for them. The birds said, 'God gave us wings to fly so we are more worthy.' The blue whale at the shore rose above the water, and said, 'I am the largest of all so who could be more worthy.' The geese said, 'We can fly and swim, we are most worthy.' The lion's voice roared, 'God made me King of the Jungle so I'm the most worthy.' The giraffe said, 'God made me the tallest to eat from the trees.' The apes joined in saying, 'God gave us hands and the ability to climb the trees, the food is for us.' The elephant said, 'God gave me the size and strength, we are more worthy.' The bear said, 'I have strength and I can climb the tree too.'

"When they tired of arguing, they decided that the food was for whomever could get it. Those in the water swam over but couldn't get ashore; the birds flew over but couldn't get the fruit off the tree. They all became angry and frustrated and began to prey on one another.

"The wise old owl called another meeting. They began to fuss and talk about the chain of command on the earth and how God planned things. 'Maybe so,' the owl said, 'but maybe he did give us a better way. I have a plan that may work.'

"What they found was, if the whale carried the giraffe and the apes to the island, and the birds led them to the ripened trees, the giraffe could get food from the branches that wouldn't hold the weight of the apes. They brought as much as they could carry back across the water in large crates. The elephants carried the large amount of food they had gathered to a clearing.

"The strange food was oblong in shape and had a thick covering. It took the claws of the lions and bears to tear it off. They chewed some of it and to the lion it was like juicy meat, to the bear it was like a fresh fish; it had a different flavor for them all. Under the outer covering was a succulent fruit with small seeds that tasted like nuts, which they all feasted on. In the center was an oval core, and inside of it was nectar that not only quenched their thirst but refreshed them with new energy.

"All the animals agreed that this food was a gift from God and that it was the cooperation among them all that made each of them worthy of it. The sun was pleased and began to shine and the rain showered them again, and they were all blessed."

After Maia finished her story, the dinner guests clapped and the General shouted, "Bravo, my dear! Well done!"

The servants cleared the table as the guests dispersed. The men retired to the parlor for cigars and cognac, while Mrs. Sherman led the women in a tour of the mansion before returning to the sitting room. All the women were educated and accomplished in their own right and ran successful businesses. The conversation soon drifted to their families. Maia was proud to mention that her daughter, Diana, was a singer with the Fisk Jubilee Singers and had traveled around the world, but she was subdued when the subject of grand-children arose.

After a while the men came into the sitting room. All the quests told the Shermans how much they enjoyed the evening and making new acquaintances. The Colemans and Robert Sherman and his wife took their leave as the end of the dinner party became evident.

"I'm sure our guests are tired to their bones, and it's only fair to give them some time to recover before we launch our next campaign," the general said with a chuckle.

The housekeeper approached Aaron and Maia and said, "I'll show you to your room." Totally worn out, Maia and Aaron were sleep before the sheets warmed to their bodies.

***

"I've been invited to a meeting with the Freemasons of Liberia to discuss business opportunities and trade in the country," he mentioned to Maia in the morning. "I don't see much cause to do it though."

"It won't hurt you to go," Maia urged. "You might enjoy yourself."

Actually, Maia wanted some private time to look around. After breakfast was served to them in their bedroom, Maia went out on her excursion. She felt the heat as soon as she opened the door. The night had been cool, but the heat of the day had already rise, despite the early morning hour. Walking through town, she saw that the streets were covered with grass and were lined in the shapes of squares, triangles, and even half-circles, but the sidewalks were clear.

She saw street markets just like the ones she had seen in Freetown, but most of the people were dressed like Americans. She walked along the St. Paul River, and the landscape was breathtaking. It was the mixture of a city within the jungle fascinated her. The houses seemed to rise up out of the mountains and vegetation. Taking it all in, she was sure that she was just a visitor and it wasn't home.

The week of meetings, dinners, parties, getting-together with old friends and making new ones went by quickly. On the first day of December, it was time for Aaron and Maia to return to Sierra Leone for the voyage back to the only home they had ever known: the United States of America.

"Maia and I thank you and your wife for the gracious hospitality you have shown us since we have arrived," Aaron said to General Sherman before they boarded the small steamship back to Freetown.

"It was our pleasure," Reginald replied. "If you change your mind, you know where you can find us."

"We certainly do," Maia said, giving Aaron a nudge.

Aaron and Maia walked along the side of the steamship and saw a black woman at the helm of the ship.

"I thank God for a place like this, where women are in charge of things," Maia said as the ship moved away from the shore.

Their feet barely touched the ground in Freetown before they boarded the *Roquelle* for the voyage to Liverpool, England. Aaron and Maia stood on the deck in the cool evening air and watched the city until it disappeared from their view. Eighteen days passed before they reached Liverpool, England, and it couldn't have come soon enough.

"I'm so tired of being cooped up on this ship," Maia said. "I've memorized every wall in the dining room and the music room."

"It doesn't bother me at all," Aaron said. "Each hour brings us closer to home, and I'm grateful to God that neither of us has come down with any of the fevers or sicknesses that they warned about before we left Savannah."

It was on the morning of December 20 that they disembarked in Liverpool. It would be another two days before their final ship sailed to New York. They collected their baggage and hired a horse and carriage to take them to the London and North Western Railway Hotel. The cold temperatures nearly sent their bodies into shock after they had langished in the tropical weather of Sierra Leone. Once they were settled they went out to see the sights of the area. A thick fog blanketed the city.

"I have never seen such magnificent buildings. They are as tall as they are broad, and some of them go on for blocks," Aaron said, impressed.

There was a mass of giant horses and carriages navigating the paved streets. Many of the carriages were so large that it took four horses to pull them. It was a stark contrast from the lush forests, grassy roads, and few horses they had seen in Liberia.

They walked along the lengthy streets, where the all the houses were connected to one another in neat rows. They saw grand cathedrals, with tall steeples that reached high into the mist, but it was St. George's Hall that gripped Maia.

"That building looks like one of the Roman palaces that I used to read about and saw paintings of in books," Maia said amazed. "It's hard to believe that regular men can build something so glorious."

It felt as if only hours had passed before the two of them stood in line to board the *RMS Etruria.*

Maia was tired of traveling, and her stomach was upset. The overcooked food of the English did not suit her. She wasn't looking forward to the rocking of the ship over the waves and in the wind for another week. However, the luxury of the *Etruria* was beyond any of the other vessels they had sailed on, and the extra comforts made the trip more bearable.

Over dinner on Christmas day, the couple reflected back over all they had seen, the people they had met, and the foods that they tasted.

"Aaron, I just want to say that I thought taking this trip was something I wanted to do for my tata, Hercules. But it has been the greatest experience of my life, and sharing it with you has made it even more precious to me."

"I'm just glad you didn't give up on me, and you pushed me to come," Aaron replied. "It has been a blessing for me to see that smile on your pretty face again."

She looked deep into his eyes and knew God was there.

When they finally reached New York, it was New Years Day. As they laughed together, Maia said, "I won't be getting in more water than I can fit in a bathtub for a very long time."

"It might be for the rest of my life," Aaron said.

Chapter Sixteen

"I thought about Diana so many times while we were gone. But now that we're back in the States, I want to see her as soon as we can," Maia said to Aaron.

Maia hadn't written her daughter because she knew they wouldn't be in the same place long enough to receive a response.

"Why don't we find a place to stay for a few days?" Aaron suggested. "It's still the holiday season. The Creole Show is based here. If they are out of town, we can find out if they're touring in a city close by."

Aaron hired a carriage to take them and their baggage to the Victoria Hotel. They had never seen so many people crowded in one place, all so busy and preoccupied with their own lives. Some coming, others going, some working, others seeming to have no direction.

"I don't know how they build such humongous bridges," Maia said, amazed at the tall buildings so close together and the bridges they crossed during the ride.

"I hope we won't have any trouble with our accommodations. Segregation is spreading in the Northern cities, too," Aaron said warily. "I've heard well-to-do blacks and celebrities can stay at the Victoria."

"At least we know we have other options across the water," Maia teased.

They checked into the hotel without incident.

"Fortunately, this hotel doesn't see any differences in the color of the money they collect," Aaron said on the way to their room.

As soon as their baggage was brought in, Aaron and Maia went out on a mission to find Diana.

In the lobby, Aaron spoke to a middle-aged man with a shoeshine stand. "Do you know what negro shows are playing in town?"

"Go down to African Broadway. Dats where all de nice shows play," he said, admiring the fashionable clothes on the couple. "Need a shine fo' you go?"

"Not now," Aaron answered. "I'll see you when I get back."

Aaron and Maia caught a streetcar to Manhattan, where they could get to the lower end of Broadway. When they stepped off, Maia bought the latest edition of *The New York Clipper* at a news-stand. She remembered it was the paper that Diana once mentioned had done an article on the show. They found a bench so they could sit for a moment while Maia searched for information on the shows.

"There's a review here that says *The Creole Show* ended its run at the Standard Theater. It's now moving on to Philadelphia and then out to the Pacific Coast for fifteen weekly bookings."

The article also said that the troupe would be leaving for Philadelphia as soon as a new orchestra leader has been hired. Maia felt her face flush with heat despite the chill on the wind. She was growing anxious that she may have missed the chance to see Diana.

"We have to get to the New York Central Railroad Station. In the last letter I got from Diana, she mentioned that Mr. Jack has a Pullman Palace Car for them so they don't have to worry about the hassle of segregated hotels when they're on tour. If they are still in New York, that's where they will be."

Maia prayed for time to be her friend. They caught another streetcar and were there in less than an hour. But the day was fading into evening, and the cold air was freezing.

"Do you know where we can find Sam Jack's Pullman car?" Aaron asked an attendant at the station.

"Gon' down these tracks, and look for the royal blue cars near the rear of the train," he told them. When they got to the door of the car, it looked like the grand entrance of a fine hotel. A porter neatly dressed in a uniform greeted them as they took the stairs up.

"Hello," Aaron said. "We're looking for Diana Portunus. She's a member in the cast of *The Creole Show*."

"Certainly, sir, follow me," the porter said.

Aaron and Maia followed the porter into the car and luxury of it took Maia's breath for a moment. They saw a small group talking in the observation area, and they exchanged quick glances without breaking their conversation. The whole car was trimmed with a rich, dark walnut, the ceilings were elaborately carved, the lighting was ornate, the floor was covered with intricately designed oriental rugs, and the seating was opulent and plush, covered in maroon velvet.

They moved through the smoking room and then the dining room, each room finer than the last, until they finally reached the sleeping area. The porter knocked on one door, and after a few seconds, it opened. Diana was peeved and prepared to ask why she was disturbed. But when she saw her family, her expression softened.

"Mama and Tata! You almost got a welcome that would have shocked you both," Diana said, pulling the door closed behind her. "When did you get back?"

"Today, we checked into a hotel, and we came straight over here to try and find you," Maia said, grabbing Diana in a tight hug.

"You two are full of surprises. I can't believe you all are really here--in New York," Diana said awkwardly, "I wish you would have written me."

"We cut the trip short in Liberia," Aaron said gladly, "This is the only home we got."

"Why are we talking in the hallway?" Maia asked. "Don't you have room for us to sit down in there?"

"Barely, Mama," Diana replied hastily. "George, can you take them to the dining room while I get dressed?"

"Yes'm, Miss Diana," the porter said.

"She's acting like she's got some man hidden in there she doesn't want us to see," Aaron whispered to Maia as they followed George back to the dining area.

"If she does, that's her business," Maia answered just loud enough for him to hear.

When the porter seated them at a table, Aaron thanked him and gave him a Liberty head nickel. Two minutes, later Diana rushed into the room and hugged them both again.

"I'm glad y'all are home safe and sound. I'm so surprised, I can't stop talking. I have so many questions. I was worried that I wouldn't see y'all again. Thank God y'all are back," she said as she sat down with them.

"How are you?" Maia asked. "I have thought about you every day and prayed that you were well. I was sorry I couldn't write letters and tell you what we saw on our trip."

"Now that you're home, you can tell me all about it," Diana said, slightly distracted.

"You look good, but you seem so different. You've changed," Maia said, touching Diana's hair. "I'm not sure what I see in your eyes."

"I'm the same, Mama, it's just I've been working so hard trying to be better."

"Well, you look like the 'Belle of the Ball,'" Aaron said. "Your mama would have had a fit if we hadn't found you."

"Well, I'm ready to hear all about your trip," Diana said as she sat back and got comfortable in her chair.

"We would need at least a week to tell it all," Maia said.

They talked for about two hours over a late dinner, with Maia and Aaron describing the ocean voyage, the tropical island, the immense mountains, and all the people they met, from members of Hercules's family in Port Loko to the old acquaintances from Savannah in Liberia. They told her about the celebration, the music, the sights, the smells, and the food. And they told her about sleeping in the hut of Zokaya's nephew.

Diana told her parents about the differences in traveling with a burlesque show and the famous people she had met, such as Isaac B. Murphy, the black jockey who had won three Kentucky Derby races, including the last two in a row. They took turns amazing one another with incredible stories of people and places since they were last together.

Then Aaron asked Diana, "What's next for you?"

"We leave for Philadelphia for a week the day after tomorrow, and then we're traveling west with stops in Chicago and Kansas City and other places on our way to California. My question is, where are you and Mama going next?"

"We're going to stay in New York and leave when you leave. But after all of the travels and the all the places we have been, we know that our home is with each other. For right now, we plan to stay in Savannah until we find some place that we like better," Aaron replied.

"Well, tomorrow I'll show y'all the town," Diana said as they shared another hug and kiss before Aaron and Maia left for their hotel.

***

It had been a New Year's Day to remember, one that would mark a new beginning to the rest of their lives. Aaron and Maia met Diana at New York Central Station after breakfast and hired a carriage to take them on a tour of the city. A steady snow began to fall adorning the sidewalks with a clean white carpet that added to the beauty of the day. They saw Wall Street, the business district, Broadway, Fifth Avenue, Harlem, and the Brooklyn Bridge. New York was full of buildings, full of people, full of activity, full of horses and streetcars moving about--much too full for Maia and Aaron. The snow had become deeper throughout the day, and they were chilled deep into their bones and ready to go inside and get warm. They had the carriage driver drop Diana off at the train station, where they said their goodbyes.

"You know where to find us, baby, and we love you," Maia said.

"Don't stay away so long," Aaron added.

"I love you, too," Diana said as she blew them a kiss through the wind.

Trains traveling in different directions carried the Liberty family to their destinations--Diana in search of uncharted successes, and Maia and Aaron to the comfort of the familiar. The rhythmic sound of the train running along the tracks lulled Aaron into a deep sleep, but Maia's thoughts ran neck and neck with the locomotive. She reminisced about the village in Sierra Leone and how different their lives were from her own. She wondered if Hercules would have felt at home there again.

Maia thought about her connections to Savannah, the good and the bad: She had raised her family there, the children that she had never known lived there, her son and mother were buried there, she had taught there, and she had written her stories there. She looked over at Aaron. He had built them a home there in Savannah, established a successful business there, and--for better or worse, it was home. She closed her eyes and felt at peace with their decision to go back.

***

In the morning when they woke, Maia could tell by the warmer temperatures that they were in the South and closer to home. When the train pulled into Savannah, they hired a carriage to carry the heavy trunk they had lugged halfway around the world back to its original location on Liberty Street. It felt good to sleep in their own bed again. Maia and Aaron spent the rest of the winter months like perennial bulbs, vegetating in the ground, waiting for the season to change and they could burst forth with new life and vitality.

When spring arrived, Aaron and Maia made time to re-plant the garden. They started cooking together, each attempting to bring some new flavor to the dish they prepared. Maia registered for classes at Savannah State College, and Aaron stayed busy with his new business partners. They lived in a way that the pressure of earning a living and raising children wouldn't allow. The beach became a favorite place for them in the summer. They would watch the waves and recollect the tense hours that they endured on the voyage to England and then to Africa.

In the fall, Maia came across an article in *The Savannah Press* about an art show at the Telfair Academy of Arts and Sciences, featuring the works of local artist Daphne Bailey. She thought of the young girl she once knew and realized she was blameless in all the happened. Maia decided that she would go the museum to see her old friend. She walked into the gallery area, and saw Daphne speaking with a potential buyer. When the man left, Maia approached Daphne.

"Hello Daphne. From the paintings here, I see that you are a very talented artist. I love your landscapes."

"You may not believe it, Maia, but I was inspired a long time ago when you use to take me on those walks in the fields to look for God. I have never stopped looking; and when I think I've found Him in a vision, I try my best to put it on canvas," Daphne said.

"I'm touched," Maia said surprised. "I guess we never realize how the things we do can affect another person's life. So, how are you? Did you marry? Do you have children, or have you found your contentment in painting?"

"I've found that the life of an artist is a solitary one," Daphne answered. "My mama died several years ago, but I'm not lonely. I feel at peace with the world around me, and my work consumes me. It doesn't leave room for anyone else."

"Well, I wanted to see you again, and your work, it's amazing," Maia said as she held out her hand to say goodbye.

"The name of the family was Elliot," Daphne said. "Mr. and Mrs. Thomas Elliot."

The words swirled around Maia's head as she left the museum. Not knowing what she would do with them, she fanned them away.

Chapter Seventeen

In late August 1893, the shadow of misfortune covered Savannah and the Sea Islands late. There was word of another outbreak of yellow fever in the city, and panic moved like the funnel of a fierce tornado, terrorizing everyone in its path. Without time to react to that news, Aaron got word from Ossabaw that a storm was brewing off the coast from a few who had come mainland. High winds had been gaining strength and speed for days, and there was no doubt that disaster would soon follow.

The relentless hurricane made landfall near Savannah on the 27th and most of the Sea Islands were totally submerged under the storm thrusts of water that flooded the city's coast. There were disheartening reports of more than two thousand people drowned, many of who Aaron and Maia had known very well years ago before coming on the mainland. Maia felt sick and took to her bed, flooded by the memories of Hercules being washed away and Apollo getting sick to his death. Aaron was drowning in his worry about Maia unable to stand his fearful thoughts of losing yet another person he loved.

The aftermath of the disasters that weighed down the city was considerable.

"It says here that the homes of 30,000 people in the Lowcountry have been washed away," Aaron read from the Friday morning newspaper to Maia. "We've surely been blessed this time," he said, but she didn't respond.

Aaron placed the newspaper on the bed and left the room. A few minutes later, Maia picked up the paper to look at the pictures. On the back page, she saw the obituary.

"Mrs. Jean Elliott, wife of prominent businessman, Mr. Thomas Elliott, passed away on August 31, after contracting the yellow fever. She succumbed at her home, surrounded by husband and surviving children, Joseph, Juliette, and Jack. Funeral services will be Saturday at the First Haven Presbyterian Church."

Instantly, Maia threw back the bedcovers and got out of bed. She had been given three good reasons to appreciate that she was not among the dead. The children taken from her at birth so many years ago were alive.

The sun was in its rightful place that Saturday. It was a beautiful morning, and Maia had a funeral to get to. She put on her dress that was the color of salmon and a matching hat. She added one of the fancy necklaces that Diana had brought back from India. Standing in front of the mirror, her reflection looked more than presentable to meet her children for the first time. She grabbed her handbag and lace gloves and went to the kitchen door.

"I've got some errands to run," she yelled to Aaron, who was working the garden out in the backyard.

Aaron smiled and waved, relieved that she was coming back to herself again. He watched as she hurried down the road and caught a streetcar to the other end of town on Bull Street.

Walking into the door of the church, Maia's eyes surveyed the sanctuary until she saw Daphne sitting in one of the rear pews on the right side. Maia took the seat beside Daphne, and they joined hands. Maia stretched and looked toward the family seated in front row of the sanctuary, but all she could see was the back of their heads and she couldn't distinguish who they were. She settled back in the pew to wait until they stood up.

It was a sweet service, with church members and friends giving condolences and anecdotes to the family. A selection was rendered by the church choir and then the three children approached the pulpit. Maia stopped breathing. She could see parts of herself: the golden brown hair and eyes; and similarities to Diana in their faces, as well as familiar gestures as they stood before the other mourners. For some reason it surprised her that they were adults with children of their own. She had always thought of them as babies but all three were more than 30 years old.

Jack, the eldest child, spoke, "We would like to thank you all for coming today to pay respects to our mother. Our hearts are heavy, knowing we have lost one of the most precious gifts God gave to us, a mother's love."

Daphne squeezed Maia's hand as they listened, and it gave Maia enough strength to hold back the tears that pushed forward for release.

The burial was in the small private cemetery behind the church. When the service concluded, Maia walked towards the family with Daphne until they stood within the range of scents from their bodies.

"My parents, Richard and Eliza Bailey, were good friends of the family," Daphne said as she extended her hand in condolence.

At the sound of their names, Mr. Elliot's whole body trembled in recognition when he saw Maia standing beside her.

"Thank you for coming, ma'am," Juliette said, stepping forward. "This is my brother Joseph, and his wife, Emily, and their daughters. My brother Jack, and his wife, Sarah, and those are their children over there. And I'm Juliette, and that's my husband, William Lowe, over there with my son, Junior."

Maia's eyes followed each introduction and absorbed the vision of all of them.

"It's good to meet you all, although I wish it were under different circumstances," Daphne replied. "This is Maia Liberty. We were raised like sisters. When we heard about your mother, we had to come; there are strong ties between us that go back many years."

They all turned and looked at Maia and then at Daphne again, wondering what the connection to their family might be.

"I hope that we will have a chance to talk at another time," Juliette said.

"I'm sure we will," Daphne answered.

The fear in Mr. Elliot's face drained, and sadness took its place as Maia and Daphne walked away.

Maia was shaken. She had stood there in front of her own children, and they didn't know her. Then she had walked away without telling them they had been taken from her. She felt the hurt of them being taken all over again. She hadn't prepared herself. She hadn't known what to say, so she didn't try to speak to them or shake hands, because if they would have been offended, it would have been more than she could bear. She didn't know what Mrs. Elliot looked like, but they bore no resemblance to the dark haired and heavyset Mr. Elliot. She had wanted to ask them if they had ever been curious about that.

"I'm so thankful you were here today," Maia said to Daphne as they stood in front of the church.

"We're both part of it," Daphne answered. "They are our blood, and the time will come for the truth to be told." The two of them shared a long and emotional embrace before they turned away to leave the cemetery in opposite directions.

Maia didn't tell Aaron about seeing her children; she didn't want to start him pining away for Roman. Besides, she couldn't put all the emotions that she felt into words or explain how it felt to see her children for the first time as adults with children of their own. How could she describe the incredible hurt she felt that they didn't know who she was and felt nothing for her? The only grief they had was for the woman they knew as their mother but nothing for the woman who was robbed of her children.

Maia thought of the grandchildren and wished that one of them would have been born with dark skin. But that would have had tragic implications for the family, and she didn't bear any bad feelings toward them. It was Eliza who did the evil to her, and now she was dead. Maia reminded herself that she should live her own life to the fullest. She started writing again and taking classes at Savannah State, while Aaron renewed his interest in politics and the black struggle.

***

In Savannah, as in the rest of South, blacks were getting sick and tired of Jim Crow standing in the way of them earning a decent living and keeping food on the table. All the black people in town were talking about how the Reverend Emmanuel K. Love had been beaten for refusing to sit in the colored section on the streetcar. At the end of the summer of 1895, Aaron sat on the veranda reading a copy of Frederick Douglass's "Lessons of the Hour" speech that he gave at the Metropolitan AME Church in Washington in January of 1894. He was inspired.

The words he read further affirmed his personal feelings after making the trip to Liberia. Douglass said, "The native land of the American negro is America. Colonization is no solution of the race problem. It's an evasion."

After Douglass died in February, Aaron started reading all of his works. Aaron felt as if he and Douglass were kindred spirits, and he wished he could have met the great man and talked with him before his death. It made him more determined to get involved and make a difference for his people.

There was a lot of talk about the head of the Tuskegee Institute in Alabama, Booker T. Washington, who was gaining influence as a rising black leader. The newspapers said he was invited to be a speaker at the Cotton States and International Exposition in Atlanta in September.

"What do you think about going to Atlanta to hear Booker T. Washington speak?" Aaron asked James after a lodge meeting.

"You go, my friend. I've already got my hand in too many pots," James said.

Over breakfast the next morning, Aaron told Maia, "I can't find anybody who wants to go hear the speech."

Maia said, "Have you forgotten who your traveling partner is? You haven't asked me if I would like to go with you."

"I didn't know if you could miss your classes," Aaron replied.

"I bet I'll learn more there than I will in class. I'd like to go," she answered.

After their early train ride to Atlanta, Maia and Aaron found their way to the exposition and the auditorium where Washington would be speaking. They were seated in the rear of a mostly white audience when Washington stood to speak. They were excited to hear what the new negro leader for African Americans had to say to the white business community.

Aaron was completely dumbfounded by what he heard. Was this the man to follow Frederick Douglass? *My ears are playing tricks on me,* he thought as he listened.

"Cast down your bucket where you are. . .making friends, keep in mind that we shall prosper in proportions as we learn to dignify and glorify common labor, and put brains and skill into the common occupations of life. Casting down your bucket among my people, helping and encouraging them as you are doing on these grounds. . . . While doing this, you can be sure in the future, as in the past, that you and your families will be surrounded by the most patient, faithful, law-abiding, and unresentful people that the world has seen. . .The opportunity to earn a dollar in a factory just now is worth infinitely more than the opportunity to spend a dollar in an opera-house."

Aaron fussed the whole way back to Savannah on the train. "I'm glad we came to Atlanta, Maia, because if I hadn't seen and heard it for myself, I would not have believed that a self-respecting black man would get up and say those things. I'm not a beggar; I have worked and fought for everything I have in my life. I don't want the white man's pity or his understanding, I want my rights as a citizen of this place, nothing more; and, certainly I won't accept less."

"Maybe he was trying to smooth over their fears, hoping that it would stop the lynching and violence. I think he just wants to us to have a way to make a living," Maia replied.

"Baby, all I heard is if the white man will throw some coins our way, we will still be his slave. I wouldn't accept any amount of money to lick another man's boot. That's why I took the name *Liberty*, because I want it all, sweetheart--in my work; at the bank; in the store; and, yes, at the opera-house. Hearing this has made me even more determined to focus on getting more political power. We aren't less than anybody. Why should we be treated like we are?"

"Things are calm in Savannah now. Why do you have to stir up more trouble?" Maia asked becoming annoyed. "I'm happy. As long as those sick bigots leave me alone in peace, I'll leave them alone in theirs."

"Things are going to get worse if we don't do something about it now, Maia."

"I don't know about that, Aaron. It looks like to me when things get riled up, black blood flows heavy in the streets and everything else stays the same."

"Maybe if we stand up for ourselves and let white blood flow, then things might change."

"It's hard to fight when you're hungry" Maia said, closing her eyes.

Chapter Eighteen

The Creole Show was a huge success. It toured for two years before the troupe returned to New York; but by the time they got there, Bob Cole, who had become the headliner, was leaving the show. Diana had become a consummate performer and was a star in her own right. The audiences loved her, but when she was off the stage, she was becoming more lonely. She started to pick up some bad habits along the way. She acquired a taste for fine wine and a liking to the warmth of good liquor to keep her company at night. She also developed an ache for David that plagued her in the middle of the night after the affection from the audience wore off.

Diana was fond of a few guys in the cast and had met a few musicians who piqued her interests, but she was hesitant to let any man get too close. There were even quite a few white men who had shown her more than casual attention, with offers of money, jewelry, and being kept in her own home, but she couldn't get past what had happened to her mama and her Nana at the hands of white men. Besides, she had enough money of her own. She swore that no white man would ever put his pale hands on her. Yet she was human and had needs. Unfortunately, she chose to find her satisfaction in eating and drinking.

"Something is wrong with me," Diana said, confiding in Belle while they riding on the train.

"What are you talking about, Di?"

"I get up late in the mornings, and then I eat huge meals of eggs, ham, bacon, pancakes, and fried pies until I can't hold anymore. Then I'm so tired, I have to go back to bed."

"It's just being on the road; it's starting to wear you down," Belle told her.

"I get these craving that I can't seem to satisfy," Diana said, sounding bewildered.

"Not even with those large helpings of barbecued meat, steaks, and potatoes that you've been eating," Belle said, teasing her.

"No," Diana said. "I eat them, and I still feel empty inside."

"You need to relax, Di. Why don't you come out with us after the show sometime and watch somebody else perform for a change?"

Diana started to go out with some of the cast members to taverns and juke joints where they could drink and relax. But she always remembered what Miss Tabby had told her about musicians, except on some occasions, when her resolve was weakened by the liquor, and she would bring some dandy who fancied her back to her room and pretend he was David.

The success of *The Creole Show* rolled on, but after their tour on the West Coast Diana was getting impatient again. She was thirty years old now and knew that her years of getting the spotlight she craved were growing short. She had her own act singing ballads, but she still wasn't the star of the show. She had hoped to get better billing after Dora Dean and Charles Johnson got married and left the company, but it didn't happened.

The emptiness deep inside of Diana was spreading, and her mind kept telling her that there was something bigger and better for her; but she didn't know what it was or where to find it. She convinced herself that if she could just get top billing in the show that she could go solo and then she would have everything that she had ever wanted and be satisfied. When would it finally be her season?

That question echoed in Diana's head as the weeks, months, and then two years passed by.

Then another year had gone by, and she was no closer to her solo performance at the Lexington Opera House in New York. She gazed at her reflection in the mirror and couldn't find the young girl who had stood in the Little Chapel singing for a spot in the Fisk School Choir. She would have never believed it if someone had told her that she wouldn't have been a star by the time she was thirty, and now she had already celebrated her thirty-third birthday.

"I'm getting bored with this routine, Belle. We've been touring with *The Creole Show* for nearly five years," Diana said after they had finished a Southern tour in the Deep South that took them to Arkansas, Mississippi, Louisiana, and Texas.

"This is close to the end of the road for me," Belle said. "I'm thinking about leaving the show."

"I hear that John wants to leave and start his own troupe," Diana said.

"I could see it coming," Belle said, "It's the nature of show business. There are always those who want to stay with the tried and true, and then there are those who want to push forward with something new. John Isham is one who pushes."

"If he does, I'm going with him. Maybe then I'll get my chance," Diana said.

Diana and the heart of the show followed John, including Belle, Billy Johnson, Mattie Wilkes, Stella Wiley, and Bob Cole. They would all be joining John's new show. He called the group the Royal Octoroons.

The change got Diana's blood flowing again. She was excited, and at last, it was her time to shine brighter. She promised herself that she would lose some weight, stop drinking, and get more rest. She still had the best voice in the company and held her own in a dance number.

Unbeknownst to Diana, John had recruited a singer named Mamie Flowers from Bob Cole's company to headline, and she later learned about the pretty young girl named Aida Overton, who would be showcased in the Cakewalk Jubilee finale. These new additions to the troupe were akin to rubbing a pound of salt in her wounds, because it was supposed to be her time. When they met for rehearsals Diana was so furious. She could have hammered nails into the floor with her feet, but somehow she kept her composure throughout practice.

"Come on, Di, we'll go by your place and have a drink to calm you down," Belle said after rehearsal.

When they got back to Diana's room, she slammed the door and pitched a fit, yelling at the top of her lungs, "Why in the name of hell would he bring some floozy in the company to put over me? He must need his head examined. I'm the one who carried the damn *Creole Show*!"

"They always put the young ones out front, Di. We must be getting old," Belle said, pouring herself a drink.

"Madame Flowers, the Bronze Melba, the greatest singer of her race," she taunted out loud. "And who am I?"

"Don't raise a fuss. You'll get your shot. They don't have the voice that you do."

"I know that, Belle, but how the hell he gonna treat me like a side dish. I should be the main attraction in the show."

Diana carried on with her ranting until she wore herself out. The she poured herself a drink and went to bed. Belle shook her head, got her bag, and left, locking the door behind her.

The Royal Octoroons opened in August at the Olympic Theater in New York to packed and approving audiences. In the theater, Diana stayed the consummate professional; off stage, she was back to her old habits.

"I feel like we've jumped out of the frying pan into the fire, Belle," Diana said when she stopped over for lunch. "If only I could have started my own company like Sissieretta Jones did with the Black Patti Troubadours, nothing could have held me back."

"That takes a lot of money, Di, and there are still no guarantees," Belle told her.

"I've got money, but I don't have the name recognition that you get from top billing. And that's what I need to go out on my own." Diana had learned over the years that it was the name that drew the crowds to the theater. "I can see it all in my mind's eye: Miss Diana Portunus, the Ebony Songbird, solo, dressed in the finest costume, standing center stage, hitting her highest note."

"Keep on dreaming, Di. That's all we really got anyway," Belle said as she poured herself another drink.

When will it finally be my season? she thought to herself. Tell me when, Lord, and I'll find the patience to wait, she would pray every day as she dressed for the performance.

After a profitable and successful run, the show went on the road to Newark, then Philadelphia, Indianapolis, New Orleans, and Cleveland. They were back in New York before Christmas.

Perseverance paid off, and, at last, good fortune smiled on Diana. Isham decided to capitalize on the momentum of *The Royal Octoroon's* success. He chose some of the most popular members of the company--Mattie Wilkes, Belle Davis, J. Rosamond Johnson, and Diana Portunus--and put them together in another company for the show. He imagined it as his greatest production to date with a run on Broadway in his sights. The third act would be an operatic finale showcasing Mattie and Diana in solos from famous operas. Diana was so thrilled that she rushed home to write a letter home.

Dear Mama, The greatest thing has happened. Everything that I prayed for has come to pass. I had been so discouraged and feeling down over the past year with my life and the show and the feeling that I was being pushed to the back for new singers after I had left the Creole Show. I never even made friends with Mamie Flowers or Aida Overton because I thought they were stealing the spotlight from me, but now I can see that them joining the company was a blessing in disguise. I'm going to do a new show, and we're going on Broadway. No more coon songs, Mama. I'm going to sing a song from the Carmen opera. It's my dream come true. I wish you all could be there for opening night. I miss you so much. Love, Diana

The Oriental American opened on August 15 in New York at the Palmer Theatre as the first all-negro cast to perform on Broadway.

"We're in another hit show, Di," Belle said when the curtain came down.

"I know what that means," Diana said, dancing a jig. "We're on our way overseas again, and I can't wait. They know how to treat stars over there."

"I can't argue with you on that, sister," Belle said, changing out of her costume.

"It feels so good when I'm out there alone on the stage," Diana said. "I sang my heart out for them tonight."

"Uh-huh, and you'll have to do again tomorrow and the next night," Belle said, laughing.

"That's exactly what I want. That's where I was born to be," Diana said, feeling blessed.

In truth, Diana had always been blessed. She was born beautiful and talented in a home where she was loved and cared for. She had never had to struggle, doors had always opened, and paths had always been made clear. She had never wanted for anything that she did not eventually receive. The cold, hard side of the face of life was a stranger to her. She had always been smiled upon, loved, and adored; but somehow, with all of her good fortune, it still wasn't enough.

With as much success as she was having in her career and in the spotlight, Diana began to taste the bitterness in mouth again. She tried to swallow it down with liquor, but it wasn't enough, even when she drank herself unconscious. When she woke, she would feel the emptiness again and tried to fill it with food, but it was no use, no matter how much she ate. Too much liquor, too much food, and too much time with men she didn't care for took their toll. Diana looked in the mirror and saw her beauty seeping out on the edges of her eyes and around her mouth. She definitely had the blues.

The men around her were never handsome enough, tall enough, or had the financial means she demanded. She measured every man she met against David, and they all fell short. They were too light, too dark, too heavy, too skinny, or they just weren't interesting. She began to wonder if she had really loved David more than she thought she did so long ago. Had she been a fool, or was it just the mystical spell of first love that held her captive. In the loneliness of one night she got up and wrote him a letter.

Dear David, You have been a constant companion in my thoughts for a long time, and I feel compelled to write to you. I must begin with my confession that I was wrong to run away from the sweet and pure love that you once offered me. I cannot tell you how many nights I have tossed and turned, hoping to find you there next to me and the disappointment I felt when you weren't there. I try to lose myself on stage, but when the show is over, I suffer with the ruminations of what might have been if I had come to you in Nashville. I want to see you again, if only to satisfy my wonderings of how you are and the direction life has taken you. I don't know if you've found someone to replace me in your eyes and heart, if you have married and have children, or if you have even thought of me all these years, but for me it doesn't matter. The show will be touring back in the states after our summer break, and when we get to Nashville, I have to see you. Find it in your heart to forgive me for my mistakes. Love, Diana

You could have knocked David over with a feather when he got the letter for Diana. He had seen her picture and name in the reviews from time to time, but he never thought he would ever see her again. He had gone on with his life years ago. He'd saved his money from the tours, gone back to school and finished his degree, opened a furniture store, and become a prominent businessman in the city.

As a former Fisk Jubilee singer, David could have had his pick of the ladies, except he had become jaded after pursuing Diana for so many years. He had married, not for love, but out of spite. He had found a woman he thought was everything Diana was not; her name was Grace, and she was dark-skinned and plain. He picked her out of crowd of women at his sister's church picnic because she seemed to be shy and uncomfortable around so many people. She didn't talk much, but after he began to court her, she was affection- ate and always kept one hand on his arm, his hand, his shoulder, a leg whenever they were together, as if to hold on to him. David loved the attention and the way she waited on his every need.

As the years went by, he resented all the things that drew him to Grace. She wasn't talented or smart, and she had no interests except for him. They tried to have children, but she wasn't strong enough. Three babies and three miscarriages convinced him that he was wrong to marry her. Despite the situation, he provided for her well with a nice home and pretty clothes; but he wasn't happy, and he blamed Diana. He knew he would see her, if only to give her a dose of her own medicine. He sent a telegram saying he would be there when the show tour came to Memphis.

David's telegram lifted Diana's spirit so high that the emptiness inside her was filled with hope, and her mouth watered with sweet anticipation. She hadn't been this eager to get on the road with the show since she was with the Fisk Jubilee Singers. *The Oriental American* played New York in September and traveled down the East Coast to Philadelphia, Baltimore, and Washington, DC. She looked forward to seeing David so much that she forgot that she had two days to visit her Mama and Tata in Savannah for Thanksgiving after the show played for a week in Atlanta. She was ready to get home and taste her mama's cooking. She had been starving herself to lose some pounds before she saw David in Memphis. She needed this time to rest up so she would look her best. No more late nights and drinking wine.

Chapter Nineteen

Savannah welcomed Diana back with the fall colors of the leaves blowing in the gentle evening winds like confetti in a ticker tape parade. It was good to be home. She hadn't seen her family for almost five years, but when they came out to greet her on the veranda, she would have sworn that they looked younger and happier than the last time she had seen them.

Her parents hugs reminded her of what it felt like to be held by someone who loved her. She wanted to linger in their arms for a while, but when Maia pulled away and said, "Come on in the house, child, we have guests that I want you to meet."

"Yeah, baby, your mama has had some help in the kitchen, and there's enough food to feed an army," Aaron added.

Diana was unpleasantly surprised. She didn't want to meet anybody. This was her family and her time with them, and she didn't want to share it with anybody.

So many people had been hospitable to Maia and Aaron when they traveled that they were happy to open their home to others. Earlier in the summer, they had invited a newlywed couple from South Carolina to stay with them. The young woman was a fellow teacher who had heard of Maia's trip to Africa from members at First A.M.E. Church and had struck up a conversation. Her name was Mary McLeod Bethune, and her husband, Albertus, a former teacher who was now a salesman, had moved them to Savannah with plans of opening a menswear shop. Mary was pregnant with their first child.

"Diana, this is Mary and her husband, Albertus," Maia said cheerfully as they sat down at the dining room table.

"It's a pleasure to meet you," Mary said. "I've heard so much about you and your singing career. Your family is very proud of you."

"Thank you," Diana said. "And what do you do, Mary?"

"I'm doing some social work right now while Albertus is starting his business, but teaching is my calling. I spent six years studying to be a missionary in Africa only to find out that they didn't want black missionaries, so it's my intention to spend the rest of my life teaching as many of my people here as I can," she replied.

"Well," Aaron said, "You can start by teaching Maia how to make this oyster stew."

They all laughed, and even Diana relaxed and enjoyed the delicious meal.

Diana finally had a chance to talk to her mama privately when Maia came to her room to say goodnight.

"Mama, I'm getting older," she said.

"We all are," Maia said, laughing.

"No, Mama," Diana said, "I'm getting older by myself, and I don't want to. I want a husband."

"When did this change come about? You said you never wanted to settle down, that singing and the stage was all you needed."

"That was a young girl talking, Mama, and I was wrong."

"Well, you've met plenty of men, girl. All you have to do is choose one," Maia said.

"That's the problem, Mama. I have never met anybody after David that I loved or would even consider marrying."

"That's unfortunate for you, my dear, because he's probably already married."

"I'm going to see him, Mama."

"Why?" Maia asked.

"I can't explain it. I just have to."

"Diana, I have been on both sides of that equation, and it doesn't solve anything. It just makes more problems," Maia said.

"I know, Mama, but I won't have any peace until I do."

"God be with you, baby. You've always been headstrong and done what you wanted. You didn't listen to me when I told you to think about this years ago, and you're not going to listen now. But I love you with all my heart, and if things go bad, I'm here for you, no matter what."

"I love you, Mama."

"I love you more," she said, kissing her daughter's forehead.

***

On Saturday, Diana caught the morning train to Memphis, Tennessee, before the curtain went up for the show. The butterflies floating in her belly weren't because she was going on stage, they were there for David. The company was playing at the Grand Opera House, and all through her performance, she could barely remember the words to her songs knowing he was there in the Negro seats of the balcony. She wanted so much to impress him. She searched and found the emotions buried deep in her heart past the emptiness to the place where her soul lived. When she sang about the cruelty of fate where true love is realized after it is lost, her words were just for him.

David watched Diana's every move. She was still a beautiful woman, and he thought her voice was as sweet and stirring as it had always been. But she was different. She wasn't that young girl who had stolen his heart; she had become a confident and glamorous woman. He wanted to hate her, but he couldn't. He had entered the opera house with intentions of humiliating her for his own revenge, but she still touched him in the space between his heart and soul where his passion lived. The question was, what did she want from him?

David waited outside the stage door in the chilled air and watched as other cast members exited and went on their way. He was looking down the street when Diana came out, giving her a chance to look at him for a moment. He made her think of a big slice of hot apple pie: good-looking, golden brown, and so satisfying. He turned around, saw her, walked over, and greeted her with a hug and a kiss on the cheek.

"It's so good to see you again," Diana said, looking into his face. "You haven't changed much except for the mustache. It's very handsome."

"Let's get out of the cold. I'm staying at the Church Hotel," David said.

"So am I," Diana said. They both smiled.

They rode in the rear of a street car to 2nd and Gayoso, where Robert Reed Church, the first black millionaire in Memphis, built a first-class hotel for colored people. They registered at the front desk, and the attendant directed them to the dining room for a late meal.

The maître d' greeted them and seated them at a cozy table along the side wall, "We're serving fried ham, mashed potatoes, collard greens, and hot biscuits tonight."

"That sounds good, thank you," David replied.

"I would love some apple pie," Diana added as she looked at David.

"Certainly, ma'am," the maitre d' said. "I'll have the waiter bring it after your dinner."

"Thank you for coming," Diana said.

"I'll always have time for an old friend," David replied.

"Friend? I was almost your wife," she said.

"You made your choice, and I had to live with it."

Diana could feel that not all had been forgiven, so she changed the subject.

"So what have you been doing with yourself since I last saw you?"

"I'm married, Diana," he said and with those words she lost her appetite.

She imagined that he was with someone, but it was a picture that she didn't like to think about. How could she have been silly enough to think that he would always belong to her?

A waiter brought the food to the table, and David continued to talk.

"I went back to school and got my business degree, and I own two stores in Nashville. I have a wife but no children. What about you? did you find the man of your dreams?"

"No, I didn't. And, honestly, I have to admit that you were and still are the man in my dreams. There was never anyone else that mattered," Diana said.

"If you had known that back then, maybe we could have lived happily ever after, but we can't go back," he responded.

"It's not that I want to go back, David. I miss you now."

"You could never accept that you can't have everything you want when you want it, Di. You are just like the rest of us. I have responsibilities and obligations that I can't walk away from."

"Can we pretend for one night that I never left you and that you still love me?" Diana asked.

David stood up from the table, knowing this was his last chance to leave without any damage being done.

"I always thought you were some kind of witch, and I was under your spell because I could never say no to you, even when you said it to me."

"Believe me, from the bottom of my heart, I regret it, and I'm sorry," Diana said.

"Come on, I'll take you to your room," David said as he offered her his hand.

David opened the door to her room and stepped aside for her to walk in. Diana turned around and looked at him with the same eyes that first possessed him over seventeen years ago. David softened. He pushed away the pain that she had caused him, along with the thoughts of Grace waiting patiently for him to return from his business trip, and closed the door.

Time rolled back in Diana's room, and they were young, carefree, and happy. They had shared the most precious time in their lives, and it had bonded them for life.

"No other man has ever treated me the way you did, David, or made me feel the way you did," Diana whispered in his ear.

"You have always been my ideal woman. You were my first love, and you've spoiled me for anybody else," David said as he kissed her.

He felt a pang of guilt, but the passion between them had aged like good liquor and was even more intense than before. Their reunion surpassed all of Diana's dreams, and she prayed that time would be her friend again and stand still for them. They stayed awake the whole night making love, reminiscing, and pretending it wouldn't be over in the morning.

***

"Goodbye, Diana," David said sadly when they arrived at the station.

"I don't want to say goodbye," Diana said to him before they boarded separate trains.

She had new power. It was if she had drunk a magic elixir; it was the most alive she had felt in years. For her, things couldn't have been better. The show was headed back north, and David had promised to come and see her again.

For David, it was much different; he was going home with fresh guilt and confusion. He had been weak and had given in to the ache that he had always had for Diana that only she could soothe. He respected Grace and loved her for being his wife, but he was never in love with her. Yet, with all the things that Diana had said to him, she still hadn't said she wanted to settle down and be his wife. By the time he arrived in Nashville, he was filled with remorse and pledged that he would be a better husband and never see Diana again.

Diana basked in the afterglow of her romantic interlude with David, and it lasted through the Christmas season as she celebrated the holidays with Belle. The 1899 New Year was fast approaching, and Diana felt optimistic that it would bring her good fortune. But they had barely sobered up from Emancipation Day festivities when John Isham announced there were to be more changes in the show.

"I can't believe that ass is moving my operatic finale and replacing it with some ragtime songs," Diana said to Belle through her gritted teeth when she showed up for rehearsal.

"Ragtime is the ticket now, Di. He says he has to do it to compete with the new stage shows that are being produced," Belle said to calm her down. "This is probably the opportune time for me to break away and go on a solo tour with my 'piccaninnies'."

"*Clorindy: The Origin of the Cakewalk* is already playing on Broadway," Diana remarked. "I'm considering leaving the company and auditioning for a role in it. I'm tired of being shuffled around by John whenever the mood hits him."

"Take your time, cool your heels, Di," Belle warned. "We can't afford to make any enemies in this business."

It was an exhilarating time for black musical performers and writers, but Diana began to feel drained of her energy and positivity. Another week passed, and she felt physically ill. Her desire to see David consumed her night and day. He had been the drug that her mind and body needed and now she was experiencing withdrawal. Her craving for him exhausted her and began to affect her performance in the show. She couldn't take it much longer. So she wrote hil a letter.

> Dear David, I couldn't wait another day to hear from you.
> The time passes, but not quick enough for me. The days
> go by like weeks, the weeks like months. I know you have
> made promises before the one you gave to me in Memphis,
> but there is a need in my soul to see you. I miss your
> presence around me, and the sensation of your touch on my
> skin. I know I am selfish, but I'm sick without you. I have
> a two-week break in March. Please say that you'll spend
> it with me in Ocean City, and I'll ask you for nothing else.
> Love, Diana

David was doing everything he could not to think about Diana but, none of it was working. He paid more attention to Grace, and she seemed happier, so what more harm could be done by seeing Diana one last time. If he stayed with her for two weeks, he would be sure to get her out of his system for good. Being with her was just a youthful fantasy he had held for too long, yet the thought of being with her made him want to run for the next train. He was her fool, and that would probably never change. The only thing left to figure our was what reason he would give Grace for being away for so long.

> Dearest Diana, I have thought of you quite often since I got home and, as many times as I have sworn never to see you again, if I had my way, I would be there with you right now. It can't be explained. I guess I haven't done a good job of washing off the voodoo dust you sprinkled over me; your smile still haunts me. I'll figure out a way to see you wherever you say and whenever you say. Love always, David

There was word that *The Oriental American* would close after the season ended, and Diana had mixed feelings about it. She knew it was time to move on, but she wasn't sure what she wanted to do. She was tired of the minstrel shows and wanted to do something serious or classical.

Her good friend, Belle, was going back to Europe, but Diana had tired of the long trips on the water and on the road. Besides, she was didn't feel well, and the only thing she could think about now was spending the last weeks of March taking in as much of the wonder tonic that David had to offer. She sent a telegram to The Henry's Hotel in Ocean City for reservations since it was still colored excursion days. She sent another telegram to David to meet her in Ocean City on March 15.

David had less than one month to come up with a reasonable excuse for a two-week absence. He considered telling Grace that he was going on the tour as an extra with John W. Works's Fisk Quartet or that an old friend was ill. Eventually, he settled on telling her that he was going to New York on business to increase the inventory for the store, and she would be in charge of everything while he was gone.

Grace was proud that David trusted her with the business, and she was eager to show him that he was justified in doing so. She could tell things were getting better between them because he had been so nice lately, and he had brought her fresh flowers when he came home from the store. If only she could give him a child, everything would be perfect.

***

The seasons were in transition as winter was giving way to spring in Maryland. The weather at the beach in Ocean City was a still a bit nippy, but it was ideal for lovers who have the heat of each other to warm them. When Diana saw David walk by the cottage window, she ran outside to meet him.

"It's so good to see you, David. I was about to go out of my mind," Diana said as she threw her arms around him and held him tight.

"It's hard coming up with lies to meet you," David said to her. "I have a wife and a business to run."

"I don't want you to think about anything else while we're here," Diana said, taking his arm and leading him inside the cabin. "As far as I'm concerned, we're the last people on earth."

"It's funny how you expect me to drop everything in my life for you now when you wouldn't give up anything for me all those years ago."

"Don't spoil our days together, David. All I know is I want to love you now," she murmured, kissing him as she took off his coat, his jacket, and his shirt.

For two weeks, David and Diana lived in a world of make-believe. He didn't have a wife or a home to go to, Diana was his wife, he was her husband, and there was no show coming to an end. They didn't count the days because for them there was no life after March was over. There was no time to waste on recriminations or disagreements. They spent every minute of the weeks together. They bathed together, ate their meals together, walked along cool beach together, and sat in front of the fireplace together. They laughed and sang the songs from the tour together; and at night, their bodies became one.

On the morning of All Fool's Day, a few hours before it was time for them to again board separate trains going in opposite directions, Diana said, "I don't want you to go back home, David. Can't we just disappear and go someplace where no one will find us? We don't have to let outside forces keep us apart. I know we belong together," she pleaded.

"It wasn't God or fate that separated us Diana; it was your thirst for fame and fortune. You didn't want to be my wife. You left, and in doing that, you threw away my happiness as well as your own, and we both have to live with that. I have my faults, but I can't hurt Grace like I was hurt. Her misfortune was loving a man who can't love her back. So I won't do this again, and please don't write me again."

"After all the perfect days and nights that we've had here, how can you say that to me?" Diana asked.

"It was all a fantasy," David answered. "Because I love you and probably always will, I couldn't resist it. But it's over, and now it's time to go back to our lives and make the best of them. We're getting too old to keep behaving like spoiled children."

David kissed Diana with the same heat that had kept her warm for fourteen days, and then he walked away.

For a moment, Diana didn't know whether to holler in anger or breakdown and cry as David disappeared into the crowd with the other passengers. But then like a true performer, she pulled herself together, lifted her head, squared her shoulders, and stepped onto the train. She refused to let David's goodbye overshadow the magical weeks they had shared together. If he couldn't resist her then, he wouldn't be able to resist her the next time she needed him. If she couldn't have all of him, she'd have to be satisfied with whatever she could get. *It might be better this way after all,* she thought to herself. She could still keeping singing and visit with him when she had time off.

***

John Isham announced at the show run-through that he would be retiring when the show finished in Philadelphia at the end of the summer. Most of the top company members had already moved on to other projects, but Diana hadn't had any offers yet, and she wasn't sure what she wanted to do. Her mind drifted to her mama's other children. They didn't have the problems that she had. They were living as whites, with all the opportunities it afforded. She could only be in negro productions, and there weren't that many top shows for negroes. She was well aware that her time was running out quickly if she was going to see her name high on the marquee.

By the end of the summer, near the close of the show, Diana was feeling the familiar malaise creeping back on her again. She had another case of the blues. She had written two letters to David, but he still hadn't responded. She started drinking and overeating again, and it was making her sick. She was tired all the time, and on the last night of *The Oriental American,* singing her song from the opera, Carmen, she fainted. The audience was thrilled with the drama of her performance and rewarded her with the greatest applause that she had ever received. Stagehands carried her backstage, and after a few minutes, she was revived.

"Are you all right?" Mattie asked her. "Do you want us to get a doctor?"

"No, I'm fine," Diana said. "I just need to eat something. I didn't have an appetite earlier."

After spending the next two days in bed without any strength to get up, Diana sent for a doctor. Late in the morning, there was a knock on the door. Diana dragged herself up to open it, and she found a toffee-colored, middle-aged woman standing there. The woman was dressed in a tweed tailor-made suit and carrying a black leather case.

"Who are you?" Diana asked impatiently.

"You sent for a doctor?" the woman inquired.

"Yes, I did," Diana answered.

"I'm Dr. Rebecca Cole," the woman told her firmly. "How can I help you?"

"I'm Diana Portunus, and I didn't know that there were negro women doctors."

"Well, I'm sure there's a lot that we all don't know," Dr. Cole said as she stepped inside.

Dr. Cole gave Diana a thorough examination and asked her, "Do you have any other children?"

"No, I don't have any children," Diana answered.

"Well, you are a little older to be having your first child, but you are in relatively good health and should have a normal pregnancy."

Diana sat in silence as frozen as a statue. *What was this woman talking about?* she thought to herself.

Dr. Cole looked close into her face and said, "You should deliver by the end of the year." Diana's head wasn't totally clear, but she had enough sense to take five dollars out of her purse to pay the doctor.

"Good afternoon, Mrs. Portunus. I'm sure your husband will be happy to hear the news," Dr. Cole said as she let herself out and closed the door.

Diana couldn't even think straight. There were other women in the shows who had gotten pregnant over the years. Some had had babies and some hadn't, but she hadn't even worried about the possibility of having a baby for over ten years. Now she didn't know what to do.

Diana looked down at her stomach and realized the extra weight wasn't just from eating and drinking. She wondered if she could hide it and keep working, but from the size of her belly, she knew that wouldn't last long. She thought about trying to get rid of it, but the doctor had said it was too dangerous and would probably kill her. She thought about going to Nashville and begging David to leave his wife and marry her; but she still had her pride, she was Diana Portunus. The words of her mama replayed in her head, and she knew that it was time to go home to Savannah.

Chapter Twenty

Diana didn't send a letter or a telegram to her mama. She didn't have the words to explain the twists and turns that had become her life. She looked around the townhouse that she had rented in Harlem, it wasn't elaborately decorated or full of personal things. She had lived out of two trunks for more than fifteen years. She spent the next two days closing out her bank accounts and packing up her clothing and mementos. She didn't tell anyone her reasons for leaving. They all assumed that she was just tired and needed to take a break.

On her last night in New York, Diana attended the opening of the *Policy Players,* starring George Walker and Bert Williams. She nearly choked on the tears she had been swallowing when she saw Aida Overton singing as the leading lady. She decided to skip the cast party afterward; it would have only reminded her of what she would be missing back home in Georgia.

Diana wasn't even thinking about the new life she was carrying back to Savannah with her as she sat on the train fanning herself in the July heat. For her, it was more of a complication or another unexpected interference in her career. Maybe it was even a punishment for letting her loneliness overwhelm her and being distracted by David. Whatever it was, whenever Diana tried to look forward, her future was all blurred. It wasn't that Diana didn't want children; it was just she had never considered her life with them. The only thing that she ever truly wanted was to be a famous singer.

Diana rode all day before she switched trains in Baltimore. All of a sudden, she had an urge to stop by and visit Miss Tabby, the warm-hearted woman she rented a room from when she first got started in *The Creole Show*. It had been ten years since she had stayed there, and she wasn't sure if Miss Tabby still had her rooming house or if she would even remember her. Diana took a streetcar to North Avenue, and before she got to the house, she could smell something sweet baking. The nausea she had been feeling some weeks before passed, and suddenly her appetite returned with added fervor.

Diana knocked on the door of the rooming house. The familiar face with white hair, twinkling eyes, and glowing teeth answered.

"Hello, Mrs. Logan," Diana said.

Before she could say anything else, the petite woman said, "Girl, I told you to call me Miss Tabby. Come on in here," she said, grabbing Diana's arm and pulling her inside.

"I know you weren't expecting me, but I just wanted to stop by and say hello on my way back home to Savannah."

"Well, you did right, and ain't no sense in you rushing off now that you here. Stay the night, and you can get back on a train tomorrow. I got a room ready."

"Thank you, Miss Tabby. I could stand to lie down in a bed tonight," Diana answered.

"Come in the kitchen, sugar. Are you hungry?" she asked.

"Yes, ma'am, I am. I don't know when I've last eaten a decent meal," Diana said.

Diana sat at the table while Miss Tabby went in the kitchen. In less than a minute, Miss Tabby returned with a tall glass of cool sweet tea and handed it to Diana.

"Drink this, sugar, and I'll get you some food."

Diana could feel the chilled drink travel down her throat and down into her stomach as she leaned her head back against the chair. The soothing coolness flowed through her veins as she relaxed and stretched out her legs.

"I seen your name in the newspaper a couple of times, sugar. Looks like you did real good for yourself," Miss Tabby said as she set the plate of cold ham, potato salad, and string green beans down on the table.

"I still got some things I want to do, though," Diana replied.

"Well, you sure are looking good, and I'm guessing you got a bun in the oven."

Diana sighed pitifully and looked down at her plate of food.

"What's the matter, sugar? Where's your husband?" Miss Tabby asked with growing concern over Diana's reaction.

"I'm not married, Miss Tabby," Diana answered.

"Well, what about the daddy, honey. He run out on you?"

"No, ma'am, he's got a wife in Nashville, and he doesn't even know. I've written to him, but I don't even think he reads my letters."

Miss Tabby sat and watched Diana as she finished her food before she said, "I wasn't fortunate enough to have children, and I always felt I missed out. You been blessed, chile. Go home to your family, and be happy. You have a baby to love for the rest of your life."

After the two women talked for a while, Miss Tabby helped Diana get settled in for the night. The sheets felt crisp and clean; and for the first time in several weeks her spirit was calm and she rested. The next morning, Miss Tabby insisted on coming with her to the train station after breakfast to see her off.

"Take care of yourself, sugar, and that baby," Miss Tabby said as Diana stepped onto the train and waved goodbye.

***

Diana did her best to keep her mind quiet by focusing on the noise around her: the train whistle, the wheels along the track, the conversations of other passengers, and the voices of attendants at each station where the train made a stop. It was mid-morning when the train finally arrived in Savannah. It had been a hot night, and her dress stuck to her skin with perspiration. Her trunks had already arrived the previous night and were waiting inside the station. She hired a negro carriage driver to take her and her baggage to the house on Liberty Street.

Diana looked around the city during the ride, and she hardly recognized it, there were more buildings, stores, and houses that had filled in the open areas in town, but there was still the sweet smell of lush trees and flowers that New York City lacked. There weren't many people ambling bout; it was Sunday, so most of them were in church.

From the time she left home, Diana never thought she would ever return to Savannah to stay for more than a week or two. But here she was back in town with no plan or timetable for when she might leave. As the carriage got closer to home, she hoped that her mama and tata were at church, too. She needed a little more time before she had to face them. When she got to the house, she breathed a sigh of relief. Her parents weren't there; and the houseguests, Albert and Mary McLeod Bethune and their baby, had moved on. She had the carriage driver bring in her trunks and take them up to her room, and she gave him a dollar for his trouble.

Diana walked through house, noticing some of the crafts that her mama had brought back from Africa. She saw a photograph of them on the wall that they must have had taken in New York. She saw a pair of glasses next to the newspaper on the table in the parlor and wondered how long Tata had been wearing them. She went outside and saw that the garden was full and well-tended. Then she walked around to the front of the house and sat in her mama's chair on the veranda and tried to see the world through her eyes.

Diana knew she was more like Aaron, always reaching and wanting more. Her mama always seemed to accept whatever cards were dealt to her in life, but Diana had to admit she'd played them well. She had been a teacher, written for the newspaper, and published two books. If she was dissatisfied with the way things had turned out, she certainly didn't show it.

From her vantage point, she saw her mama and tata long before they saw her. It cheered her up some to see them happy with each other as they walked up the street hand in hand.

"Diana?" Maia called out as she saw her sitting on the veranda. "Child, we didn't know you were coming. Why didn't you send us a telegram?" Maia rushed up the stairs with Aaron close behind, and Diana stood up and gave them both a tight hug and kisses on their cheeks. "Is the show playing somewhere close to town, sweetie?" Maia asked.

"No, Mama, the show ended after the season, and I haven't decided what I want to do next," Diana answered.

"Well, you must be living good, baby," Aaron said. "You've put on some weight."

"Leave her alone. She looks good," Maia said, bowled over but delighted to see her daughter.

They all sat down outside for a few minutes and talked about the weather and how hot it had been, how good the garden was doing, and what happened at church service that morning. Maia noticed that whenever Diana talked, she looked away, up to the sky, down at her feet, or out into the street. Aaron could tell something was wrong, too, but he decided to let Maia handle it.

"Well, you ladies are going to have to excuse me," Aaron said, standing to his feet. "That service was long, and the meal the sisters served was just as heavy. I believe I need to lay this body down for a while and help it recover."

"All right, I'm going to sit out here with Di and see if we can catch a breeze or two."

Aaron gave Diana's shoulder a quick pat before he opened the screened door.

"Diana, tell me what's happened," Maia said as soon as the door shut.

"I've been thinking that I might come home for a while. I've really missed y'all," Diana said.

"That's good, baby. I'm glad you're here. Now tell me what's happened."

All Diana wanted to do at the moment was cry, but she fought her emotions and began her story. "Mama, I told you the last time that I talked to you that I wanted to see David. Well, we saw each other at Christmas in Memphis, and then we spent the last two weeks of March in Maryland. I was so happy, and I know David was, too. I thought maybe he would divorce his wife, and we could be together again, but I haven't heard from him since."

"I'm not surprised, Di. I told you the man was married, and that is a very complicated relationship. He can't just say 'wham, bam, thank you, ma'am,' and leave his wife for you."

"Mama, I'm having a baby!" Diana yelled.

Maia didn't think that there was anything that Diana could do or say that would shock her, but she sat there in shock for a few moments before she could respond.

"Child, I know this is not the way you expected things to be, but it's not the worst thing that could have happened. You know your tata and I are here for you and will help you in every way we can."

"Mama, I want David. It's his child, and he should be with me."

"You don't have the right to expect anything from him, Di. You knew he was married. Besides, you didn't want him when you could have had him. You went and did everything you wanted to; now you have to think about somebody else, and it's that baby you're carrying."

Diana let her tears of frustration cover her face, knowing that there wasn't much she could do to change things for the next five months.

Aaron was happy about the news when Maia told him.

"It won't hurt us to have some new life in this house," he said. He thought about Apollo, who would have been a grown man with a family of his own by now, and Roman who was nearly seventeen. "I told that girl years ago, if she didn't go get that man, she was going to end up by herself. Now, she has waited too late. It don't make much difference to me. If Diana don't want to raise the baby, I'll do it myself."

Aaron and Maia did their best to keep Diana's mind on other things. They invited some of her old friends to come by and visit; they went on picnics; they shopped for baby things; and they even took a trip to Ossabaw Island, where they went for a swim. But Diana couldn't stop pining away for David. As the next month rolled around, she was even more determined to tell David about the baby. She sent several telegrams to the store and wrote two more letters.

Unfortunately for Diana, Grace had continued to work at the stores with David after his return from Ocean City. She had had her suspicions about the trip because no additional inventory had been ordered or delivered, and David didn't want to talk about the trip or any of the meetings that he had attended. Her suspicions were confirmed when she intercepted the telegrams for David at the store.

She promptly disposed of them, along with the letters that came later to the house and kept a sharp eye out for any others.

Judging from David's behavior since he returned from Ocean City, she could see that he had not chosen Diana over her. But she was determined that he would never know about the baby if she could help it. It was the one thing that might convince David to leave her since she had not been able to bear him the children he wanted. She loved on David as much as he would allow her and prayed that she, too, would get pregnant before this other baby was born.

As the months passed, Diana grew bigger and more irritable. She looked at her reflection and was disgusted. How could she ever pull herself back together enough to stand before an audience after this? Her longing for David had turned to anger, and she swore that he would never be a part of her child's life after treating her so badly. She even had evil thoughts about falling on her stomach and hurting the baby.

"Keep counting your blessings, child," Maia told her whenever she saw Diana sulking.

But all Diana could think about was that she should be singing the lead in *The Policy Players* instead of Aida Overton or Abbie Mitchell in *Jes Lak White Folks*. They were both only teenagers, but how could she compete with youth? She thought about how she looked when she was their age with even more talent, but the opportunities for negro women then were fewer. Aida and Abbie had more chances and more time to see other doors open. Diana was starting to believe that she had suffered the misfortune of being born too early.

When the time for the Thanksgiving feast came, Diana had stopped going out any further than the backyard.

"I don't want you all to invite anybody here for the holiday," Diana said, giving instructions to Maia and Aaron, "I feel like a cow, and I don't want anybody to see me like this."

"You've never looked more beautiful, baby. Stop worrying yourself," Maia said.

By the time the Christmas season had begun, Diana had stopped coming out of her room.

"Come on downstairs, and get some fresh air," Maia pleaded with her, but she refused.

Aaron and Maia were losing their patience with Diana.She was about to become a mother, but she was behaving like a spoiled child.

They were all about to go crazy when on Sunday, New Year's Eve, after they'd eaten a late lunch Diana screamed out, "Mama, help me! The pains have started."

Maia ran up to her room, and Aaron grabbed his coat to get help.

"I'll go next door and borrow a carriage to go fetch the doctors," Aaron said as he rushed out the back door.

The Drs. McKane, Cornelius and Alice, were a couple Aaron and Maia met after the two had come to the church to speak about funding for a colored hospital and nurses training school a few years back. Aaron had been a strong supporter, and they had eaten dinner together on many occasions, when they had traded stories about their experiences in Liberia. The McKanes had emigrated there on the voyage in 1895, but had returned one year later when Alice had become ill. They were around the same age as Diana.

"Come and get us when Diana goes into labor, day or night," they had told them.

"Relax, Diana," Maia said, holding her hand. "Aaron has gone to get the doctors. Turn on your side so I can massage the small of your back. You know, baby, I loved the song you sang in the last show. Would you sing it for me? It will take your mind off of the pains."

Diana started singing, there was no sense in complaining or being uncooperative. This baby was coming today.

She stopped suddenly between the chorus and said, "I'm sorry, Mama, for acting ugly and being disrespectful. I didn't mean to treat you and Tata that way, I was just so hurt that David didn't want me or our baby."

"It's all right, baby. We understand. We love you, Diana, no matter what you do. You are a part of me, and this baby coming is a part of you, and we're gonna take care of both of you," Maia assured her as she rubbed the side of her face.

The pains started again, and Diana started singing again. She and Maia sang, massaged, and cried until late in the afternoon, when they heard the carriage in front of the house.

"Thank God," they both said at the same time.

Maia was as tired as Diana when the doctors finally arrived, and she took the opportunity to ease down to the kitchen to eat a few bites while they examined Diana. The piece of bread with butter and the cup of water refreshed her so she poured a glass for Diana and carried it with her back up the stairs.

The doctors worked well together. They took turns caring for Diana, giving each other time to take a break downstairs with Aaron. All of them could hear the changes in Diana's songs, mixed with intermittent screams of pain as they intensified with each hour.

"Babies come when they're ready," Cornelius said matter-of-factly. "They won't be rushed no matter how long it takes."

Around nine o'clock, Aaron started to get anxious, so to keep busy, he decided to cook some food for everybody to keep busy. It had been a long afternoon and evening that looked as if it would extend into the night, and none of them had eaten a decent meal all day. He went into the kitchen and prepared some rice, black-eyed peas seasoned with ham, warmed the greens that Maia had prepared, and fried some corn bread.

As midnight approached, the singing faded, and only Diana's exhausted screams could still be heard downstairs. Maia was seated on the bed with Diana propped up against her when the two doctors directed her to push. In one long note, Diana pushed, and the baby was born three minutes after midnight on New Year's Day 1900. Cornelius cut the cord and tied it.

"It's a boy, Diana," Maia said. "You have a son."

Aaron rushed up the stairs behind the cry of the new born baby.

"He's beautiful," Alice said as she wiped the baby's eyes and laid him on the bed next to his mama. "Monday's child is fair of face."

Diana looked at the baby in her arms, her child, and he looked back at her with maple-syrup brown eyes. He opened his mouth, and she couldn't believe that she had actually given birth to another life; the very sight of him amazed her. He was golden brown--like the crust on an apple pie--just like David, looking more like his father than his mother.

"Have you thought about a name?" Maia asked.

"Caesar, Mama, his name is Caesar Portunus," she said before she collapsed back on the pillow and fell asleep.

Dr. Alice and Maia cleaned and dressed baby Caesar, and he fell off to sleep. Maia wrapped him in the blanket she had made for him and then placed him in the oak bed that Aaron had built especially for him.

"We'll let both of them rest for an hour before he needs to get his first feeding," Dr. Cornelius said.

Downstairs in the kitchen, Aaron toasted the occasion with wine. "This has been my favorite day--January 1, Emancipartion Day-- and I've celebrated it for 26 years. On this day, we have been blessed again with the greatest of gifts, a new life. Here's to Caesar's good fortune."

Maia and the doctors feasted on the meal Aaron had cooked for them and drank to the New Year until daylight. As tired as they were from the day's events, it was only adrenaline and pure happiness that kept them awake.

Maia woke Diana to feed the baby, and when Maia picked Caesar up from his crib, a smile that came from deep within her soul spread across her face as she held her first grandchild. Then she remembered that there were others.

"A child is a real blessing," she said as she watched Diana breast-feeding, recalling the others at the funeral, where she could only look but not touch.

Whenever Maia tried to think about the experiences she had missed with her children or what her life might have been like if they had not been taken from her, a tidal wave of grief came over her and she had to clear her mind lest she be consumed. She hadn't even had the opportunity to give them names. Her thoughts drifted to Daphne. Her children were the only family Daphne had left on earth, and they didn't even know she was a sister to them. For a minute, Maia considered confronting her children and telling them the truth, but she thought better of it. It would be stirring a hornet's nest, and she would probably be the one who got stung.

***

Diana was having a rough start taking care of little Caesar.

"I can't do anything right for him," Diana said to Maia. "He keeps on crying all the time."

"Babies are supposed to cry sometimes. It strengthens their lungs," Maia told her. "Your problem is that you've never taken care of anyone else besides yourself in your life."

Maia and Aaron were her left and right hands, taking such joy in keeping the baby clean and occupied. By the time the seasons had begun to change and Diana's 38th birthday had passed she began to get restless. She loved Caesar very much, but she didn't see why her life had to stop just because he had been born. She was ready to get back on stage again and the only thing that slowed her down was that she hadn't lost all of the extra weight she had gained.

Diana started doing calisthenics and going for long walks, and by the time Caesar had his two front teeth, she had gotten her confidence back. It was just in time, too. A telegram had arrived from George Walker in New York about a new production called *Sons of Ham* that he was putting together with Bert Williams, and there was a singing part for her.

Diana was ecstatic. She thought they had forgotten all about her while she down there in the Lowcountry. Maia watched her as Caesar crawled around on the floor in the parlor while Diana read the message. Diana had already finished reading it but was trying to find the words to tell her Mama that she would have to get back on the road.

"What is it?" Maia finally asked.

"It's a producer saying there's a part for me in his new musical," Diana answered.

"When will they need you to come?"

"Rehearsals start in a few weeks so the show will be ready for the new season in August."

"I know it will be hard for you to miss this opportunity, but you can't be in two places at one time," Maia said.

"Are you saying that you and Tata won't take care of Caesar for me while I go to New York? This could finally be the role that will get me to where I can go out on my own and make a career for myself."

"What I'm saying, child, is that you are a mother now, and you have to let this baby get on his feet before you go gallivanting across the country chasing that pie-in-the-sky dream of yours."

Diana was totally outdone. She wanted to just pack up her things, take Caesars, and go; but she knew she wouldn't have time to take care of him properly, and she really couldn't trust anybody but her mama and tata with her baby. Diana decided to bide her time and enjoy the months with Caesar, because when she left, she would be gone for a while. She started giving him all of his baths, combed his hair, dressed him, took him on her long walks, and carried him around as her mama did her.

Diana and Caesar smelled and touched flowers, sat under shade-trees, played in the grass, and dug in the dirt of the garden. When Caesar got four more teeth, Diana fed him small bites from the table. She joined him when he played with his fingers and toes, loving the cute little laugh that came all the way from his tummy. She was there when he first said "Mama," and it made the whole family cry. Diana and her child were practically inseparable, and she never thought she could love anyone as much as she loved her son. Then, on Christmas morning, as the family sat in front of the fireplace, Caesar stood up.

Chapter Twenty-One

New Year's Day was a day of celebration in the Liberty home. Not only was it Emancipation Day, it was Caesar's first birthday.

"I can't believe our boy is one year old already," Maia said, during Caesar's morning bath.

"The months have gone by faster than I thought they would," Diana said happily, wrapping him snugly in a towel.

"Your tata and I have planned a big party to celebrate," Maia said. "He's invited his Mason brother, James Sims, his business partner, Albert Jackson, and their families, and I've asked my editor, Sol Johnson, and his family to come. We are going to have a huge feast."

Maia spent the whole day cooking and preparing the meal, Aaron spent the day playing with Caesar, and Diana spent her time wondering how she would tell them she was leaving again.

"That's a fine boy you have here, Diana," Sol said as they ate and drank around the table.

"We're all so proud of him and her," Maia said, pleased that her family was there together.

They drank a toast with all the hope that's felt at the turn of a new year, and no one was happier than Diana. The heaviness in her chest was gone; she was free again. She could start thinking ahead. It was mid-season in the theatre already, and there was no need to rush. Besides, it was probably cold and dreary in New York City right now. Diana made herself a silent promise that by the day she turned 39 year old, she would be back in Harlem.

When the cool winter weather began to break in Savannah, Diana sat down to talk with her mama and tata.

"It's time for me to go back to New York if I'm going to prepare for the next theatre season," she announced as they were eating breakfast one morning.

"What about Caesar?" Maia asked.

"Mama, I only need two years, time enough for me to get where I want to be, and then I'll come back for Caesar."

"You don't think this baby needs his mama for two years?" Maia asked.

"I'll visit as much as can. But Mama and Tata, this is my last chance to make it."

"Baby, you have made it. You have performed all over the world, and you're already a famous singer. We're proud of you," Aaron said.

"Tata, I feel like there is more for me," Diana said, begging them to understand.

"It's never enough for you, child. Every time you get to your destination, you choose another one farther away," Maia added.

Aaron could see Diana was getting distraught, and he empathized with her frustration and dissatisfaction. "Go on and go if you need to keep chasing that dream, but remember everything you need is right here in front of you."

Caesar started to cry as if he understood the adult's conversation in front of him, and Maia could only shake her head in dismay.

Diana didn't care if it took her a week to get to New York or how many trains she might have to catch, she was on her way. She missed her little son, but she would make him proud of his mama.

She had heard that Walter Smart and George Williams had a group called The New Octoroons performing at the Unique Theatre in Brooklyn, but she definitely didn't want to go backward repeating her days with The Creole Company.

She had thought about trying for a spot with The Black Patti Troubadours, but there wasn't any chance for her to be the main attraction with that troupe, since Sissieretta had formed the group herself. Why couldn't she form her own group? She had money, but Diana didn't want to gamble with her own hard-earned dollars.

By the time she got into Harlem, she had decided to give herself a few months to look up her old friends and get her bearings. She thanked God that she hadn't given up her townhouse.

***

In Savannah, Maia and Aaron enjoyed having Caesar and watching him grow. One hot summer day in June, they were sitting on the veranda as Aaron was reading the paper.

"Peek-a-boo," Aaron said, raising the newspaper and then hiding behind it again.

Caesar stood in front of him and giggled with delight in the game.

"He's so good-natured," Maia said. "He loves to laugh."

"Ahh, hell, there's a story here about another lynching in Georgia," Aaron said, becoming engrossed in the article.

Caesar wanted to continue with the game, and in his frustration, he grabbed part of the newspaper and ran over and gave it to his Grammy.

"I see you're not going to be ignored, are you, little one?" Maia said, laughing at what he had done, until the obituary announcement of Thomas Elliott caught her eye.

She read the announcement closely but said nothing to Aaron. Instead, she gave the paper back to Caesar and watched her grandson make a mess of it. There was so much hatred and segregation spreading through Savannah that she dare not bring any calamity into the lives of her children by showing up or by revealing that she was their natural mother. Moreover, she had little Caesar to think about.

On the other hand, Daphne had also seen the obituary, and once again, she was a mourning friend of the family at the funeral. She went unnoticed at the service and was tempted to confront the Elliott family, but she knew it wasn't the appropriate time or place. It was hard to imagine them as babies looking at them now; they were middle-age adults with children who were nearly grown. It was then that Daphne decided she would write a letter to all three, Joseph, Juliette, and Jack.

Dear Family, I start this letter with that greeting because we are indeed related by blood. My father, Richard Bailey, was the heir of a rice plantation on Ossabaw Island before the war. It was when I was about three years old that he became obsessed with a young slave girl and brought her to live at the mansion at Bailey Estates in Savannah. She was like a sister and friend to me for many years before he took her as his concubine. She bore him three children that were, in essence, snatched from her womb and given to a childless woman, married to a business associate on the other side of Midtown. You three are those children. Unbeknownst to you, you all have met your mother. She is a well-known writer in Savannah, Maia Liberty, and she stood beside me at your mother's gravesite. I have no other motives in this revelation other than to tell the truth. So many wrongs have been done to so many people that I have no illusions of making them right. Mrs. Liberty has known about you all for twenty years and has made the sacrifice to remain silent and not interfere in your lives. She asks or expects nothing from you. I myself am not that unselfish. I would like all of you to come to my home for dinner for the Fourth of July. Yours truly, Daphne Bailey

Daphne never received a response to her letter, but on the evening July 4, the Elliott children showed up at Bailey Estates. Daphne invited them to sit in the gazebo under the large tree, where she had cool drinks waiting for them.

"I took the initiative and spiked them a little; I hope you all don't mind," she said.

They all looked at one another, speechless, as they searched for the words to begin the conversation.

Joseph started it, saying, "How do we know that this is true or that this is not some type of extortion?"

"I don't need any money and neither does Maia Liberty, and there is no earthly reason for us to create such a lie." Daphne went further: "I wanted you all to know that while you grieved over the deaths of your parents, there is a woman who has grieved for her children for the better part of her life."

"I would have preferred not to know. It doesn't change any-thing," Joseph replied.

"Oh, but it does, Joseph. Your whole perspective has changed because now you know who you are. Since you all have received my letter, have any of you looked any closer in mirror, at one another, or at your children?" Daphne asked.

"Miss Bailey, in all honesty, there have been times when I wondered if we may have been adopted. There was no resem-blance between us and our parents, but I never thought they would take another woman's children," Juliette said.

"Your parents were good people who offered the children of a young slave woman refuge. If not for them, I don't want to think about what might have happened," Diana said.

"How much black blood do we have?" Juliette asked.

"Your mother was the also the child of a slave and her slave master. That makes you quadroons and your children octoroons," Daphne answered.

"This is all a pile of horse shit, and I don't want to hear anymore about it!" Joseph said angrily.

"There was another child," Daphne said, "And she has the same blood as you all. She was born after the war started and was raised with your mother. Her name is Diana Portunus. She's a singer and an accomplished performer in New York City."

"Does she know about us?" Juliette asked.

"Yes, Juliette, she only found out about you all after she was grown, but she has known for quite some time."

"What about our father?" Jack asked.

"My father, our father, Richard Bailey is dead. He died many years ago in England. I have no explanation of how things were back then before the war or the evil that men do. I can only assure you that he loved Maia very much during those years," Daphne said.

There were more questions, and after a while, feeling enough had been said, Daphne asked, "Will you all be joining me for dinner?"

"No, thank you," Joseph said promptly. "We all have previous engagements and can't stay."

Joseph stood on his feet and ignored Daphne's extended arms for an embrace, but Juliette and Jack rose and gave her sincere hugs. Daphne watched them walk to the entrance and leave hurriedly in their carriage.

***

Time passed and the seasons changed and Caesar changed with them. He grew taller and more steady on his feet and had a thick head of curly hair, and when he laughed, he showed his whole mouth full of perfect teeth. However, his second birthday came and went with much less fanfare than the first and without the presence of his mother.

Diana hadn't come back to visit as she had promised. She stayed on Maia's mind when her 40th birthday came around and they hadn't heard from her. Maia wondered how her child could stay away from her son for so long. She hated the idea that Diana was missing so much of Caesar growing up, and Maia knew better than most that once those years are gone, a mother can never get them back.

Life continued on with its twists and turns, and then something that Maia had never thought about happened on Easter Sunday. It was a cool day, and Caesar had the sniffles, so Maia decided to skip church services.

"You go on, dear, and say some prayers for us," Maia said as Aaron rose from the breakfast table.

"I always do," he replied as he grabbed his jacket to leave.

Aaron was in a rush to speak with the Men's Council at the church about Richard Young, a young black man accused of the murder of a white man. He had heard from their neighbor that morning that there had been another lynching last night, and he prayed it wasn't Richard.

It was around noon, and Caesar was sleeping when Maia heard a soft knock on the back door in the kitchen. She saw through the curtains on the window door that it was a white man, and her heart jumped. What was this about, and why was he at her back door? There wasn't one person in town whose nerves weren't on edge.

Concerned, Maia slowly opened the door and saw clearly that it was Jack Elliot, her youngest son. Her mind began to race trying to catch up to her heartbeat. Maia had not even dared to let herself think about the possibility of this day. She wondered who had told Jack but realized that it could only have been Daphne. She could never forget their faces from that day at the cemetery; they were engraved in her memory. In his hands, Jack held a bouquet of pink and white tulips.

"These are for you," he said.

"Please come in," Maia said and offered him a chair at the table.

"Miss Daphne wrote us and when we met she told us about everything. I have wanted to meet you for some time," Jack said.

"I'm very happy to see you again," Maia said, looking into his eyes and seeing her own.

"My brother, Joseph, can't accept it, and my sister, Juliette, fears that it would break up her family, so they couldn't come here with me."

"I understand, and I don't blame them," Maia said. "It's a diffi-cult situation. What made you decide to come?"

"Ma'am, I am a veterinarian, and I see births of offspring almost every day. The relationship between the mother and baby is a mir-acle and fundamental to me at the same time. It's the precious and simple gift of life, and I want to thank you for that. I also know that the love and protectiveness of a mother is instinctive. I thought about how my wife would feel or any of God's creatures would react if their children were taken from them, and I knew how you suffered, so I wanted to say I'm sorry for that."

"None of that blame belongs to you, Jack. I don't have the words to tell you how much you have touched my heart by coming here. I have loved and missed all of you from the day each of you were born. I have prayed for your safety and happiness, and I thank God that all of you are well. You all were taken from me, but today you are a gift to me again, and for that I thank you."

The two of them had so many questions for each other. He told Maia about where he grew up, the kind of people the Elliot's were, things he did in high school, where he went to college, and how he met his wife. Maia told him about growing up at Bailey Estates, going back to the island during the war, getting married, coming back to Savannah, Apollo's dying, teaching, and writing her books. It was only Caesar calling for her upstairs that gave them pause.

"I guess I better go, ma'am," Jack said. "I don't know when I'll see you again."

"Don't worry about that, my dear. You came today," Maia answered as they gripped each other's hands before she walked with him to the back door.

Maia was so full of emotion when she got up the stairs to get Caesar that she cried more tears on his shoulder than he did on hers. She tried to think about whether she should tell Aaron about Jack coming by, and then she thought better of it, supposing that it would just open up old wounds. When Aaron got home from church, he could see that the extra rest had done them both a lot of good.

"Where'd you get the flowers?" he asked.

"Daphne got them for me," Maia answered quickly.

"No telegram from Diana?" Aaron asked.

"No, not today."

"If we don't hear something from her soon, I'm going up there to bring her back. I love the boy, but it ain't right."

***

Diana wanted to write home to her family and she wanted to visit them. But she hadn't found any decent roles, and they wouldn't see any reason for her to stay in New York. She wasn't ready to give it up and come home. The problems were the race riots that were popping up in the city and the attacks on black entertainers that were slowing down the amount of work.

The new word on the street was that top music writer Will Marion Cook was collaborating with Paul Laurence Dunbar on a new production that would be starring George Williams and Bert Walker. "I promise, you'll have a part in my next play, Diana," George had assured her after she missed out on *Sons of Ham*.

Diana's complaint was that she was tired of working in the shadows of other performers; it was her time to bask in the spotlight. She had been patient but her time was running out. She could see how most of the women she had started out with, the ones who had worked their asses off for a negro woman to be respected on stage, were being pushed to the side for starring roles by producers to make way for the younger women singers.

The new musical, *In Dahomey*, opened in September at the Globe Theatre in Boston. It was the best production starring the Walker and Williams team to date. Diana's role in the play wasn't exactly what she had hoped for; she didn't get to play the part of the leading female singer. She and Abbie Mitchell, Marion Cook's wife, did get small but worthy singing parts in the musical; and Diana accepted her role gracefully, knowing it was her own actions that had taken her out of line, and that she would just have to wait her turn again.

The starring roles for the women singers were given to Aida Overton Walker and Lottie Williams, the wives of the starring men. Diana was disappointed, but the musical was top-quality, and she wanted to be a part of it. And with the way things were going, she was glad just to get to work.

Diana's consolation was that, *In Dahomey* was destined to play on Broadway. It opened at the New York Theater on February 18, 1903, and was a monumental success. After 53 performances, the show was headed overseas to London, England. Diana knew that her mama and tata would think that she had lost her mind and had abandoned Caesar, but this was what she was born to do. David was right, she thought. She had given up any chance for a husband and family years ago. She decided to send her parents a short letter.

Dear Mama and Tata, There is nothing I can say that can express how much it means to me that you are caring for Caesar and allowing me this time to do what I feel I am driven to do. I can only say thank you from the bottom of my heart. I regret that there's no way for me to be all things to the people I love and be true to myself, but I love you both, and I love my son. I will be going abroad for some months touring with In Dahomey. I may be wrong for the decisions I have made and still make, but I am happiest when I'm performing. I would be back there to visit as soon as I can. Soon Caesar will be old enough to come to live with me in New York. Love, Diana

It was the first time that an all-negro cast had performed in a full-length musical in Britain. *In Dahomey* toured all across England for seven months as the most popular show in London, with the cast giving a command performance for the Prince of Wales's birthday at Buckingham Palace. Diana felt the adoration that she first felt with the Fisk Jubilee Singers. The tour moved on to Scotland, and the musical was so well received that what she thought would be a six-month tour abroad stretched well over a year.

It was the end of August 1904, when the troupe returned to the States and opened at the Grand Opera House in New York. The successful run sparked another tour that would take the musical production to American cities from coast to coast for another forty weeks. Before the run of *In Dahomey* ended in the spring of 1905, they had given 1,100 performances. Diana had sent handfuls of telegrams home to Savannah, but the reality was, she had been gone for four years.

"We're going to move quickly to capitalize on the success of *In Dahomey*," George told the cast, "We're going to follow up with a major production called *Abyssinia*. In the interest of time we're going to use the same cast members. Diana, you'll have the lead role this time."

It was kismet. Diana had been patient, and her time had finally come.

"This show will be elevated to a higher level, with lavish costumes and an extravagant set of waterfalls and live animals that will include a camel, a lion, and live asses," Bert added.

They opened in February 1906 at the Majestic Theater with Diana having a starring role as the wife of the African King, Menelik. The show opened with a bang. It was another smash hit, and Diana relished the spotlight, but it was not to last. Providence delivered another cruel moment as white audiences shunned and rejected the high-quality comedy, and the show closed in August after only 31 performances.

Diana sank low in despondency. Just when she had gotten the role she had been waiting for, the chance to show the world her real talent, it disappeared. Why was there always something that kept her from the full bounty of success? Fate would hand her the fruit, let her take a bite and savor its sweetness, only to snatch it away. Diana's loneliness was magnified, she missed her family, and she missed her baby.

The words of Bert Williams's song repeated over and over in her mind,"When life seems full of clouds and rain, And I am full of nothing and pain, Who soothes my thumpin', bumpin' brain? Nobody."

Diana woke up early the next morning, packed a small bag, and boarded a southbound train to Savannah.

Chapter Twenty-Two

Savannah was in the midst of racial turmoil as negroes were protesting the overbearing presence of Jim Crow. The city council, for several reasons, was revisiting the old fight to increase segregation on the streetcars. Sol Johnson, editor of *The Tribune,* called for community leaders to mobilize at the beginning of September to organize their strategy for the battle. The first meeting took place at the First African Church, with representatives from the business community, along with ministers from various denominations.

"Good evening, gentleman," Sol announced, standing behind the podium at the opening of the meeting, "We are about to take a stand against segregation in Savannah, and this campaign requires a level of commitment to achieve success that we have never demonstrated before. It's going to be a long, tough battle. We will now take nominations for the leadership of this fight against Jim Crow."

"I nominate Aaron Liberty," James Sims shouted.

"I concur and also nominate Rev. J. W. Carr, and Rev. J. A. Lindsey," Sol affirmed. "Are there any other nominations or objections?" There was a brief moment of silence before Sol started the applause for the newly elected leaders that would organize the boycott against streetcars.

"I know that you haven't had time to prepare a strategy, but would any of our new leaders care to provide us with a word of encouragement?"

Aaron rose to his feet and approached the podium.

"For all of my life, I have wanted to be an instrument to improve our lives and opportunities as black people. I pledge to you all tonight that I will hold nothing back in the forefront of this under-taking, and we will be victorious. In this boycott against segregated streetcars, remember that with every step we walk, Jim Crow is under our feet."

Cheers and applause broke out in the room after Aaron finished speaking. This was what he had dreamed about. At last, he was in the position he desired, and he vowed to make a difference. He had finally gotten the validation that he had sought so long ago.

"I'll be behind you with full backing from *The Tribune*," Sol said after the meeting adjourned.

"I appreciate that," Aaron said. "I'm sure I'll need some of that tonight when I tell Maia."

Aaron saw the light in the kitchen when he came into the house. He walked in to find Maia washing up the dishes and Caesar doing his lesson at the table.

"I'm going to be serving as a leader in the new streetcar boy-cott," Aaron stated bluntly.

Maia finished cleaning as if nothing had been said. She dried her hands on her apron, took a deep breath, turned around to face him and said, "Be careful, Aaron, you don't stick your neck out too far. The support you need to do this might not be behind you."

"The purpose of the leader is to show our folks which way to go."

"I understand that, honey, but there's going to be a lot involved with the boycott: the inconvenience, the intimidations, and the threats. Are you all ready for that?" she asked with her eyes fixed on Caesar.

"I have to be because we're moving forward. We're going to submit a proposal for the integration of the streetcars to the city council as soon as possible and hopefully they'll accept it."

Aaron sat down at the table and was explaining their strategy from the meeting when they heard the front door open. The two of them paused for a moment as the footsteps came closer to the kitchen, and in walked Diana. A hush came over the room, and Caesar, who had been occupied practicing his letters looked up to see what was wrong.

Maia searched for words, but she was so stunned that all she could utter was, "Diana."

Aaron stood up from his chair, startled, and said, "We didn't know you were coming. Is everything all right?"

Diana's eyes were fixed on Caesar, and he looked back at her in confusion. Seeing this boy sitting at the table forced her to confront the years that she had lost with him. Maia could see the emotions building up in Diana as her body began to heave.

"It's been a long time, baby," Maia said in a low voice, trying to soften her shock.

Diana couldn't take the way Caesar looked at her as if she were a stranger. She wanted him to run over to her and give her a big hug to show his mama how much he had missed her, but he just sat there wondering who she was. Diana insides were broken further, and it was more than she could bear, she fell to the kitchen floor where she stood and passed out.

Maia helped Aaron get Diana to the couch in the parlor; and after about ten minutes, they were able to revive her. Caesar stood back and watched the dramatic scene from the middle of the floor.

"Caesar, this is your mama. She's come back home," Maia said to him.

Caesar could only look at Diana with fascination. His grammy and grandy had shown him pictures and talked about her to him all the time, told him where she was traveling on the road and what shows she was touring with, but to him she was still a stranger.

"Where are your manners, boy?" Aaron gently scolded.

Caesar walked over to Diana, held out his hand, and said, "Hello, ma'am."

Diana burst into hysterical tears; it seemed as if nothing she ever did worked out or got her the love that she wanted. Aaron took Caesar by the hand and led him upstairs to bed.

"Calm yourself down, Di," Maia said. "It's late, and it's been a long and chaotic day. Go on upstairs, and we'll talk in the morning."

Diana ambled slowly up the familiar stairs blinded by tears and weighed down with despondency. Her instincts guided her to her old bedroom, and she fell across the bed fully clothed and pleaded for sleep to overtake her. Being conscious caused her too much pain.

Maia sat on the couch and closed her eyes, trying to gather her thoughts and shake off the drama of the evening. After a while, she opened them and saw Aaron standing there in front of her.

He reached out his arms to help her up and said, "Will you take a walk with me?"

Maia smiled, and that released the tension of the day. They went outside for a long, quiet walk where they could breathe in the crisp air of the fall night to relax before they went to bed.

***

Diana slept late into the morning, but she felt better when she finally came down to eat. Caesar had already gone to school, and Aaron had gone to meet with Rev. Lindsey and Rev. Carr to prepare the proposal for the city council on the issue of the streetcars.

"Good morning, my dear," Maia said as she gave Diana a hug before she sat down.

"I'm sorry, Mama. I didn't mean to come here raising all that fuss last night. I didn't even know I was coming until two days ago. I just couldn't take it anymore."

"What was it that you couldn't take, baby?" Maia asked patiently.

"I finally got where I wanted to be all my life. I was in the spotlight, Mama, and then it just fizzled out. I have worked so hard for so long and given up so much, and now I don't think it was worth it," Diana said.

"Look here, child, you have had the opportunity to travel all over the world as a Fisk Jubilee Singer. You were among the first black women who could get on stage and look good. You have sung in musicals all over this country and overseas, you have made a lot of money, you've had the love of a good and handsome man, and you got a wonderful son to show for it. Why are you sitting here singing the blues? Count your blessings, baby!"

Maia left Diana in the house to make her own meal. She was tired of hearing her complain about her life when she had been so fortunate. It reminded her of a story she had written many years ago about a peacock named Prosper.

Prosper was born in tropical in forest in India, the only egg that hatched after a hailstorm came and destroyed the rest. His mother, Carla, loved him with all her heart and always told him how special he was. He was a handsome thing, with a magnificent tail, and his mama told him so every morning. Prosper would strut through the forest, and whenever he saw a group of other birds, he would show off and dance. It was cute when he was young, but as he got older, the other animals were annoyed and started to ignore Prosper.

He started to feel like he wasn't special anymore and would stomp around all upset.

One day, he saw a flock of flamingos wading in the water, and he became angry. Why do they have to be so colorful, and why can they swim and fly? The next day, he saw a family of swan swimming gracefully in line in the river and got even madder. Why do they have to be so attractive? Why do the canary and the nightingale sing better than me? I'm the one who's supposed to be special. He started to feel ashamed of himself, he had behaved so badly. He wasn't the best bird in the forest. Every other bird had something that he didn't have. He began to sulk and stay alone by himself.

One day, he sat in tree feeling sorry for himself while his mother foraged around looking for food. High above the ground, he saw a wild tiger running toward her. In an instant, he flew down and lifted his mother up to safety just in the nick of time. Unfortunately, the tiger was quick enough to tear away part of Prosper's handsome tail with his teeth.

Prosper was devastated. He thought he had lost all that was special about him, but all the animals admired him after that. They were so proud of him for saving his mother's life at the risk of his own. They told him so, and he was humbled by it. Prosper knew then that it wasn't his splendid fan that made him special, or the way he could dance and strut. It was because of who he was inside, and that made him proud.

***

Maia sat outside until the afternoon when Aaron returned with Caesar from school. She loved to see the sight of the two of them walking up the street to the house. Aaron joined her on the veranda while Caesar stayed in the yard amusing himself, kicking and chasing the leaves.

"The decision has been made. The council voted to segregate

the streetcars. Rev. Carr and Rev. Lindsey and I will be meeting again to go ahead with the boycott," Aaron told Maia, sitting down beside her. "We stopped it with the boycott in 1899, and now is no time to back down."

Maia didn't voice the reservations she had about Aaron being one of the leaders in the protest. She had never questioned his judgment, and she knew it was important to him to help black people fight for equal rights in Savannah. It was what he always wanted.

"It's one thing to have segregation forced on you, and then it's another thing for you to go out and pay for it," he told Maia. "We have power in where we spend our money."

Diana watched them all through the window. She was tired of knocking her head against a door that only opened halfway. She was going to stop and take some time and get to know her son. Here he was going on seven years old, and she didn't know anything about him, what he liked to do, his favorite food, what scared him or what made him laugh. She didn't even know the size of his clothes.

Diana could see that her mama and tata had taken good care of him. He was tall for his age, and he reminded her of David, except he was a bit lighter in complexion. Diana decided to take it slow and earn the love and affection that he had given her freely as a baby. She walked out and greeted her tata, and then she walked down to Caesar.

"Do you like school?" she asked.

"Yes, ma'am," he answered.

"That's good, baby. Can you write your name?"

"Sure, that's easy," he said proudly.

"Well, come inside and show me," she said as she took his hand, and they walked up the stairs into the house.

Maia smiled as they went by and nodded her head in approval.

***

Halfway through the month, the boycott went into operation, and the absence of negro passengers was felt on all fourteen streetcar lines. Nevertheless, it wasn't easy. Negro hack drivers helped many of the boycotters get where they needed to be, but police were arresting anybody who stood in one place too long. Then there was word of a race riot in Atlanta on September 22, when a mob of whites went through the negro business district attacking hundreds of boycotters, adding more fuel to the fire and strengthening the resolve of the boycotters. By the end of the month, the streetcars were nearly empty.

Aaron was encouraged and spoke boldly at the meetings. "Brothers and sisters we don't have to submit to segregation and accept disenfranchisement as we have been told in the so-called 'Atlanta Compromise.' Unity is a powerful weapon, people, and nobody can stop us from using it except ourselves."

The boycott had hit Savannah Electric hard in the pockets, and they were using informants and buying the support of a few black ministers. Unfortunately, fear and intimidation proved to be a formidable weapon against the boycott; and the inconvenience for the protesters was also having an effect, but the boycott muddled along through the winter.

"This is so frustrating. What is wrong with us?" Aaron said to Sol. "Our support from the clergy and the professors at Georgia State Industrial College is falling off. They keep riding the streetcars."

"They're nothing but buzzards," Sol replied angrily. "That's the name I give them in *The Tribune* when I refer to them and anyone else who rides the streetcars."

"I can't believe that Bishop Turner actually broke the boycott and rode on the segregated streetcar," Aaron said flabbergasted.

The unity that gave them power was being split from every direction. A mass meeting was called on March 24, 1907.

Aaron spoke at the end and did his best to encourage the protesters to stay resolute. "This is only the beginning of our struggle, brothers and sisters, and we have many fights ahead. We can't afford to lose a battle this early in the war. Our enemies will try to turn us against each other to weaken us so we must stay united."

Aaron walked home from the meeting deep in thought, searching his mind for a way to build up the faltering campaign. Instinctively, he began to feel danger or an evil presence in the air around him. Suddenly, before he had time to react, a large cloth was thrown around his head, and someone landed a heavy blow to his back and then to his head.

"Who are you?" Aaron shouted as he turned around to defend himself, punching and kicking in the air around him, searching for any target. Many of his blows connected with flesh.

Aaron fought with the ferocity of a tiger, but he was being hit with so many kicks and blows all over his body from something that felt like a stick. Another blow to his head sparked a bright light behind his eyes. All Aaron knew to do was to keep fighting, and any man who dared to come close enough to lay a hand on him would surely suffer for it.

"Fight me like a man, you cowards!" he yelled just before he was pushed and knocked to the ground.

Aaron continued to swing his legs and arms with the fervor of man who had fought his whole life. Then there was another hard blow to the back of his neck, and the hot pain that burned throughout his body went cold. He was numb, and then the shadows of the men that he saw standing above him faded.

Maia was writing at the dining room table, and Diana was reading a story to Caesar, when they was unnerved by a frantic knock on the door.

"Oh Lord, have mercy!" Maia said as she opened the door to see Sol and another man she didn't know carrying Aaron.

Maia barely recognized her husband's swollen face covered in blood. She heard Diana scream and soft cries from Caesar.

"I've already sent for a doctor, Maia. Show us where to lay him down," Sol said between quick breaths.

Maia didn't say a word but led them upstairs to their bedroom; she was dazed, as if she had been hit with a blow similar to the ones Aaron had suffered. When the doctor came into the room, she backed away and looked out the window while he examined Aaron.

After a few minutes, the doctor went over to Maia and said, "He's alive for now, and he may survive, but I don't know how bad the brain has been damaged. But I feel it's severe, and he will probably be paralyzed or crippled at best. I've given him some medicine for pain, and he'll probably be in and out of consciousness for tonight."

"Thank you, doctor," Maia said quietly. I'll send for you if we need you."

Maia went down the stairs to send everyone home. "You can all go on now. Aaron is resting, and there's nothing more to do tonight."

Back in their bedroom, Maia looked at Aaron and thought about the day she saw him walk up to the school, so tall and strong. Then she remembered how he looked in his formal attire the day they got married, so handsome and proud.

"You could always make a bold statement without uttering a word," she said, standing over him.

Maia stiffened her back and walked out to the bathroom. She reached under the sink for the wash basin and filled it with warm water, and then she searched in the cupboard for a brand-new face cloth. She took them and walked back into the bedroom, where Aaron lay unconscious. She gently took off all of his soiled cloth-ing, taking care not to hurt him. She washed the blood from his face, and then she kissed it. She washed his neck, and then she kissed it. She washed his chest and kissed it. Finally, she washed his arms and kissed them.

Maia washed and loved on Aaron from head to toe. She rubbed the wash cloth over his hair until it was clean. Then she ran her fingers through his hair, and her eyes were fixed on the beauty of the silver hairs as they were caught in the rays of light from the lamp on the nightstand. She cleaned his hands and feet and clipped the nails, and then she covered his wounds and rubbed his whole body down in lavender oil.

Maia looked in the closet and found Aaron's finest suit. She dressed him in it, taking care that every button was done and that his shirt collar was straight. She shined his shoes and put them on his feet. She stood at the foot of the bed and looked at him and was satisfied with what she saw.

Then she began to speak, "I love you, Aaron. I love you as my husband, I love you as the father of my children, and I love you as the man you have proven yourself to be."

She walked over beside him and kissed him long on the lips. Then she put her pillow over his face and held it. She placed her other hand over his heart, and she held it there until she could no longer feel its beat. Maia put the pillow back in place on her side of the bed and then left the room.

***

The funeral service was held at the First African Baptist Church, and there was standing room only.

"Allow only thirty minutes for people to view Aaron's body before the casket is to be closed," Maia instructed the undertaker.

She sat on the front row of the church with Diana and Caesar and watched as the long line paraded across the front. At the viewing,

Maia saw families for whom Aaron had helped build homes in Ossabaw, his Masonic brothers, business associates, friends they had made over the years, old students of Maia's, and Sol Johnson represented the *Tribune*.

"I'm so sorry for your loss, Maia, truly I am," Daphne said as she came up to give her condolences, with Jack close behind.

"Thank you both for coming," Maia said, struggling to hold on to her composure, feeling the tugs to her heart.

All the speakers were respectful and complimentary, and then Diana walked to the front and sang a song written by the Johnson Brothers, James Weldon, and J. Rosamond called "Lift Every Voice and Sing." Everyone in the church was transfixed. It was as if she was accompanied by angels from heaven. Maia tightened her arms around Caesar and let the tears flood her eyes.

Maia buried Aaron Liberty at Laurel Grove Cemetery next to her mama, Rachel Liberty. It was difficult for her to believe he was gone. She spent most of the day in their bedroom, thinking, writing, and taking her meals there, but not sleeping. It was much too lonely in there at night, and she preferred to sleep in the guestroom they had for her mama.

"Don't you worry about anything, Maia," Rev. Simms assured her when he and Albert Jackson came by. "We plan to look after Aaron's portion of the business as usual."

"I'm so sorry this happened," Sol Johnson said when he came in. "I promise you we'll keep working hard to sustain the boycott."

Maia was devastated that even after Aaron had lost his life fighting against segregated streetcars, more blacks had started to riding them. She swore that she would never set foot on another streetcar for the rest of her life. For his whole life, Aaron had only wanted to help his people have the rights they deserved. They had sacrificed so much, and no one seemed to care.

Epilogue

Diana looked at her mama sitting out on the veranda, where she and Aaron had spent so much time talking. She didn't know how her mama kept going after all the grief she had suffered in her life. Now it would only be harder on her when she and Caesar had to leave.

"Come on out here and talk to me," Maia said, seeing Diana standing behind the door.

"It's hard for me to see you sitting out here without Tata," Diana said, sitting next to her.

"I know, baby, but we knew that one day it would be either him or me sitting here alone. I'm at peace with it now; he died doing what he always wanted to do. I've been sitting here thinking about my life, the times I saw God and the times I couldn't. Now I know God was with me the whole time, through the good and the bad. He doesn't go in and out of our lives; we are the ones that go away from Him."

"If God is always with us, why is there so much suffering, Mama? Why can't things work out the way we want them to?"

"We only complain through the rough times; the smooth times we take for granted instead of being grateful. That's the mistake I don't want to see you make, Diana. Don't run away from the sunshine in your life. You'll just run straight into a storm."

"I'm not running anywhere, Mama," Diana said, standing up. She didn't want to hear any more about the decisions she had made.

"I hope not," Maia said, reaching for her hand. "Because as many times as my heart has been broken, when I look at you and Caesar, I can still see we've been blessed."

"I'm glad you can see that, Mama, because what I see is a lot of blues," Diana whined as she pulled her hand away and walked back into the house.

A few days later, Jack came by again for a short visit to see Maia. He wanted to give his condolences to the family and tell her how sorry he was for her loss.

"Is there anything I can do for you?" Jack asked.

"Yes," Maia answered. "Get me a horse."

Before the week was over, Jack had a horse sent out to the house. The horse was chestnut with white marking on both of his sides. When Diana brought Caesar home from school and they saw him in the backyard, she was shocked, but Caesar was thrilled. Maia had already had the shed fixed so the horse could stay in there.

"What do you think we should call him?" Maia asked them over dinner.

"Mama, you don't know the first thing about taking care of a horse," Diana told her.

"Why don't we call him Pegasus, after the winged horse?" Caesar suggested after they had considered a few other names.

"That's perfect," Maia said. "Those spots on his sides are where the wings should be."

As they finished their meal, there was a knock on the door. Maia's hearrt heart skipped a beat the way it had for the last month whenever anyone knocked. Diana went to answer the door and Maia and Caesar followed her into the foyer. When Diana opened the door, Maia knew who it was before the young man opened his mouth to introduce himself. He was Aaron's spitting image.

"Hello. Pardon me for interrupting y'all's meal. I'm Roman Nelson."

"Please come in," Maia said. Diana looked him up and down as she shut the door behind him.

"I heard about Mr. Liberty's passing, and I had to come. My mother was from here, and she knew him. Her name was Eve," Roman said.

"I never met your mother, but I know who you are," Maia said. "Have you eaten yet?"

"No, ma'am, I haven't," Roman replied.

"Well come join us at the table," she said. "This is my daughter, Diana, and her son, Caesar, and we're glad to meet you."

They sat back down at the table, and Diana prepared a plate of food for Roman while Caesar hung on his every word.

"My mother run off with another man when I was thirteen," Roman told them. "I ain't seen her since. My papa read in the paper about Mr. Aaron Liberty being killed, and he told me that he was my natural father."

"Yes, he was, and he loved you more than you'll ever know. He wanted to be a father to you and raise you, but it wasn't possible under the circumstances," Maia told him while he ate.

"I'm sorry I didn't get the chance to know him," Roman replied.

"How about yourself?" Maia asked. "What do you do to make a living? Do you have a wife and kids?"

"I'm a bricklayer, ma'am," he told her, sounding exactly like Aaron on the day they met. "But I haven't found a wife yet."

"Well, you are welcome to stay here with us for as long as you like, Roman. And by the way, would you happen to know anything about horses?"

"Yes, ma'am, I do," he laughed, puzzled by the question.

"In that case, you came to us at the opportune time," Maia said, laughing. And then Diana and Caesar laughed, too.

Later, Maia went outside to look for God up in the dark blanket of the night sky. She dug her bare feet into the moist earth below her and looked high into the faraway stars. They sparkled in the heavens, where they had always been, never wavering, even as she suffered through turbulent winds and devastating storms.

Standing as strong as the evergreen trees that had lined the forests of Ossabaw when she was a young girl; Maia--like them--had remained resilient through all the changing seasons of life, weathering the sun and the rain. The elements had served to nurture her as she matured, spreading wider and reaching higher as each branch of her family sprang forward. She lifted her arms up in triumph in the midst of the cool evening air that surrounded her.

"I see you, God," she said softly, knowing that as long as the stars held their place up there in the galaxy there would be no end to the blues and the blessings.

BROWN REFLECTIONS

A New Season
Blues and Blessings, Part Two

Diana can't give up on her dream and the hope of seeing her name lit up on the marquee, she goes back to New York to find fame and glory. Maia is determined that the Liberty family legacy will survive in her grandson, Caesar, but the young boy goes through his own seasons of good times and bad after he meets his father, David, and his wife, Grace, in Nashville. He looks for his escape in the service, and World War I escorts him into manhood before he makes his way back home. Savor a taste of history through this family's blues and blessings before and through the Great Depression, the Civil Rights Movement, and feel the beat of the rhythm and blues of Jefferson Street in Nashville, Tennessee.

A Reflection
What a Difference A Day Makes, What about 100 Years?

Change is often described as evolution. This evolution is a slow process of change in a population that is spread over many generations that introduces many variations as we adapt to our environment. What are the results of the evolution of black people over the last 100 years? What have been the catalysts for the changes or evolution? How have we evolved economically, socially, educationally, politically, and artistically? Has this process of change been a 180-degree transformation, have we come full circle, or is it more likely that we have detoured on some tangent from an obtuse angle? These are the questions I hope to answer by retracing our history over the past 100 years.

Martin Luther King Jr spoke of reaching the Promised Land and dreamed that we would "overcome" as a people, that we would all be assured of our unalienable rights. Has the majority benefited as a whole in a normal distribution, or have the results been positively skewed for only a select a few? There is always a range in the strides toward a particular destination. Some have taken a more straightforward route, others have taken less-traveled routes, and then the incessant wanderings of those who have lost their way. Langston Hughes's poem asks what happened: "Has the dream been deferred, or has it dried up like a raisin in the sun?"